A NOVEL BY

MACK STOUT

Unintended
CONSEQUENCES

ONE MAN'S BATTLE WITH IRRESISTIBLE FORCES AND
IMMOVABLE OBJECTS

Unintended Consequences: One Man's Battle with Irresistible Forces and Immovable Objects

R. Francis Thompson
100 24th Street West Suite 1-1100
Billings, MT 59102.
rf.thompson32@gmail.com

ISBN: 979-8-9899173-0-3 (E-Book)
ISBN: 979-8-9899173-1-0 (Paperback)
ISBN: 979-8-9899173-2-7 (Hardcover)

Book Cover Design and Interior Formatting by 100Covers.

This and other titles by Mack Stout are available in print at Amazon.com and other major retailers.

For more information, visit www.mackstout.com, where you'll find entertaining blog posts and news about new books. You can also sign up for my list and get my free eBook, MACK STOUT GOES THERE.

A NOTE FROM THE AUTHOR

Thank you for your interest in this book. I wish to give you a fair warning that this is not my usual style of writing. To be honest, I am concerned that some may find this story disturbing. If you are offended by explicit language and what some would consider strong sexual content, I urge you to set this aside until you have had an opportunity to reevaluate your relationship with the facts of life. I am aware that there are those who see literature that is sprinkled with words that start with the letters c, f, p, and s and will dismiss it as pornography. Such people see what they believe, and it says more about them than it does about the material. People like sex, and if that weren't true, neither you nor anyone you know would be here.

It is not my intention to appeal to prurient interests or to shock and disturb anyone. This is the story of a man who struggles with feelings that are too often judged by society to be inappropriate or indelicate. These feelings are no less real to some people, and I believe that this story deserves to be told. I hope you will view it in that spirit. If not, Helen Hunt in the publisher's office is the person in charge of customer complaints and issuing refunds. So, if you are looking to get your money back, you can go to Helen Hunt[1].

—M. S.

---

1   Or maybe I meant go to hell 'n hunt.

Dedicated to all who struggle to find understanding, connection, and acceptance.

"For thereby some have entertained angels unawares."
- Saint Paul, or whoever the hell wrote the Book of Hebrews

FOREWORD

By Southern Diane Marie

The story you are about to read begins with the author, through his main character, asking the question, "Why does something as natural and healthy as sex produce so much guilt and shame?" This question is powerful and thought-provoking. Over the last four years, I have talked with countless men from all over the world, and we have discussed this topic. What I hear consistently across the board is men want to feel special, sexy, and desired by their spouse or partner. They want to share intimacy and fantasies with them. So many men don't experience that feeling. These men go on to feel guilty or ashamed for having sexual desires that are completely normal, natural, and healthy.

Allow me to introduce myself. I'm known online as Diane Marie, a social media personality. You may know me from YouTube, Instagram, X (Twitter), Twitch, or one of my private sites. I wear many hats, such as wife, mom, content creator, product promoter, and live streamer. I could go on and on. I am most known for my Bra or No Bra videos on YouTube.

Unintended Consequences: One Man's Battle with Irresistible Forces and Immovable Objects is a book I believe so many men will connect with, especially men over the age of 35. Men chat with me every day on my private sites. So many of them share stories with me about how they don't have intimacy at home with their spouse or partner. They tell me their lady is embarrassed or isn't interested in being intimate sexually. They do not want to betray them. It is normal to want sexual intimacy with another person. We are human, and having hormones is part of that. Ponder this: Is it considered cheating if a man chats online with women? Where is the line drawn? I think it is beyond the scope of a foreword or even one book to answer that question. An individual or couple must set boundaries for where the line is drawn.

I offer a nonjudgmental, discreet, comfortable place for men to ask me questions about anything, share fantasies, and enjoy the fantasies I share. Some men are inspired by me to spice up their bedroom life. They like having access to a woman they can ask, without judgment, how to please the lady in their life. The conversations I continue to have are about how they want sexual intimacy with their spouse or partner, to please them, and to have fun in the bedroom! Most of all, they want understanding, connection, and acceptance.

Mack first saw me on my YouTube videos. Then, he began messaging me on one of my private sites. I enjoyed chatting with him about his writing and my business. We shared an interest in fantasy and exploring ways to express that. I shared with him how, through my business, I have learned the importance of people having a healthy fantasy life. I want those who join me to feel comfortable and feel that they have found a safe place to have sexual desires, fantasies, and curiosities.

Mack shared with me that he is a writer. I have read the other books that he has published. One thing that is consistent with his writings is his wicked sense of humor. He has a way of looking at life and situations that, even though they may not be funny in and of themselves, he finds a way to bring out the comedy. We can all use a good laugh now and then.

Among the writing genres he shared with me were erotic stories. He sent them to me. I read them and thought they were sexy, erotic, and fun. I suggested that he find a way to publish these stories. I have to say he found a brilliant way to add these erotic stories to his novel.

This novel is about a gentleman in his fifties who is struggling with his thoughts of sexuality due to societal attitudes that can be repressive and judgmental.

The main character in the book, Alex, is like so many of the men I have and continue to chat with on my private sites. These men are average, everyday men from all walks of life and every type of career you could imagine from all over the world. Just like Alex, they are looking for a way to be turned on and release sexual tension, which is completely normal.

Mack has such a way with words. I laughed when I read the name he came up with for the site that substitutes for OnlyFans. When he referenced it by its initials, I wondered if this was part of a gag. Then I asked myself how long I had known this guy. Of course, it's part of the gag. Wordplay is his superpower! I would go so far as to say he is a cunning linguist.

He once told me that a novel is a work of fiction, but many times, cloaking reality in storytelling is the only way to tell the truth. Like his other books, this one has a serious message, but it's presented with a healthy dose of snarky humor. Be prepared to laugh, cry, and have your preconceived notions challenged as you follow Alex on his journey of illumination.

I am thrilled to be a significant part of this story. I'm pleased with how Mack portrays me and with the opportunity to collaborate with him. Over the past year, we have worked through numerous drafts and revisions to get it just right. Our hope is that you will enjoy reading it as much as we did in putting it together.

—Diane Marie

Diane Marie is a social media personality with a presence on many well-known sites such as YouTube @DianeMarieSouthernDianeMarie, @ dianemariesoutherncharm X(Twitter), Twitch, Instagram, LinkedIn, and allmylinks.com/southerndianemarie

PART 1 // UNDERSTANDING

CHAPTER 1

"The unexamined life is not worth living."
– Socrates

Why does something as natural and healthy as sex produce so much guilt and shame? I wonder how many men my age grapple with this question, as I did, sitting in the doctor's waiting room, preparing to undergo my annual physical. Since I didn't bring my phone, I needed to occupy my mind somehow. I made a practice of traveling light for these checkups. It always begins with the weigh-in, so I wore lightweight clothes and carried no extra items in my pockets.

As an alternative to wrestling with deep philosophical issues concerning sex, I picked up a magazine with an article about people leaving the corporate world to sell artisanal products like pickles, beef jerky, and salsa. The idea is appealing: to ditch the rat race and gain a semblance of freedom and independence. But it also meant giving up the security of a full-time salary and all that goes with it, like health insurance, so I can come here once a year to keep tabs on my slowly deteriorating body. At last, the woman with the clipboard stepped through the door to the waiting room. "Alex Anderson?" she called out.

On the way to the exam room, we made a stop at the scale. This part depressed me. I have been struggling to maintain a healthy weight for years, and it is becoming a losing battle. It seems I gain a pound or two every time I make this visit with my doctor. I don't consider myself obese, but I will admit my six-pack is well on its way to becoming a keg. My doctor is a man pushing 60 years old and skinny as a rail. I wonder if he is getting as tired of hassling me about my weight as I am hearing It. For all I know, he might think my weight management issues are a character flaw if not an outright moral failing.

The checkup went fine, with no significant issues. The doctor was quite thorough, right up to the point where he put on his one-fingered glove and told me to lean forward and think of my favorite politician. He then asked if I had any other concerns. I wanted to bring up one thing. "I'm getting to the point where I need to ask about treatment options for… erectile dysfunction," I said. It's an issue I have dealt with in recent months, and I chalked it up to the fact that I am approaching my fiftieth birthday.

"Yes, it happens," the doctor said. "Although I believe you could mitigate that if you mind your weight a bit."

Well, he said it. The 'W' word. Of course, he meant to say the 'O' word. I knew what was coming next. "Still working on your diet and exercise program?" he asked, like a trial lawyer who never asks a question to which he doesn't already know the answer.

"You are still trying to make me give up everything I enjoy in life so I can live longer, aren't you?" I said. "If I do things your way, the net result will be that when I'm 90, I can look forward to an extra year and a half in a nursing home at 10 grand a month. None of us are getting out of here alive. Besides, the world's major religions tell us we're all better off dead."

"That is some rather arcane logic," he responded.

"Just getting old and cynical," I replied. "Now, about those treatment options…"

***

Having accomplished that unpleasant task for another year, I decided I owed myself a cup of coffee and a muffin. I scheduled my checkup for early Friday morning, enabling me to skip breakfast, and I took the rest of the day off from work because I could. I have a favorite place to go when I need to think and unwind. It is called Roasters & Readers, a coffee shop annexed to a bookstore. Those who hang out there on a regular basis call the establishment R&R. The place is owned by an elderly couple who believe the old ways are best. It serves an eclectic bunch of hipsters and professionals, many of whom work in the lower downtown area of Denver.

Sitting there, drinking my coffee, I thought about my upcoming wedding anniversary. My wife Roberta and I are nearing the end of our second decade of marriage. Like most couples who have been together that long, we have our ups and downs. My perceived need for ED meds is only a symptom of a bigger problem.

Roberta and I have had our issues over the years, some of which involved raising kids. When we got married, Roberta was a widow raising two boys, Freddie, age 12, and Jason, 10. I had never been married and had no experience with kids, but that changed in a hurry. When I married Roberta, I wanted the security of a stable relationship, but I was unprepared for how uptight she could be about relationship matters, by which I mean sex. I admit my inhibitions didn't help the situation, but it has been a tough go of things most of the time. I have always had particular itches I felt I needed to scratch. One time, I ventured a bit too far, and it caused a rift. I still don't like to think about it, much less talk about it.

While that situation looked like a total disaster and betrayal, I maintained my conviction, then as now, that since I have been married to Roberta, I have never had sex with another woman, never touched another woman in a sexual way, never even kissed another woman. That is as true today as it was then. I guess I believed that made it possible for me to say I never cheated on her, but I'm not sure she is convinced of that reality.

Sitting in R&R, I had some time to kill. I decided I would use my day off to play a round of golf. My brother Todd will be here soon, and we like to play a few rounds together every year. He became an avid golfer after he moved to Ohio, and I took it up to have a way to connect with him. I have managed to become proficient enough at it that I can break 100 as often as not. That's satisfactory for most golfers as long as prize money isn't involved.

I used my free time to browse videos on Y'allScreen. I found one by a lady giving a talk at a TED conference. Her topic is about how sex workers create a human connection. I found it intriguing, no doubt, due to the taboo nature of the topic. This lady, who called herself Nicole, explained that as a sex worker, she often spent time with clients who felt isolated and lonely. She stated that men would pay for two, three, or more hours of her time. They might have sex, which she pointed out, on average, only took about five minutes. So, she posed the question, "What are they really paying for?" I agree with her assertion that it is understanding, connection, and acceptance.

Nicole went on to talk about how men are expected to 'man up' because 'big boys don't cry.' She quoted a statistic that eighty percent of suicides are men; she said some of her clients credited her with convincing them not to take their own lives. I must admit that the things she said about how men are expected to behave rang true to me. In the world I occupy, men keep a stiff upper lip, second place is the first loser, and life boils down to every man for himself and God against all. The issue of how you deal with your feelings is seldom addressed in any meaningful way.

It reminded me of my own experience with a sex worker. It came in my mid-20s at one of the legal brothels in Nevada. Being a single guy in Las Vegas with time on my hands, I drove under cover of darkness out to the rural desert area where such places can operate. I went to the door unannounced, and someone escorted me to the parlor. A group of young ladies came out, stood in a line, and introduced themselves by name. I swear to God, I didn't remember a single one of their names as they called them out. I saw one I liked and said, "Her." She took me to her room, and we went through the negotiation. She launched into a discussion of the 'menu,' stating that prices started at $1,500, at which I froze until she continued, "On down." I started breathing again. Keep in mind, this was in the mid-eighties when every casino on the strip had at least a couple of two-dollar Blackjack tables. I ended up spending a few hundred dollars and had a memorable experience. She was a gorgeous lady and super nice. She could tell I was out of my element, and she still made it happen.

I would have taken a fair amount of grief from people I knew if they found out I went to such a place and paid for the experience. I rationalized it by concluding that you always pay for it, one way or another. I started to wonder if patronizing the oldest profession is such a bad idea.

***

The following week, I took an afternoon off to drive out to the dairy farm I grew up on to visit my brother Todd. It would be a mini-family reunion. Todd's son Blaine and 12-year-old grandson Jimmy made the trip with him this year. Roberta was going to spend the evening with her group of girlfriends, so I figured this would be an excellent time to spend an evening with Todd. We only get to see each other when he makes his annual trip to the farm from his home in Steubenville, Ohio. I looked forward to these trips from one year to the next.

Todd is the only one of my three older brothers I ever felt close to, and to be honest, I idolized him. However, the time I could spend with him as a kid was an all too brief experience. When I started school, he moved to the other side of the state to start college. After that, I only got to spend time with him when he came home for Christmas break or a few weeks in the summer, but during those times, he needed to work to earn money for college. He got some of those jobs with the help of our oldest brother, Randy, who worked as a foreman on a road construction crew. But some of those times early in my life still bring back fond memories.

When I got to the farm, Todd was sitting home with Jimmy while Blaine was out riding his horse. They all enjoy the peace and quiet of the farm. Todd bought the place after our parents divorced, and Mom continued to live there until she passed away a little more than 10 years ago. Now, he rents out the barn and pastureland to neighbors, and he comes for a visit for a few weeks every summer.

I asked Todd if he had heard from either of the older brothers since we last spoke. "Not often," he said. "Dean will call to chat from time to time, but I seldom hear from Randy. He's a hermit these days. Have you talked to them?"

"I haven't spoken with Dean in quite a while," I said. "Randy called me out of the blue a couple of months ago, and we talked. To be more accurate, he talked, and I listened while his beer-soaked brain rambled on about how we aren't a close family. I told him that's because half the people in this family think the other half are assholes, and half of them are probably right."

"You might have a point," Todd said with a grin.

While I sat there, Jimmy came in from the other room with a question. "What's a Johnson?"

Todd was caught off guard. "Ah, well, it's ummm…" he stammered. "Why do you ask?"

"I texted one of my friends back home, and he said something about his Johnson. It didn't make sense."

"Well, it's that thing…" Todd looked at me like, *Help me out here.*

"It's like an Anderson, only smaller," I said, pointing to the zipper of my jeans. "A little-known fact."

"Oh," Jimmy said. "Why do they call it that?"

"Well," Todd said. "Some people find it embarrassing to talk about… you know."

"Yeah," I added. "Those f-wording s-word heads are really starting to p-word me off."

Jimmy rolled his eyes. "You guys are weird. I'm going outside."

"I see there's one family tradition that's still intact," I said to Todd.

"What's that?"

"Not being able to talk about… you know," I said. "Do you remember a book that a doctor wrote in the seventies? It was called *Everything You Always Wanted to Know about Sex but Were Afraid to Ask.*"

"Yeah, I think Randy owned a copy," Todd said. "I asked to borrow it, but he said it disappeared."

"That's because I beat you to it. I'm not sure I ever mentioned that fact. I kept it for a while in my room, stuck away in my bookcase. One day, Mom cleaned out my room, and that book grew legs and disappeared. Nothing was ever said about it."

Without a doubt, Mom believed sex was not a suitable topic for youngsters to explore. As for the practical side of sex education for kids, I'm not sure how she conceptualized it happening other than hoping it might be delayed as long as possible. I think she wished there was some angel of wisdom who could get the job done. Although I doubt she associated sex with angels.

"She was sure uptight about it," Todd said. "I guess that's just how people were back in the day."

"You don't have a clue about Mom, do you?"

"What do you mean?"

"After the house you grew up in burned down right before I was born, they built this one slapdash over the years," I said. "The wall between these two bedrooms is paper-thin. I'll tell you this much: I never heard the bed shake, but I heard a lot of discouraging words spoken in that bedroom. I shouldn't say anything more," I went on. "But if there is anything to what I'm thinking, you couldn't handle it. Nobody in this family could. Forget I brought it up."

I held some suspicions about our parents' relationship, of which I didn't have evidence or proof, but if true, they would explain a great deal about our family dynamic.

CHAPTER 2

"Marriage is the death of hope."
– Woody Allen

Driving to work at Crypt-Tech Software Systems the next morning, I dreaded another day of writing one-off programs to move records from one database to another. Crypt-Tech is the third such company I have worked for in the past 15 years, each one being worse than the one before. My boss is a micro-managing bean counter who makes the job feel like being in prison, only with less autonomy and empowerment. I would love to find something else to do, but this is what I trained for, and I am stuck here due to the need for pay and benefits. I'm not sure what kind of work would ever give me a sense of purpose and satisfaction, but from my upbringing, I always regarded those things as secondary considerations. Something that had constantly been hammered into me was the idea that you needed to have a job, a real job. Not some fanciful idea about pursuing your passion or changing the world. No doubt, the fact that my parents grew up during the Great Depression influenced my thinking, as they stressed the importance of financial security. Despite those concerns, I'm ready to chuck it all, set up a kiosk by the side of the road, and sell artisanal pickles to make my way in the world. I figured I paid my dues with a job for all these years, and I'm ready to have a stress-free existence.

I usually make the trip to LoDo via Colfax Avenue from my home in Lakewood. Due to some construction blockages, I opted to take the freeway to work this morning. Now, I'm stuck in a rush hour traffic jam that came at me seemingly out of nowhere. It is incredible to me that the majority of the freeway system around Denver was designed and built before marijuana use was legalized in Colorado. You might have difficulty convincing an out-of-state visitor of that fact.

Sitting in the snarl of rush hour traffic, my radio was tuned to one of the conservative talk show hosts who dominate the airwaves on the AM dial. I will admit that I tend to hold conservative views, but I reserve the right to think things through. Many of my liberal friends would say that a conservative think-tank is a contradiction in terms. Unfortunately, many of my conservative friends don't do much to refute this notion. My friends and family primarily consist of wingnuts, both left-wingnuts and right-wingnuts. I once explored the idea of becoming a Libertarian, but my research into it left me puzzled. Libertarians say they are social liberals but fiscal conservatives. Who pays for all the social liberalism they support? It's often not the people being socially liberal. The only thing that chaps me more than the intellectual arrogance of liberals is the provincial pompousness of conservatives.

Being disenchanted with talk radio, I switched the channel to seventies rock. I was greeted by Sonny and Cher singing *I Got You, Babe*, about a couple going through life hand-in-hand, no hill or mountain we can't climb because I got you, babe…It made me think about Roberta and all the romantic feelings we used to have. I wondered where those went and when.

***

On Saturday morning, I was relaxing over a second cup of coffee, thinking of going to R&R to work on some ideas for my blog. Roberta, not being a fan of coffee, put on some water to heat for tea. "Did you remember the couples conference at church next week?" she asked. It has been on my radar, but I was hoping to find a way to duck out on it.

"Yeah, do you still want to go?" I asked, knowing her answer would be, "Of course."

"Christy and John went last time, and they said it was great," she said, referring to a lady from her Bible study group and her husband. "I don't think it would hurt to spend a little time working on our relationship."

Our relationship, indeed, needs a shot in the arm. I also acknowledge that my enthusiasm for church attendance is low. Those two circumstances appeared to be inextricably linked. Roberta and I have attended church on a regular basis the entire time we have been together, but I'm now ready to pull back a bit, to the extent I could do so without it becoming a source of friction between us. It has been said that the fastest growing religious identity group is the "nones," mostly millennials who check none in the religious preference box. Not far behind are the "dones," those who are older and have been active in churches for a while but now are leaving. For me, it comes down to the fact that I have followed intellectual pursuits most of my life. I am not down with the way many churches want you to check your ability to think at the door simply because critical thinking is antithetical to their worldview. So, for those and other reasons, I decided I was ready for a bit of freedom from religion.

Around mid-morning, I went over to R&R to hang out and think. One way I deal with the stress of my job, and in recent times, the stress of home life, is by writing. I have written a couple of self-published memoirs and am trying to get my blog the attention it deserves. I went to work trying to come up with a relatable and engaging topic. I have been told you should write about what you know. Something that holds your interest and gives you an outlet to discuss your passions. The thing is, I'm not a person who expresses passion about much of anything—part of growing up with relatives who felt it their duty to squelch creativity.

I considered doing a blog about sports. I thought about the one and only World Series played here in the early 2000s. Our team, the Rockies, had a fantastic run at the end of the season, winning 20 of their last 21 games to win the National League pennant. Leave it to us to build an open-air ballpark a mile up in the Rocky Mountains without thinking that the beginning and end of the baseball season can have brutal weather. During the home games in the series, the phrase 'colder than a witch's tit on the shady side of an iceberg' was spoken more than once. But for the most part, the club is usually all but mathematically eliminated from post-season contention early, often around the time their short-season minor league affiliate in Grand Junction starts play around mid-June. I'm pretty certain I don't want to engage people over their closely held beliefs about their favorite sports teams. I have learned that arguing with fans in an online forum is like wrestling in the mud with a pig; you both get dirty, and the pig likes it.

Another thing I might blog about is dysfunctional families. I have no shortage of experience in that department, as my conversation with Todd the other day reminded me. My parents didn't get along at all. They ended up getting divorced, ironically enough, within days of my twenty-first birthday. I have joked that they waited to make sure neither one of them had to risk getting custody of me. I figured out a long time ago that I was an accident when I came along. Todd was 13 and just starting high school. It must have been a shock.

The two oldest brothers, Randy and Dean, have always been, well, different, for lack of a better word. I don't have much to do with either of them. They have both been openly hostile toward me. Perhaps Todd and I bonded because he appreciated that I took some of the pressure off him since he was no longer the youngest.

Randy left home at an early age, by some accounts, at Dad's invitation. He developed street smarts and learned to make his way in the world by eating the other guy's lunch. To say Randy is a reprobate scoundrel is like saying Tom Brady can toss a football, which is to say it is his defining characteristic. He tried to pull me into some of his schemes, but I kept out of them. I felt that just because he was comfortable living his life one step ahead of the sheriff, it in no way obligated me to do so. But I also knew he had it figured out that if anyone was going to get caught, it wasn't going to be him.

Dean is almost as bad. He is headstrong and belligerent. He divorced his wife a dozen or so years earlier and had been married and widowed since. His first wife was a bit fanatical over religion. She once encouraged her pastor to have a talk with Dean to try to put the fear of God in him. Dean responded by telling the pastor, "Every time that goddam bitch gets religion, she's impossible to live with!" Not one to mince words, that Dean. Both he and Randy were off doing their own thing, with varying degrees of legality. That's pretty much the way it's always been.

Todd was the only one who appeared to have his act together. He graduated college, got a good job, worked hard, invested wisely, and retired relatively young. He lived his life halfway across the country from our home growing up, but he had purchased the dairy farm we grew up on and spent a few weeks there every year during his summer breaks from being a middle-school teacher. His wife seldom accompanies him on these trips. She feels she is above the rabble that live out west. I'm sure Todd is okay with being left to enjoy his happy time.

Todd's son Blaine also had some issues in his marriage. He and his wife got divorced not long after Jimmy was born due to some mental health issues she had. Apparently, she wasn't cut out to handle raising kids, and Blaine was left with sole custody of Jimmy.

For my part, it goes without saying that being the youngest of four brothers would always be like going through deep shit on a short horse. What made it even more weird for me was that a couple of them had kids my age. Imagine being an uncle at the kids' table at Thanksgiving dinners. It gave me a unique perspective.

One thing I do know a thing or two about is cats. I have always been a cat person. When I started dating Roberta, she had cats, too. The older of the two she had when we started dating was named Mittens. She was a gray cat with a white face and paws. She had a sweet disposition. Roberta had rescued her from the animal shelter as a kitten, about six months old at the time.

I have always believed you can form accurate opinions about people based on whether they like cats. For example, Mark Twain loved cats, as did Beethoven and Albert Einstein, among others. Some notable individuals who despised cats include Hitler, Atilla the Hun, and, um, well, Hitler—just saying.

So, it might be worthwhile blogging about cats. I'm sure many people can relate; pets are trendy, after all. So, I decided to start a blog page called Life with Cats, where I would describe the zany antics of our furry friends. There was a running joke between Roberta and me that we referred to some of the misadventures with our kitties as CATastrophes. We have a cat we named Valentino because we adopted him on Valentine's Day. He was an adult cat in the rescue shelter, and he immediately bonded with us when we saw him there. So, we took him home, and he fit right in.

One of Tino's quirks is that he will wander off when we let him go outside. It got so bad that we had to put a name tag on his collar with our phone number on it so people around the subdivision would know that we needed to come and pick up our cat.

I published this post and waited to see how it would be received. To put it mildly, it didn't set the world on fire. There weren't any really negative comments; it just didn't capture people's imaginations. A few little old ladies and others from my demographic cohort thought my adventures with Tino were cute and charming but nothing of real substance.

***

Friday evening, Roberta was sitting on the sofa with Mittens curled up in her lap. The needle inserted between Mittens' shoulder blades transported the saline solution under her skin. We had been doing this for Mittens for a few weeks since her kidney function had started to diminish, and for a while, it seemed to help. Now, I could see Roberta had her doubts. She wasn't alone. Valentino was sitting beside her and would reach a paw toward Mittens in what appeared to be a comforting gesture. For their reputation of being independent and aloof, cats can be remarkably empathetic. They can always tell when one of us is not feeling well. Now, it was time to care for Mittens. "Do you think it's time to let her go?" Roberta asked.

"Let her go? As in…?"

"Put her to sleep."

I knew what she meant, but I wanted her to say it anyway. "Maybe," I said, realizing there was no point in postponing the inevitable. I was sitting in a chair holding Ginger, our new seal point Siamese cat who had wandered into our yard as a stray some time ago and made known her intention to adopt us. Three cats were the most we ever had at one time, but it appeared we were heading for a reduction in the feline population.

"I mean, look at her. She's not grooming anymore, and I can tell she doesn't feel good. This isn't the quality of life she's used to," Roberta said. "I'll call the vet in the morning and see when we can take her in."

We scheduled the 'procedure' for Monday at a time when I could take a long lunch break and be with them. We both wanted to be there for her, and we arranged for a private cremation so we could give her a proper burial. The veterinarian who attended us remarked that Mittens had a long, happy life. She recalled the times over the years when we brought the cat in for checkups and shots, and she always seemed to be a happy, healthy cat who has lived to a ripe old age. "If there is such a thing as reincarnation, I want to come back as a cat and live with you two," the vet remarked.

After the vet administered a sedative to Mittens, she fell asleep before being put to sleep, which is the standard procedure. "This is the hardest part of my job," she said before leaving us alone in the room for as long as we needed. As hard as it was for me to experience it, I'm sure it was harder for Roberta. She had Mittens longer than she has had me.

A few days later, the veterinary office sent us a card acknowledging Mittens and included a story about the 'rainbow bridge,' where all pets go when they leave this life. It is touted as a place where they are restored to perfect health and happiness, waiting for the time when their special person comes to be reunited so they can cross the bridge to a blissful afterlife. It sounded like hogwash to me, but I get the need for some people to have the hope of seeing their beloved pet again. To make matters worse, on the radio one evening, I heard the song that came out a few years earlier, a remake by a Hawaiian man singing *Somewhere Over the Rainbow* with a lilting melody and an ethereal feel to it. It made me break down and cry.

Between losing Mittens and the lackluster response to my cat blog, I needed a change of pace. In any event, it looked like I would have to find a more provocative route if I wanted to hit the big time with my writing. I had an idea of what I needed to do and decided that the time had come. If they want controversy, that's what they will get.

CHAPTER 3

"Many a true word hath been spoken in jest."
– William Shakespeare

One topic I make every effort to distance myself from is abortion. I find it is best to permit myself the luxury of a private opinion on the subject. But for the sake of getting noticed as a writer with strong opinions, it would prove to be useful. I tried to frame my argument based on logic rather than emotion, but I feared I had the more difficult (and less popular) position. Still, I gathered my thoughts and assembled them in the shape of a blog post that looked like this:

Some Thoughts on a Major Social Issue

People like to go on and on about their rights, but I never hear anyone talk at length about responsibility. In my mind, if you are going to engage in an activity with a somewhat predictable outcome, your choice is made. Own it. Being of a conservative mindset, I think the core principle is to err on the side of caution. If life does begin at conception, there are consequences. The problem is you can't make the other side see the irrefutable logic of this position. But kick over a nest of sea turtle eggs and watch what happens (hint: they lose their shit).

However, I feel those who favor exceptions for rape and incest are being inconsistent. If your argument is for life beginning at conception, how do you rationalize punishing the child for the sins of the parent? Have the courage of your convictions. I am all for exceptions for the life and health of the mother, and there are possibly religious grounds for them. Too many people take their theological position based on the notion that if they were God, that's the way they would do it. However, people aren't God, and for that, I say 'Thank God.'

Some say you search in vain to find monuments to the greatness of those who can't or won't set aside their own selfish concerns for the sake of the greater good. One thing is certain: if you fight it out in the realm of emotions, it will never be resolved. You end up with more polarization and divisiveness.

I took a good look at what I had written and realized it was enough to make me rethink my position. I figured it would generate discussion, so I published it. Before long, I got taken to task by a lady who, I am guessing, is not a native English speaker. For one thing, she seemed to have the idea that my name was Sebastian, but she butchered the spelling. She said that because I am a man, I didn't have a valid point of view on the subject and would I please STFU? I couldn't let it pass without responding with a personal message:

Thank you for commenting on my post. It's good to know people are interested in my topics. While I respect your right to your opinions, let me tell you a story about a woman I once knew who found herself in an unplanned pregnancy. She was in her mid-40s at the time, as was her husband. She loved kids and was looking forward to the addition to her family. Her husband did not share her joy at the prospect. Their other kids were growing up and moving out, so he did not want to be raising a kid until he was 60. He insisted she 'take care of it' and move on. The woman stood her ground and had her child. The woman was my mother, and if the old man had his way, I would not be here to be enlightened by your towering intellect. So, which one of us should SHUT THE FUCK UP?

I waited for this person to respond to my message. While I waited, the talk radio landscape devolved into a cesspool for conspiracy cranks over an alleged 'deep state,' a global pandemic torpedoed an already shaky presidency, an insurrectionist mob stormed the U.S. Capital over a big lie, and the Supreme Court, because it could, issued a decision that overturned Roe v. Wade. But my blog was starting to attract some attention, and it wasn't as difficult as I thought. I still made every effort to steer clear of the abortion issue and politics in general, which left religion and sex as options. I thought religion might be a topic I was able to remain somewhat neutral on. Since I had the typical indoctrination into protestant theology early in life, I had lately started to question some of those beliefs. Try that in a community of true believers and watch what happens (hint: they lose their shit). In any event, I thought I could be objective about it.

On the work front, I left my previous job with Crypt-Tech. I started doing contract work in health insurance claims processing. I also had a couple of non-profit organizations I freelanced with, helping them out with small data processing programs. Not a great way to make a living, but it would do until my writing started to pay the bills. At least this way, I can work remotely and somewhat pick my hours.

I started thumbing through the list of videos on Y'allScreen, which was my default escape mechanism. It had become semi-addictive of late. For supposedly being meant for amateurs to upload clips of themselves crashing skateboards or teasing their cats with toys and laser lights, I was finding there are a lot of high-quality content providers out there. I started out searching for belly dancers. It's something I have always been attracted to. I happen to have always liked women with trim midriffs who didn't mind showing them off. It probably started when I was young, growing up around cowgirls and farmer's daughters who often wore shirts they would pull up and tie in front.

Perhaps owing to those searches, along with videos I had stumbled upon, like the one featuring a sex worker from a while back, the algorithm pegged me as someone who would be receptive to seeing more, shall we say, adult-oriented content. I got a lot of recommendations for this channel from a Nevada sex worker who called herself Alice Modicum. I assumed it was a nom deplume since people in that space never use their actual name.

She was a cute, bubbly lady who projected a sex-positive attitude, like a lot of the channels I subscribed to. I was fascinated by people who were open to their sexuality and were not inhibited or uptight about discussing it. How different from my reality that was.

There were a few ladies in the sex worker space who had channels, not all of whom were as polished and wide-ranging as Alice. Many of them appeared to want to vent about the shabby treatment they got from potential 'clients' who would nit-pick about prices and services. I think a lot of them brought this treatment on themselves by their attitude without realizing it. Some of the comments on their videos were brutal. One such comment on a video by a lady who appeared rather skanky and brassy waxed poetic. It carried the title 'Ode to a Hoe' and started with:

Shall I compare thee to a (truck stop) urinal?
Thou art more grody and more festering.

From there, it started to get nasty. A short time later, her channel was taken down. I guess not everyone is up for such abuse.

One thing Alice mentioned in one of her videos is that before becoming a full-time sex worker, she worked as an instructor in a BDSM club in New York. It got my attention, as I have long held a fascination for this realm, which is quite possibly also related to an influence from my past. The problem is, with the conservative crowd I run with, I would be crazy to make mention of it. Alice usually appeared provocatively dressed in the thumbnail photos for her videos. I was becoming intrigued as to whether Alice Modicum might be an outlet for the exploration of this curiosity.

***

When Todd and his crew came for the annual visit, we decided to go to a Rockies game. Baseball had all but shut down for a couple of years during the pandemic. It was good to enjoy an afternoon at the ballpark, even though one thing which remained consistent was my team's disturbing habit of getting their butts kicked. I have been a Rockies fan for so long that I think of fantasy sports as a hit with runners in scoring position.

After the game, we went to a sports bar for drinks and a bite to eat. My great-nephew Jimmy, the one I had given an anatomy lesson to a while back, had just finished his first year of college. He had played football in high school and had shown some promise until he blew out his knee and never got enough playing time to attract the attention of recruiters. I asked him if he missed playing.

"I can't say I do," he said. "Football wasn't much fun in high school. We lost more than half of our games. What stinks is, lately, they have been a whole lot better."

Without realizing it, Jimmy had opened a door I was pathologically incapable of not walking through. Todd and Blaine knew it and glanced at each other with a look that said, "Oh boy, here it comes."

"Now let me get this straight," I said. "You're saying when you were there, the team sucked, and after you left, things got better. Okay, now think about that, Jimmy."

Jimmy got that look, as if he desperately wanted to crack a smile, but there was no way in hell he was going to give me the satisfaction. I live for that look. "Glad I could provide some clarity for you," I said with a smirk.

"You suck!" he said. We all had a hearty laugh, sort of at Jimmy's expense, but he took it in his usual good-natured way.

It was a light-hearted moment in a family that has had all too few of them recently. We've had more than our share of tough times lately, as if things aren't bad enough for me at home these days. These past six years have been unreal, like a fog of war experience. My brother Dean passed away a few months back. We had never connected in a meaningful way. He and I didn't see eye to eye on much of anything. He appeared to be mellowing a bit in recent years. We spoke occasionally but seldom about anything substantial. When I got the call that Dean had passed, it was a surprise, but I can't say it was a shock. It was what it was.

Our oldest brother, Randy, had also died about five years ago. If Dean and I were not on the best of terms, Randy and I were totally estranged. When he passed, his daughter wrote his obituary, which I thought was the most self-serving load of crap I had ever read. She was basically reiterating his belief that he was more sinned against than sinning. I read her comments as a thinly veiled swipe at the family for the shoddy treatment we gave this saintly man who would give anyone the shirt off his back. If I could have put my two cents worth in, I would have added that he never did anything for anybody that he didn't expect to come back to him in spades.

My marriage to Roberta had passed the quarter-century mark, and our relationship was becoming a hodge-podge of ho-hum. I can't deny things were rough between Roberta and me. We had plenty of difficulties with the boys and in our own relationship. I felt overwhelmed by parenting challenges. Things got to the point where we had to do some counseling with a family therapist. As far as our sex life was concerned, we had entered the once-a-month club, and that was pushing it at times. I honestly wasn't feeling it, and I can't be sure she was either. I know a lot of people who, if they were in our shoes, would have bailed out and gone their separate ways years ago. I'm not sure what was keeping us in it other than the stigma of a failed marriage and the judgment of people we know, particularly the church crowd. I'm not at all sure it's worth it.

We have had our times of trials and tribulations like any married couple. I was starting to feel that Roberta and I were becoming adversaries in the relationship department, a feeling I never thought I would have to deal with. I was starting to wonder if there was an angel of wisdom out there who might help me deal with all these conflicts. At least I had a steady diet of Y'allScreen videos to distract me. I figured Roberta wouldn't be pleased if she saw some of what I was watching, but really, how much harm could it do? Really.

***

In an attempt to learn more about some taboo subjects related to sexuality, I subscribed to Alice Modicum's Y'allScreen channel. I knew I would catch hell if the wife saw me watching it. But Roberta is less than enthusiastic when it comes to conversing about such topics, so I could either repress it or look elsewhere. Alice was matter-of-fact in her view of what a healthy outlook on sex was all about. I found myself being drawn in by her, though I found her presentation a bit grating owing to her exaggerated cutesy voice and mannerisms. She also pointed out the fact that she stood a mere four feet eight inches tall. She had no discernable physical augmentations. Simply cute, petite, and sex-positive. Well, it was enough to hold my interest.

One of the offerings at the brothels that I heard Alice mention on her streams was the Girlfriend Experience or GFE. This is something for which clients pay top dollar, and they will engage the services of a lady for a whole day or perhaps an entire weekend, paying out the wazoo for the thrill. We are talking about five and six-figure paydays for the ladies who excel at this skill. One might only hope the sex lasted more than five minutes.

At one point, Alice said she was scheduling sessions for her next tour at the brothel she worked at. She suggested that anyone wanting to spend time with her send an email describing what they were interested in doing, and she would do her best to make it happen. I was intrigued. What if I could present my deepest, darkest fantasies to someone who wouldn't judge me for wanting something a little bit off-center? On a whim, I decided to send her an email describing all the things I would like to do with her if I were somehow able to get to her location.

Alice had a presence on a site called Just Our Intimacy, where she could say and show things she couldn't get away with on Y'allScreen. Other Y'allScreen providers caught my eye. Many of them also had pages on Just Our Intimacy. It appeared they used Y'allScreen as a pointer to their real side hustle on JOI.

One of those whom I started following was Diane Marie. I found her on Y'allScreen in a video in which she was modeling a sexy golf outfit with the teaser title *Bra or No Bra*. It was a fun presentation in which she made a production out of removing her bra to show the effects of her appearance in the outfit.

Diane described herself as a wife, mother, and MILF. She had built a site where it was safe to discuss fantasy situations. Unlike Alice, Diane was not an actual sex worker in the sense of actually having sex with people who found her sexy, which, at the time I discovered her, numbered in the tens of thousands. I would describe her as part of the NATO alliance, as in, no action, talk only. But that's okay; the talk was stimulating, and she did a lot of it while nude, so there's that. She was quite approachable and friendly. She posted a video every morning where she would discuss a fantasy situation, and she almost always made a point of taking her boobs out so her followers could feast their eyes. It cannot be overstated how sexy she looks with bare breasts, IMHO.

On Diane's private site, we can exchange direct messages, and we got into some lengthy discussions. I asked her how explicit I should be in describing my fantasies. She said I could be as explicit as I wanted and that she created this site to be a safe, nonjudgmental area for expression. I was intrigued, so I dashed off a quick scenario where we would have an encounter that would culminate with us in a private pound session where we can, as I recall putting it, 'fuck like sex-starved forbidden fruit addicts who are married, but not to each other.'

A while later, she responded with a voice clip in my DM, saying she enjoyed what I had shared with her, and she loved the line about fucking like sex-starved forbidden fruit addicts who are married but not to each other. Hearing her say that was stimulating, and I have to admit it piqued my interest.

I was in the mood to explore the possibilities with Diane some more, so I sent her a new fantasy situation. I started typing into the app:

I ring the doorbell and hear a voice from inside the house telling me to come in. I don't see anyone, and as I walk in, I see a door slightly open and a light on inside. I step in and find you there in the bathroom in a skimpy negligee. I'm somewhat stunned but amused at the same time. You let the garment fall away, leaving yourself clad in only a pair of thong panties. You give me a playful look and say, "Is that a pipe wrench in your pocket, or are you just glad to see me?"

I smile as I reach into my pants and whip it out. "It's a pipe wrench," I say. "I'm the plumber you called. And I'm glad to see you. What can I do for you?"

"I saw your ad on TV, and I thought I could use your services," you say. "Things are all backed up, not flowing the way they should."

"We'll have to do something about that," I tell you. I walk over to you, and we embrace and start kissing. I spin you around and let my hands roam over the front of your baked body. It builds up to a hot and heavy session that could lead to only one thing…

At that point, I decided to hand it off to her. I hit send on the message. Only after I saw the post did I spot the typo. I tried to pull it back, but there is no way in this app to edit or even delete a post, so I sent another message:

"BTW, I meant to say your naked body, but I'm guessing you knew that."

I heard back from her in a short while.

"LOL, no, I didn't pick up on that right away," she said.

"It had been a long day of errands and responding to messages, and I was tired and not thinking about it. It wasn't until I saw your follow-up message that I figured out it wasn't about my being sunburned or something."

I decided to have some fun with it. I sent another message that I was sure would leave no doubt:

"I bend you over and plunge my naked manhood into your naked womanhood, and the naked juices flow as we collapse in a naked heap of naked flesh, and you nakedly writhe in naked spasms of naked lust, and I'm left gazing in amazement at your naked body. There, I think I have established there is a certain amount of nakedness involved." I hit send and waited to see her response.

Soon, she messaged me back:

"LOL, that was hot. I'm a little confused, though. Were we supposed to be naked?"

Oh, she's good, I thought. I liked her sense of humor.

For whatever reason, I decided to send Alice Modicum another email and ask about her virtual offerings. She wrote back and said she remembered the message I sent her before about some of my ideas along the BDSM theme and that she would be interested in chatting about it. She sent me a rundown of online session availability and prices for what she called 'virtual dates,' complete with a list of packages that could be purchased as a block of time at a reduced per-hour rate. Even that wasn't what I would call cheap, with the most economical package approaching four figures. Still, I was more than a little intrigued and decided I would get back to her.

Little did I know, I was about to grab a tiger by the tail.

CHAPTER 4

"A writer is a world trapped in a person."
– Victor Hugo

At breakfast one morning, Roberta told me about an amusing incident from her weekly Bible study group. She and her BFF, Eileen Tudor-Wright, met at the home of another lady in the group, Christy Hannity. Christy's hubby was going in for a colonoscopy the following day, and he was making the necessary preparations. Eileen got the idea to stage a group prayer gathering for him, complete with a 'laying-on of hands' to the area in question for added moral support. For as uptight and traditional as Eileen could be, I had to give them props for having the sense of humor to do that and the awareness of it being pretty darn funny.

***

Despite how much I enjoyed my occasional DMs with Diane, one thing she would not do is chat one-on-one in real-time, either on webcams, Zoom meetings, or any other form of instant messaging. She explained that she didn't have the time. I understood that and also the strain it might put on her personal life. She said if I was looking for something more interactive, I might try engaging the services of a sex and relationship coach. I thought about it, but I wasn't sure if it would be helpful since the person I am in a relationship with would most likely not be interested in such an arrangement. Roberta had her own views on what constituted a proper dialog on relationship matters, and it was most definitely not with a third party who might talk about actual sexual situations.

Diane suggested if I were interested in getting in touch with my own feelings and responses, I investigate a type of provider called a sexological bodyworker. "Wow, that's a mouthful," I replied.

A short time later, Diane messaged me back: "If you're lucky, you might find one that's more than a mouthful," she said, adding some LMAO emojis. That's what I get for messaging someone with a sense of humor like mine. Diane sent me a link to a directory of these providers.

I did some research on it and found there is an association to which these practitioners belong. I clicked the link to the online directory and found a bunch of them listed. There were people of every imaginable size, shape, and state of gender fluidity. I saw some terminology I wasn't familiar with, like somatic sex coaching, which they say means pertaining to the body. There was a block of items that most of them listed, like kink-positive, fantasy exploration, BDSM, boundaries and communication skills, pleasure mapping, masturbation coaching, virtual sessions, and something called the wheel of consent. I scrolled through the listings, and one caught my attention, to say nothing of my eye. She calls herself Sophia Angelique, she/her. I felt drawn to her for some reason. I bookmarked her and decided she might be someone with whom I could work.

***

Winter was fighting to muscle its way in on fall, and it appeared fall might give up early this year. As I sat in R&R one afternoon, I saw a lady I had become acquainted with, an Asian lady named Sue Nami. She often came alone, but from time to time, she was with a man I assumed was her partner, lover, shack job, call it what you want. Sue struck me as a bit of a radical politically, like she never met a liberal cause she didn't love.

As the snow piled up outside from the late autumn blizzard that decided to dump on us, Sue sat looking at her iPad with an annoyed look on her face. "These idiots!" she said.

"Excuse me," I said, glancing in her direction. "Is something the matter?"

"All these people who deny climate change," she said. "Whenever there is a snowstorm somewhere, they tell climate activists they don't know what they are talking about. They don't understand the difference between weather and climate. What's the word when they mix it all up?"

"Conflate?" I suggested.

"Yes, they conflate weather and climate. They are not the same thing."

"Right, I've heard those arguments. They say climate is like personality, and weather is like mood, something like that," I offered.

"Exactly," Sue said. "It's not rocket surgery." I looked at her a bit quizzically. "Was that a non sequitur?" she asked.

"More like a mixed metaphor," I offered. "But I know what you mean." I threw in a comparison of my own. "Kind of like the way some people conflate love and sex."

Sue looked puzzled. "What do you mean? They're the same."

"Really? You think so?" I asked. "I'm pretty sure they're not." Now, I had to think of an example to prove my point. "Remember back in the early 2000s when some pop-tart woke up in a Vegas hotel room having just married a close friend? She said she wanted to see what it felt like to be married. It made me want to shake her. If you want to know what it is like to be married, you have to get out of bed and face the day year in and year out because you stood up and made a promise that you would. That's when you find out what it feels like to be married." I'm not sure Sue was picking up what I was laying down, but I knew only too well from my experience with my own family, marriage, stepkids, the whole ball of wax.

I looked across the way and saw my friend Stu Pidasso. He is the manager of the bookstore here, and his favorite section is the one on religion. I have known Stu for years. He is cut from the same cloth as the aging boomer couple who own Roasters and Readers. No wonder they chose

Stu to manage the place. He's a firm adherent of traditional evangelical fundamentalism, along with young Earth creationism. Stu lives with his significant mother. Actually, it is more accurate to say she lives with him since he is gainfully employed. His tribe was very much into constitutional principles, though they couldn't really quote any part of it other than the first and second amendments, and then only in paraphrase. The fact is, Stu has no shortage of education; he just never let it go to his head. He is, without a doubt, the most ignorant educated person I know.

Stu was busy setting up a display of the latest book by his favorite evangelist, Dr. John Daniel. Stu told me about hearing Dr. Daniel talk on the radio recently, where he told the story of a man who was out on the town on business and met a woman in a bar. They ended up in a motel, and you know. Well, the guy wakes up the next morning, and the woman is gone. He goes to the bathroom and finds a message in lipstick on the mirror saying, 'Welcome to the AIDS family.' "Isn't it sick?" he asked. "What happens to this guy? Will he give it to his wife? What a mess."

I told him this is a well-known urban legend which never actually happened. Plus, it doesn't work that way. But I also know Dr. Daniel and people of his ilk would never pass up a chance for heavy-handed moralizing, and truth be damned. I had actually been a fan of this particular preacher at one time, but I found way too many examples of this playing fast and loose with the facts that I became put off by it.

***

The next day, I decided to get in touch with Sophia, the sexological bodyworker whom I had located with Diane's help. She is in her mid-to -late 20s, about five feet six inches tall, slender but shapely, with long, honey-blonde hair and hazel eyes. Her nose is slightly upturned, and her lips are somewhat heart-shaped and look deliciously kissable. She offered a free 30-minute Zoom call to get acquainted and see if her services would be a good fit for me. She operates out of the Los Angeles area, and she stated she is willing to do sessions online or in person. Since I don't have a reason to get out to LA, I decided that online would have to do. Sophia specializes in something she refers to as somatic sex counseling, and the sky's the limit as far as the topic of conversation is concerned, drawing the line at kiddie porn.

"That is a good line to draw," I said. "Tell me more about what somatic sex counseling means."

"Somatic means pertaining to the body," she explained. "In a session conducted in person, it can involve one-way touch, as in me to you, or online, I would guide you through the sensations of self-touch and the results of that."

"Sounds a little outside my comfort zone at the moment," I said. "I'm not sure I would even be down with sending someone a picture of my junk. I'm about as uptight as they come."

"Then what can I help you with?" Sophia asked.

"I just need someone to have a rational discussion with about all of these taboo subjects so I can figure out if I'm normal," I told her.

"We can work on it," she replied. "Doesn't your discomfort with talking about sex get in the way of expressing passion in your relationship?"

"Oh, you have no idea," I said. "The simple truth is passion has never been part of my life in any sense of the word. It has a lot to do with my weird family dynamic growing up," I told her. "Being the youngest, I was subjected to a lot of harassment by my older siblings and, to no small extent, their spouses and kids. I think they felt threatened by the fact I still had the potential to surpass them in life. If I were to exhibit a passion or even enthusiasm for anything, it would be discouraged pretty quickly. I guess they figured putting me in my place would make them look good by comparison. So, I've always been pretty guarded about revealing what interests me."

"Can you elaborate on that?" Sophia asked.

"It always appeared to me that things that were perfectly fine for everyone else in the family to do or say became a cause for comment if I did them," I went on. "Maybe it was my position as the youngest in the family that made me a target for the others, and perhaps I was more sensitive because of it. I always got a lot of ribbing and snickering comments from my brothers and their kids if I displayed any romantic inclinations toward anyone. Still, they had wives and girlfriends; hell, a couple of them had both at the same time, but no one said anything about that."

"What kind of work do you do?" she asked.

"I'm semi-retired from the tech industry," I responded. "I occasionally do some freelance work for non-profits that I think are worthwhile. I never enjoyed that career, but it was what I trained for, and I drifted along for several years. Lately, my interests have turned toward writing. I have a blog, and I enjoy coming up with engaging narratives and stories."

I can see the gears start to turn behind Sophia's eyes. "If you are uncomfortable talking about your sexual feelings, could you write about them? Say, come up with a story that brings up those topics and lets you control how you present it?"

"I suppose it might be a thing," I said. "I admit I have enjoyed reading erotica, more than watching it in movies."

"Do you watch porn at all?" Sophia asked.

"Nothing you would call hard-core," I stated. "I'm okay with adult-oriented movies if they have some discernable plot. I have sufficient respect for good storytelling that I will resist efforts to subvert it. Hence, a lack of interest in run-of-the-mill porn. I guess I would say I'm into eroticizing situations more than objectifying people."

She continues. "Can you tell me about something that turns you on?"

"What use would you make of such information?" I ask.

"I might try to turn you on," she replied.

"It's not inconceivable that you could do that; just not sure why you would want to."

"That's my job," she stated. "So, tell me, what does Alex Anderson find sexy?"

"Well, for one thing, belly dancing."

"That's an easy one. I am actually quite accomplished in that art form. I even have an outfit. Would you like to see it?"

"Sounds intriguing," I say. "Does it show your belly?"

"Yes. And my legs," she added.

"Well then, definitely."

"Great, sit tight, and I'll get changed."

When she reappeared, she was stunningly beautiful. Her skirt was slit up both sides, revealing a pair of long, shapely legs, and the top showed just the right amount of cleavage. Her abdomen was breathtaking; she started some simple music playing, and I sat transfixed as she began to move. She performed some basic hip lifts followed by a shimmy, followed by belly rolls. She has an absolutely magnificent stomach. I found myself getting turned on involuntarily. And by that, I mean hard. She was clearly enjoying her ability to use her body to express her sexuality and the fact that I took notice. I found myself wishing I was there so I could reach out and feel her tawny skin, caress the flatness of her beautiful stomach, and kiss her belly button. I could get lost in her navel, never to be heard from again, and I wouldn't care.

"You are magnificent, truly lovely," I told her as she concluded her presentation.

"Thank you," she said. "Now, you owe me a story."

CHAPTER 5

"The mind, once stretched by a new idea, never returns to its original dimensions."
– Ralph Waldo Emerson

I sat staring at a blank screen, trying to come up with a story like Sophia asked. It made sense to approach it this way. I can make it about anything I want to and involve characters who would be different from people I would typically talk to. People I would feel comfortable talking to about things which made me extremely uneasy. Here, I can be with people who wouldn't judge me, and I would let it all out.

I tried to think of a situation I could use. I recalled an incident from years ago before I met Roberta when I was in a 'gentlemen's club' setting and became friendly with a dancer at the club. I pranked her once in a playful way and got a laugh from her, and we hit it off. Perhaps this could be a springboard for my tale. I don't recall her name, but for purposes of this narrative, it's not important. I'll call her Allie. In the process, I would create an alter ego that would be my voice. In addition to bringing out some of my deep-seated longings for airing some of my repressed sexual feelings, I could delve into some of my closely held beliefs about my family and other issues from the past that have become stumbling blocks for me.

I debated about writing this story using my real name but decided it wouldn't hurt since it would be written for an audience of one. Overall, it sounded like a sensible approach, so I dug in.

Confessions
By Alex Anderson

Allie is a bright, ambitious young woman with a goal and a plan. For now, her plan involved getting a job, and the only thing she could find was serving cocktails at a roadside tavern called Big Dick's Midway Inn. She was trying to support herself and save up enough money to start her own business someday. Her idea was to open an online store to sell artisanal pickles. Her dream of Internet billionairehood was within her grasp. Everyone should have a dream to work towards.

The Midway Inn didn't have a great reputation. It was more or less an open secret that it was a low-rent whorehouse. There was a well-known joke around the area about a man who told his friend that you could go to this place and for twenty bucks, they would give you a sandwich and a beer and take you in the back and get you laid. The friend asked the guy if he had ever been there, and he replied, "No, but my sister has."

As for Big Dick, he is not one to show his face. In fact, some people doubt he even exists. Others swear he does and will assure anyone who will listen that he lives up to his name in more ways than one. He trusts the day-to-day operations of the business to his assistant, a loathsome son of a motherfucker named P. Oliver deFleur, whom everyone calls P.O. for short.

Allie was working her shift one evening when P.O. pointed to the stage where the strippers were working and told her she was on in five minutes. "Oh, no," Allie said, "I'm not a dancer, I'm a waitress."

"You're whatever I say you are, you little cunt," P.O. said. "Now strut your boney ass out there and get naked by the end of the third song." Allie shrugged and got psyched up to put herself on display. Not that it was a big deal. She had put a lot of work into her body and didn't mind showing it off.

Thus began Allie's career as a dancer at Big Dick's. As she got more accustomed to her new role, from time to time, she noticed a man who appeared to be paying considerable attention to her. He was different from most of the guys at this place. He wasn't grabby or leering like a lot of the customers who would hang out around the stage. He would watch appreciatively as she did her routine; he was always polite, and he tipped well. He would usually go off to a table in the back, have a drink or two, and walk out. He always came alone, and he always left alone. It made Allie curious.

On this particular evening, Allie was feeling apprehensive. She was in danger of not pulling her quota for the week, an outcome which could have dire consequences. As she took the stage for her first set, she saw the man she had noticed before, but this time, he was sitting front and center by the stage. She welcomed the chance to have his attention. She shed more and more clothes and started playing to him to get his attention. But for some reason, he seemed oblivious to her presence. She was confused, so she made herself more available to him. She got down on her knees in front of him and arched her body back so he would get a good look at her lean legs, her undulating belly, and firm breasts. Still, he didn't appear to notice. His blank stare settled on nothing in particular. Allie was determined she was going to get a rise out of him one way or another. She reached out and took his glasses off; she placed them under her boobs and lifted them up. Still nothing. She folded up the glasses and rubbed them on her crotch, smearing them with her girl goo. She pressed her nipples in the center of each lens and placed them back on him. Suddenly, he sat bolt upright and, with a look of wide-eyed amazement, shouted, "I CAN SEE, I CAN SEE!" He grinned and gestured with a look of "Got you" as Allie sat back on her heels and playfully swatted at him. They shared a good laugh as those around the stage applauded the miracle they had witnessed. The man stood up and placed a couple of bills on the stage and went to his customary table in the back.

Allie decided it was time to get to know him. After she gathered her tips and put herself back together, she walked over to his table and said, "Hi, I'm Allie."

"Craven Moorehead, pleased to make your acquaintance," he said and invited her to sit with him. "I guess now is the time to ask what someone nice like you is doing in a place like this," he said.

"I could ask the same of you," Allie replied.

"Then this would be the part where I tell you about how my wife doesn't understand me," he said. "When I come here, I can escape to a fantasy land where there are sexy, attractive people who aren't threatened by sexuality and can jettison all the hang-ups and inhibitions."

"Is that what you are looking for here? Sex?" she asked.

He shrugged. "Is it possible?"

"Well, let's just say that sign over the bar isn't as much of a joke as some people would have you think it is," she said. He looked at the sign she pointed to, which read LIQUOR UP FRONT, POKER IN THE REAR.

"Intriguing," he said with a chortle. "But I'm not that kind of a guy."

"Too bad," Allie responded with a wistful sigh. "The thing is, I need to come up with $1,500 by morning, or P.O. is going to take it out of my hide, and that is putting it nicely."

Moorehead reached into his pocket, pulled out a roll of bills, and peeled off 15 of them. He slid them across the table under his hand. "And what can that get me?" he asked.

Allie looked astonished. Then she thought about it. "Are you a cop?"

"No," he said, shaking his head.

"Good, because right now, I would do anything for that," she said.

"Great, come over and paint my house," he smirked.

"Seriously, what are you thinking?"

"We can just talk."

"Really. Talk," she said. "About sex?"

"Considering I'm not remotely comfortable talking about sex with anyone I know, yeah, it would be stimulating."

Allie glanced across the room and saw P.O. peering at them from his perch near the end of the bar. "Alright, but to keep up appearances, I would feel more comfortable if we go back there," she said, pointing to the beaded curtain at the back of the room.

"Fine," he said as he released his hold on the cash so she could pick it up.

As they made their way to the back, Allie looked over at P.O. and gave him the signal to let him know she was going to be busy for a while. P.O. scowled at her but nodded and waved her off. They went to a room with a bed, a couple of chairs, and a small table and sat down. Allie tried to think of a good way to start the conversation. "Do you want to tell me about the first time you had sex?" she asked.

"Oh, gosh, I haven't thought about that in ages," he said. "I remember I was terrified. It was late at night, it was dark. I was alone…" A grin slowly spread across his face.

Allie buried her face in her hands and groaned. "I can see this is going to be a long night," she said.

"Yeah, that's an old joke, but so am I," he said. "My mom always used to say, 'There's no fool like an old fool.' Of course, she was talking about my dad."

"So, sex never came up in your family?" Allie asked.

"Well, I'm here, and I have three siblings, so it came up at least four times. All of our birthdays are in the late summer, so what does that tell you?"

"That there were some cold winters back in the day?" she responded.

"Yeah, I hear that a lot. But considering our age range spans two decades, it might be safe to conclude winter isn't all that was 'frigid' back then." He continued, "Mom had no use for men. I always thought it was because my dad was such a jerk. But over the years, I've suspected she preferred women but couldn't act on it. At that time and place, people did what was expected of them, which was mainly to get married and raise a family. She appeared to be a happy person, but I'm not sure if she ever found the fulfillment she was looking for. Believe me, it's not something I can bring up at a family reunion.

"I am a little bit more open-minded than most people I know," he went on. "My wife is more set in her ways. I have a few kinks to work out while she's industrial-strength vanilla. I messed up once in a situation that looked way worse than it was. I had a hard time forgiving myself for making her feel like she wasn't good enough. Maybe I never actually did." He started to think maybe he was laying it on thick, so he tried to lighten up a bit. "Did you know researchers have identified a link between a certain food and a sharp drop in libido?" he asked her.

"What food would that be?" she asked.

"Wedding cake," he replied.

Allie smiled and shook her head. She was starting to see he used his sense of humor to cover up some deep sadness which he was either unable or unwilling to express, but she could tell it was there. "What happened?" she asked.

"With my wife? It's complicated. Our biggest problem is communication. It isn't easy to express things when you feel repressed and guilty. I've done things out of a need to explore, which could have been thought of as cheating, though at the time, I didn't think it was. I suppose there is a way of looking at it that makes it appear to be so. That is the way she chose to look at it. From my perspective, it was kind of like having ulcers without being rich and powerful because I got all the grief with none of the supposed benefits." He continued, "It was rough for a while. Forty years of wandering in the wilderness would be preferable to what it took to get back to square one."

"Why did you stick with it?" Allie wanted to know.

"Because I said I would," he replied.

"Not because you love her?" Allie asked.

"That too. Probably... mostly that," he said. "I still believe in marriage, even though most people nowadays think of it as little more than a government registry of friends with benefits. Maybe I'm only being stubborn, like wanting to show that I succeeded where so many others haven't."

"Like your parents?" she asked.

Moorehead nodded. "My wife is a good person," he continued. "We have had our ups and downs over the years. I was ready to walk away not long ago, but something happened, and it appeared like she was trying to reconnect. I'm not sure what her issues are; they might be religious hang-ups, body image issues, or past traumas. Any number of things, I guess," he said.

"Do you have any of those issues?" Allie asked him.

"You could say that. When I come here, it's different. When I talk to you, I can assume you are comfortable with your sexuality since that is what you put forth. I feel safe, like this is a judgment-free zone."

"Well, you don't appear to be judging me for what I do," Allie said. "Whatever you call that."

"Some might call it 'sex worker.'"

"Is that what I am?"

"It's a thing. The first time I thought about it in that way was after I saw a Y'allScreen video. It was a lady giving a TED talk about the way sex workers make a human connection with people who otherwise wouldn't have an outlet for those feelings. The gist of her talk was that, as a society, we have some seriously flawed ideas of what it means to be a functioning adult, particularly for men. I started to see how important connection can be, and how it was a legitimate need being fulfilled. It started to sound pretty good to me."

"Are you happy?" Allie asked him.

"Content might be a more accurate description."

"Is that enough?"

"It will do. How about you?"

"You would think there should be something more to life. But this place isn't a great environment," she said.

"I think you would be fantastic as a 'sex worker,'" he said. "But if you are serious about it, there is only one place in this country you can ply that trade in the open, and that's Nevada."

"Tell me more," she said.

"Well, they call places like these ranches or brothels there, and they're legal."

"Have you ever been to one?"

"No, but my sister has," he grinned.

"You're terrible," she said.

"You have no sense of humor," he shot back.

"I think I proved otherwise out on stage."

"True enough," he said. "Actually, I have been to one of the ranches, though it has been more years ago than I care to think about. In those days, $1,500 could get you the ultimate party package. Now, it gets you on a waiting list to start the negotiation."

"And you know this because…?" Allie teased.

"Suffice it to say I do my research," he replied. "Hey, I can dream, can't I? Anyway, you might want to look into it. I think you would be successful if you were serious about it."

Allie decided she would think about it.

They talked for a long time. He enjoyed the experience of having a mature conversation with an intelligent, attractive lady. As it was getting toward morning, Allie asked if there was anything else he wanted. He shook his head. "You've been great. I do appreciate you spending time with me."

"There must be something I can do to earn my keep," she said. "Would a kiss be okay?"

He thought long and hard about it. "Maybe."

This is incredible, Allie thought. He had paid her all this money, and she was practically having to seduce him for a kiss. "I want to kiss you," she said. He nodded. She kissed him, and he let himself be kissed, for a while. Then he started to kiss back. Eventually, he took ownership of the kiss, and Allie allowed herself to be kissed. When it was over, he looked at her and smiled. It was a sad smile, like when you know you are seeing a friend for the last time. He took the remainder of the roll of bills from his pocket and placed it in her hand.

"Do give some thought to Nevada," he said. "I think it would do you good. You might want to do it sooner rather than later. Otherwise, I'll keep coming back, hoping to find you here, and we both know what would happen."

"Would that really be so bad?" she asked.

He took a deep breath and let it out with a sigh. "I don't know. I honestly don't know. I just know I should go home."

He leaned over and kissed her cheek, noting that it tasted salty. Allie watched as he walked across the parking lot, got into his car, and drove off into the reddish-orange sunrise.

Allie thought about what Moorehead had told her. She was tempted to make the break but didn't know if she could muster the nerve to make it happen. She thought about the human connection she had made with the man and how important it appeared to be to him. It occurred to her there might be more important things than stripping for strangers and turning the occasional trick. Maybe even more important than artisanal pickles. She felt she needed a sign, something that would tell her for sure it was time to move on. It wasn't long before it came. Someone came bursting in the door to the main entrance. "BIG DICK'S COMING, BIG DICK'S COMING!" they shouted. People started to scatter. Allie had never seen the place empty out so fast. She started to leave when P.O. stopped her.

"New girl's gotta stay; that's what he's here for. Now get back there," he growled, pointing to the beaded curtain.

Allie waited in the corner by the bed to see what would happen next. Suddenly, the door burst open, and an enormous man stepped in, hardly able to clear the top of the doorway without ducking his head. He looked like a mountain man on steroids, with a bushy beard and long hair, wearing a flannel shirt and dirty jeans. He took one look at Allie and growled, "Take your clothes off and get on the bed! I've only got time for a quickie, and I'm gonna get what I came for."

Allie complied, and in no time, he was on top of her, all three-hundred-plus pounds of him. What he did barely qualified as a wham, bam, thank you, ma'am, and afterward, he gathered his clothes, pulled what cash he could find from his pockets, and tossed it in front of her on the bed. As he raced to get dressed, Allie thought he wasn't all that bad and said, "Hey, what's the rush? I'm game for a rematch if you are."

The man turned to her with a look of wide-eyed panic on his face. "Are you out of your mind? Big Dick's coming!" he said and bolted out the door.

Nevada, here I come, Allie thought.

THE END

CHAPTER 6

"Oh, what a tangled web we weave when first we practice to deceive."
– Sir Walter Scott

"Wow, I did not see that coming," Sophia said as she began telling me about her experience with the story I had written for her. "So, this three-hundred-pound mountain man is afraid of Big Dick. That's hilarious."

"Oh, yeah, that part came from a beer commercial I saw ages ago. My superpower is I never forget a good joke. I will find a way to use it somehow," I told her.

"Well, I guess I better watch out so I'm not the butt of any jokes," she deadpanned. I almost had to bite my fist to keep from issuing a snide response, and she knew it. Damn, she's good.

"I assume you are Craven Moorehead," she said.

"For pretty much my whole adult life."

Sophia lowered her chin and peered at me over the top of her reading glasses. "In the story," she said.

"Oh. Yes."

"It's engaging and fun to read," she went on. "I couldn't put it down. Curious how you told it from the lady's point of view."

"She's more interesting," I offered.

"Don't sell yourself short," Sophia said. "But also, there is a lot to unpack here," she continued. "I would like to cut right to the chase. Do you really think your mother was a lesbian?"

"I can't say with any certainty, but there were a lot of signs which appeared to point to it. At a minimum, she had to have been asexual." I noticed Sophia writing in her notes. I continued. "My parents didn't have anything even remotely resembling a healthy marriage. There were rumors that Dad was having affairs. Mom would tell me in kind of a joking way that Dad was going off to see his girlfriend at the pasture association office, but I never thought anything of it. But she had sort of a general animosity toward men. Maybe Dad wasn't getting his needs fulfilled in that department. Tell me something, do you think sex is a need?" I asked her.

"Well, it's a basic human function. Some would go so far as to say it's an essential human function. What do you think about it being a need?" she asked me back.

"I think if it is, there are a lot of people in a sad state of affairs, and often through no fault of their own," I said. "Some people just don't feel the same as their partner, for whatever reason. It's true that Mom didn't hold men in high regard. I don't know of anyone ever suggesting she was same-sex attracted, but she never failed to comment when a pretty girl caught her eye. I think she might have been trying to drop subtle hints to me when we were together in later years without coming right out and saying it. After she and Dad got divorced, she used to refer to herself as a 'gay divorcee,' which maybe wasn't as clueless as she might appear to be.

"In terms of my own experience learning about sex in my youth, it was practically non-existent," I went on. "I never got the lecture about the birds and bees from my parents concerning the biological realities. Mom was a pious woman and would never be caught dead having anything to do with something as crass as sex. She figured the less said on that topic, the better. If she had decided to take the opportunity, she would have summed it up as bees sting and birds will peck your eyes out if they have a chance, so best to steer clear of it."

"So, there was an avoidance of the topic of sex altogether?" Sophia asked.

"Yes, it was taboo for sure," I said. "I remember one time when I was a pre-teen being in church with her one Sunday, and they showed a movie about a young couple who had gotten themselves in a bind and didn't know what they were going to do about it. As I recall, the beauty of the 'act' was expressed through interpretive dance. I couldn't tell you what the outcome of the story was, but I remember being thoroughly puzzled about the whole thing. Days later, and it shocks me now that I could be this clueless, I said to Mom, 'I didn't think a girl could get pregnant until she was married.'

"'Well, they're not supposed to!' she snapped and brought the discussion to a screeching halt. I couldn't make any sense of it. It was similar to what Dr. Masters of Masters and Johnson fame reported when he counseled young couples who were heavily influenced by their religious upbringing and thought all they had to do was 'lie together' to start a family. I guess mom's attitude was the best way to keep kids out of trouble was to keep them ignorant. That always works so well.

"If it was the case, it's possible Dad had no idea what he was getting himself into when he married her," I continued. "I'm sure it wasn't long before it became apparent to him it was going to be infrequently, as opposed to in frequently." That got zero reaction from Sophia. "It's not funny, but it makes you think," I offered. Judging from her response, it makes her think it's not funny.

"Is it true about your sibling's age range and the birthdays being in late summer?" She asked.

"Yeah, the folks' wedding anniversary was in October. Randy came along late the next July. So, if you run the numbers, things look pretty normal. But it was three years before Dean was born and another five years for Todd. I didn't come along till 13 years after Todd. The last three of us have birthdays between the end of August and mid-September, and it's more than 21 years from oldest to youngest.

"Anyway, Mom had a disdainful attitude on the subject of sex. I think that led me to believe women generally don't like sex. Mom seldom talked about it other than to drive home the point that it was something to be regarded as distasteful," I continued. "I'm sure it's the reason I find it difficult to talk about it openly.

"Something else I remember Mom saying," I continued. "One day, apropos of nothing, she told me that of all the girls in her family growing up, she was the only one who didn't 'have to' get married. It struck me how proud she was to be able to say so."

I went on, "I will say, if my suspicions are correct, it would make it a lot easier for me to forgive my dad for being the way he was. He pretty much shut everyone out, especially me. I have reason to believe he didn't want me around at all."

"That's heavy," Sophia said. "What was your relationship with your mother like?"

"We got along great," I said. "Other than my brother Todd, she was the only one who I felt really cared about me at all."

"Tell me about your wife. What's her name?"

"Roberta. One does not call her Bobbie," I said.

"Is it a non-negotiable with her?" Sophia asked.

"Pretty much," I replied. "I once asked if she would prefer Bertha, but that didn't go either."

"Understandable," she said. "But I get it. Try calling me Sophie and see what happens," she said with a wink.

"Noted," I said.

"So, what can you tell me about this incident which caused a problem between you and her?"

"It was something stupid. I was into photography at the time. I found a site where models go to promote themselves. One of them lived close by, so I contacted her and made arrangements for a shoot. She was willing to pose in bondage gear in various stages of undress. There was nothing at all sexual between us; it was understood to be a photo session, nothing more. But, unbeknownst to me, Roberta was reading my mail. It led to some dark times."

"Is this the deep sadness there is an unwillingness or inability to express?" Sophia asked.

"Not entirely."

"Care to elaborate?"

"Not at this time," I said.

"Moving on then. You are into bondage? Things like BDSM and kink?" Sophia asked. "What is the genesis of that?"

"I would say it goes back to some of my dad's smut collection and the fact I am the youngest in the family. He had a lot of what were called 'sweat' magazines; some people called them men's adventure magazines. There were all these stylized covers done in elaborate drawings, which showed women bound and threatened with all kinds of dire straits. When he started piling them up, it wasn't so far removed from WWII, so the bad guys in these depictions were often Nazis or Asian types. Since I was the low man on the totem pole, so to speak, I was intrigued by the feeling of being the one with all the power in that situation. It got my juices flowing if you take my meaning."

Sophia kept writing in her notes. "Does Roberta share any of these interests?" she asked.

"We don't appear to share much of any interest in sex-related matters these days," I said. "Our relationship is kind of stale and boring. Once, I tried to spice things up with some movies which veered into soft-core porn, as in brief nudity and couples that got it on in a highly suggestive but simulated way. From her reaction, you would have thought I poisoned a kid's puppy. It was some time before she would even speak to me.

"Another time, I started to watch this show called *Mad Men*. I thought we might at least talk about the relationships in it. The problem for her was that the lead character had relationships with women other than the one he was married to, and she excused herself from the room and wouldn't participate. She doesn't deal well with stories other than where the romance is sweet, and the characters are chaste. Otherwise, she gets spooked by it. I think she has a lot of religious hang-ups about it."

"Is she aware God created sex?" Sophia asked. "At least this is what I hear from religious commentators."

"God may have invented sex, but people invented sexuality, it would appear," I added. "Most of the good folks from the church crowd want to keep it at arm's length and then some."

"Getting back to the story," Sophia said. "Who is Allie? Is she someone you know, like a muse or something? You appear to have some emotional connection to her."

"She isn't anyone in particular," I said. "There was a situation from my past involving an exotic dancer in a club that I developed a rapport with. The incident with the glasses actually happened. But as far as 'Allie' is concerned, I don't even have a clear picture of her in my mind. In my dreams, she would be medium height, with dark hair, a smooth complexion, and shapely in an all-natural way, if you know what I mean. Otherwise, I doubt I could pick her out of a lineup."

"What's this about artisanal pickles?" she asked.

"Well, it is basically a symbol for freedom," I replied. "Like something that is frivolous and gives you a way to make your way in the world without carrying the weight of it on your shoulders."

"A nice dream, at least," Sophia offered.

"At least I can dream about something," I said.

***

At dinner one evening, Roberta brought up the prospect of selling our house and buying something smaller. As we have finally become empty nesters, we no longer need a lot of space. We had been using the spare bedroom as an office and work area of sorts for the past few months.

She was also interested in exploring the possibility of becoming snow-birds and spending winters in Arizona. Living high in the Rocky Mountains, winters can be bone-chilling. I was never fond of winter weather, but it had been a long time since I worked a job where I had to spend time outdoors. "So, what are you thinking?" I asked.

"We can get a place half the size of this one, and it would be big enough. We might have to rent storage space for a while, but this is a lot more house than we need."

I was seeing her point. I didn't relish the thought of paying on a mortgage for another ten or twelve years as I was getting ready for something that would give me more flexibility. "What about an RV?" I asked. "A lot of people do that full-time. It would let us go to a warmer part of the country in the winter and explore options where we want to go the rest of the year."

She appeared ready to explore the idea. The big question was whether we wanted to get a motorcoach or a towable, like a fifth-wheel trailer, and a truck big enough to pull it down the highway. We had some research to do.

CHAPTER 7

"If you always do what you always did, you'll always get what you always got."
– Henry Ford

One day, I was sitting in the coffee shop, and it occurred to me I hadn't seen Sue Nami in a while. I figured maybe it was her week to stand up to the gun lobby. It sounded like something she would do. She is a nice person; she has some radical ideas or ways of doing things. This appears to be the leftist mentality. They want to change the world right now, while conservatives want to change people. The net result is the same, but the conservative approach takes longer.

I started up a blog post about how people tend to pigeonhole various groups into their common characteristics. To use conservatives as an example, many people believe that if you identify as conservative, you must be a certain way; you like NASCAR, that old-time religion, and guns. I have never been a fan of guns. Not that I am against them. I understand the Second Amendment crowd who advocate for the freedom to bear arms (or is it to arm bears?). However, I am at a loss to figure out how a bunch of liquored-up hillbillies with gun racks in the back window of their pickup trucks constitute a well-regulated militia. Still, I understand that when guns are outlawed, only outlaws will have guns. I would say if the hazards of modern life are such that I may be thrust into a situation where I would have to kill or be killed, I might sooner stay home and binge-watch Law and Order and the FBIs. I know some people who say they would rather be judged by twelve than carried by six. The fact remains, I have zero confidence in the legal system to have my back if I ever had to blow somebody's shit away, even if it was some asshole who desperately needed it.

If you are going to carry it, you had better be committed to using it. I've heard of those who become timid at the wrong time, having the weapon taken away and used against them. There is a little touch of irony if you like that sort of thing.

I have been told men commit suicide at a rate of 4 - 1 compared to women. It's possible the number of attempts is closer to even, but men tend to be more successful. The reason? Men use guns.

Too many people, I fear, use guns as a substitute for guts. Or, as I like to say, the bigger the Smith & Wesson, the smaller the Johnson.

I can only imagine how many people I might piss off if I posted this. And some of them have guns. I decided I had better let it cool for a while before I hit publish.

***

I eventually got back to Alice Modicum and decided to purchase a block of time. I still didn't have a plan of what to do, so I thought of another story idea involving a schoolgirl theme.

She sent me a schedule of rates, which called for a significant price break on her hourly rate at the three-hour level. I decided to go for it. What the hell, I figured. It was a chance to talk to someone who knew about things I was interested in and might make it happen. I let her know I was interested in the top-tier package. "All right," she replied. "Will you be purchasing using Zelle or Venmo?"

"Venom," I replied. Wait. A typo. "Venmo. Damn autocorrect," I emailed back.

"Great," she said. "It was a great movie, though, LOL. When would you like to get together?"

I knew there would be logistical considerations. I had to find a time and place where I could be online and inconspicuous. "How about next Tuesday afternoon?" I responded.

"Great," she replied. A few minutes later, she said, "Wait, let's do Wednesday; I just remembered I have a riding lesson on Tuesday."

"Fine," I replied. Wednesday it would be.

***

After I reread the piece I wrote about guns, I decided not to pull the trigger on it (Haha, see what I did there?), but I still thought the time had come to shit or get off the pot with finding a niche for my blog. It would have to be something that I have enough of an axe to grind over that it would motivate me to make regular and frequent posts. I knew one thing that would provide an endless stream of angst: people like my friend Stu Pidasso and their off-the-wall beliefs, especially those who adhere to a literal interpretation of scripture. The morons who think you have to take every word in the Bible at face value are a special kind of whacko. Think about how language and our knowledge of scientific facts have evolved in the 3000 years since it was written.

Religion was something I could at least formulate opinions on, both good and bad. I got the standard religious training with Sunday school and a steady diet of TV preachers Mom always wanted to have on. I listened attentively, and a lot of it took hold. I also did some inquiring on my own, and some of what I uncovered contradicted much of what I had been told. It came from a radio preacher who was from a different denominational tradition than we were, and it was refreshing to get another perspective. He was big on pointing out that many closely held beliefs people have are nowhere to be found in scripture. The takeaway was that you have to be careful and not simply believe what someone tells you, no matter how much you might trust them.

Stu sees things through the lens of judgment and condemnation of anyone who doesn't see it his way. He is so busy seeing the speck in the other person's eye that he can't see the stick up his own ass. Granted, it's a bit of a paraphrase, but it is a valid one. In addition to being a religious nut case, Stu also had some political views, which tend to run me out. Once, when I was visiting him at Thanksgiving, I was attempting to make small talk and asked if he had any preferences for the day's NFL games. He proceeded to launch into a rant about how he didn't watch pro football anymore because of all the players who took a knee during the national anthem. Well, it sucked the joy out of anything that might happen the rest of the day. It is as if by taking the simple pleasure of watching a game on TV away, the terrorists have won. I felt like pointing out that playing the national anthem at sporting events was not constitutionally mandated, so maybe to avoid controversy, they can skip it. Honestly, there are times he aggravates me so much I want to introduce his skull to the fat end of a baseball bat. But it wouldn't be worth the trouble it would cause me. Besides, it would be a shame to ruin a perfectly good bat.

Some would say the church he goes to is a cult. I believe it is more like an inbred sect. I asked him once if he couldn't find a church closer to home, but he said he had to go farther away to find one he liked. I wanted to ask if that was defined as one where they hate the same people he does.

I decided to pursue an angle of discussions on religion where I would debunk a lot of the closely held beliefs of people who only believe what they are told to believe. I decided to call it 'The Devil's Advocate.' It should be easy to sustain, I thought, writing about how people have so many misconceptions about religion and the meaning behind scripture. I knew I could get some traction out of poking holes in there.

The Devil's Advocate begins

Some observations on what passes for religious thought, which in itself may be the ultimate oxymoron.

Religious folks tend to be excessively uptight about sex. I wonder if it has to do with the idea that many times when the word sex or sexual appears in the Bible, it's often paired with the word immorality. A lot of it appears to come from the writings of Saint Paul, who is credited with writing the majority of the New Testament. He might have an agenda there, enough that it might occur to someone to wonder if maybe Paul wasn't getting any and wanted to make sure those who were didn't enjoy it. There is a verse in scripture that talks about salt losing its saltiness. What happens when sex loses its sexiness? It invariably does when the religious crowd gets hold of it. It's as if you can be deeply religious, or you can have a passionate and uninhibited sex life, but you can't do both at the same time.

When it comes to erotic literature, they like to point to the Song of Solomon as the gold standard. In actuality, it is half a dozen pages, which, to me, are as dull as dishwater and about half as hot. Oh, and by the way, it is attributed to a guy who is reputed to have had 700 wives and 300 concubines. Has anyone ever run the numbers on that? What if he had 300 wives and 700 concubines? Would the wives feel a bit slighted? Gotta wonder. Compared to the millions of pages of erotica published every year (hell, every day), they are clearly outgunned. Still, I would opine that it doesn't get much raunchier than the first couple dozen or so chapters of Genesis. There is some heavy stuff going on there. Like the story of Noah. No, not that story. I mean the one from years later when he is making wine and has a bit too much one evening and passes out naked on the floor of his tent. Noah had three sons, Ham, Shem, and Japheth. Ham wanders into the tent and sees Noah lying there and proceeds to tell his brothers he has seen their father naked. He is immediately banished to the furthest reaches of the civilized world for this atrocity. Oh, and by the way, didn't Noah and his family pretty much make up the entirety of the civilized world at this point since everyone else got wiped off of it recently? Still, it was a big deal for some reason. Well, there is a school of thought that says that old Ham didn't just look. Given the prevailing attitudes of the day, it might be understandable they would consider such a thing an abomination. But writers and interpreters who got hold of the story may have thought it needed to be sanitized a bit for consumption by the faithful. Again, just a thought.

One thing I will give to Christianity is that it doesn't discriminate on the basis of academic credentials like so much of the world does. The downside is you see a lot of flakey ideas put forth since anyone can sound off on a topic they feel strongly about.

There are a lot of brain-dead notions that go into the whole religious idiocy thing. Like the prohibitionist mentality with alcohol. I know people who think they will be kicked out of the holiness movement if they put a splash of cooking sherry on their stir fry. Of course, it does no good to explain to them what little alcohol there is in it burns off when you cook it. They see what they believe.

Then there is my wife's close friend, who takes a very traditional worldview. She is all about the patriarchy and all that goes with it. She won't put a bite of food in her mouth until the man of the house has said a few words over it. If the actual man of the house isn't available, she will enlist the closest available reasonable facsimile. People like her appear to treat religion as a bunch of hoops they think they have to jump through to show other people how religious they are. They talk the jargon and exhibit symptoms of a neurological disorder when the worship leader takes center stage, and it's all for show. It's enough to make me cringe when I'm around her. The license plate on her car displayed the scripture reference John 8:32. This is one I happen to have committed to memory: "You will know the truth, and the truth will set you free." In her worldview, the man is the head, and the woman must be submissive to his authority. In my mind, she is given to a lot of vain displays of religiosity, which I quite honestly don't hold with, and I can cite scripture to support my reasons. I also have always held the belief that it takes more than the biological fact of possessing a penis to make someone qualified to be in charge. Things like wisdom and character come to mind.

Many religious fanatics are sensitive to perceived persecution. What they don't realize is that they bring persecution on themselves by being insufferable assholes about it. I like to make a point of wishing them happy holidays at Christmas time to see the veins in their necks bulge. I have been known to throw in a very merry solstice and a debauched Saturnalia for good measure. It occurred to me I might do a future Devil's Advocate post about how so many of our Christmas traditions are co-opted from pagan fertility symbols. What's that they say, learn not the way of the pagan? Oh, what fun I would have with that.

I published this dissertation and waited to see what would happen. It didn't take long before some lively debates were being waged in the comments. The neat thing was people generally went after each other, and I could sit back and observe.

***

Roberta and I decided to get serious about our search for an alternative living arrangement, which, as we had discussed earlier, might include living in an RV. We knew we would have to do serious research, and the sooner, the better. Fortunately, the go-to option, as usual, was Y'allScreen. We looked and found a wealth of videos on every imaginable topic, from the type of unit to possibilities for camping, RV resorts, and boondocking.

We made the trip out to the recreational vehicle superstore, RVs R US, and were taken to a waiting area until the next available sales representative could see us. Soon, we were greeted by a cheerful, gregarious, and extremely large man with a name tag on his shirt that said Emerson Bigguns. He asked what our plans were for the RV experience. We said we were thinking about downsizing our living quarters and traveling seasonally to where it is a bit warmer in the winter.

"Have you considered RV living full-time?" he asked.

"Well, I've heard people do that, but is it really possible?" I asked.

"There are those who do it, but it is definitely not for everybody. It does have advantages, though, like not having to worry about your home if you are away for extended periods. What type of RV did you have in mind?"

"We are just getting started with the search, so I guess we need an education on the pros and cons of the various types," I told him.

He launched into a spiel on the major divisions in the RV world. "To begin with, you have your towables, consisting of either a travel trailer like Airstream or fifth-wheel trailers that connect to a mechanism in your truck box. Do you have a truck?"

"Yes, we have a half-ton Nissan," I stated.

"You might need something along the lines of a three-quarter ton dually, especially if you go with one of the big fifth-wheels that would possibly be something you could live in for any length of time."

Roberta chimed in, "Let me guess, those aren't cheap," she said.

"Now you are starting to understand the RV world; good for you," Emerson responded.

"So, what's the alternative?" I asked.

"You would be looking at a coach of one kind or another," he said.

"You're saying there is more than one type of those, too, I take it," I said.

"Bingo," Emerson replied. "First, you have the Class A bus type coach, then there are the Class C campers, which is basically a cabover bolted to a heavy-duty truck chassis."

"Is there a Class B?" Roberta wanted to know.

"Yes, those are the conversion vans, basically," Emerson replied. "Sort of the low end of the camper space," he added.

"Then why isn't that called a Class C?" I asked. "They should classify them in a logical order, you know, conversion van, Class C. That would make more sense."

"Do you want to make sense, or do you want to go camping?" he grinned.

"I have to choose one?" I asked.

"Oh, you have no idea," he stated. "Anyway, I see the two of you in a Class A. We have some with slide-outs which give you an unbelievable amount of living space and an incredible amount of storage as well. The Class C might be a fallback option if you decide to keep the house."

I could see we had a lot of thinking to do. Emerson loaded us up with brochures and pamphlets enough to keep us up nights for weeks. I liked his easy-going manner and decided that when the time came, he would be worthy of getting our business.

CHAPTER 8

"There's a sucker born every minute."
– P. T. Barnum

"I'm going out shopping this afternoon," Roberta announced as I sat at my desk, going through the comments on my blog from earlier. "On my way home, I'll stop at the store and pick up something for dinner. I have some coupons from their flyer I want to use."

I stopped and stared at her for a moment. "You realize you have an app you can use to clip those sale prices, right?"

"Oh, yeah, I never thought about it. I'm used to clipping coupons, I guess," she said.

I was stunned. "The nineties called; they want their Rolodex back," I muttered as she turned to go.

"Did you say something?" she asked.

"Nothing, see you later," I said. I caught a break there, as I had my session with Alice coming up, and I was wondering how I would keep from being conspicuous with my laptop. I figured this way, I should be in the clear.

I thought I would use the time to find out what kind of situations we might explore in the realm of fantasy creation. It was stimulating thinking of having someone I could connect with on that level. It is always so hard for me to find someone who shares my interest in off-center sex, but if anyone could, it would be her. After all, I'm sure she encounters all kinds of interests and experiences, and it shouldn't be weird or unusual. As the time got closer, I waited with bated breath. And waited… and waited…

Well, after a while, I figured I had missed a step. She must be waiting for me to do something. Maybe I needed to let her know I was ready. I sent an email. No response. I waited. No response. I was starting to wonder what was up. It was like being in limbo and not having any control over the situation. After what I considered to be a reasonable amount of time and what an average person might consider an abuse, I decided to put some thought into what we might discuss when and if we connected at some point. Of all the options bouncing around in my head, the schoolgirl scenario seemed appealing.

Later that evening, I got an email from Alice. She said she got called away to a meeting in Vegas and thought she had sent me an email to let me know, but for some reason, it didn't go through. She suggested we try again at the same time next week. Great, I thought, only another week to end up right back where I am now.

At least it gave me some time to think of something we could discuss or act out. One thing she mentioned is that one of the props they have is a desk, which can be used for schoolgirl scenarios. I can only imagine. Since I had recently had some success with story writing, I decided I would apply this talent to come up with a scenario we might try out sometime.

Payne and Pleasure
By Alex Anderson

Allison was sitting through her last class of the day, Advanced Biology, which was also her favorite, due mainly to the teacher, Mr. Payne. He was tough but fair and always encouraged his students to do their best. He has an easygoing manner and can be quite funny at times. He even has a funny name. His first name is Darrell, and his middle name is Bruce, so you could say his name is Darrell B. Payne. It was an inside joke in the school that by the end of the term, you would know the truth of it. The neat thing about Mr. Payne is that he knew the joke and thought it was funny, too.

The fact was, Allison really liked Mr. Payne, and, unlike many other students in this girl's academy she attended, she had an advantage that enabled her to do something about it - the age of consent. Because of a learning disability she had early in primary school, she was held back and had to repeat a grade. Although, as it turns out, her learning disability was actually a teaching disability on the part of one of her teachers. This teacher was more concerned with form over function, and Allison paid the price. Since many other students in those days had the same problem, this school ended up enrolling many of them. Allison never wanted to get preferential treatment for this situation, as she wanted to fit in with her classmates. So, she was perfectly content to be subject to all of the rules and regulations that other students in her grade had to follow. Besides, she was petite and short for her age, so even though she had turned 18 at the beginning of this semester, she could easily pass for 16.

On this day, Allison was struggling with a problem that had nothing to do with school. She was finding it hard to concentrate, even with Mr. Payne going through the lesson that day. After the final bell rang, the rest of the class moved out, and Mr. Payne asked Allison to stay for a bit.

"Allison, you appeared to be distracted today," he said. "Is everything all right?"

She appreciated that he noticed her struggle. He always showed such concern. She would have liked to believe it was because he really liked her, but she knew he cared about all his students. She welcomed the opportunity to discuss this with Mr. Payne. He was such a good listener. She felt like she could talk to him about absolutely anything. "Yesterday, I had a situation that freaked me out a little," she said. "A boy I know came up and said he wanted to kiss me. No one had ever said that to me before, so I thought it was nice. I let him kiss me, and while he was doing it, he reached under my blouse and touched me on my... my boobies," she said.

"I see," said Mr. Payne. "It's probably none of my business, but did he touch you over your bra or under your bra?"

Allison's face turned red. "I wasn't wearing a bra," she said, looking a bit sheepish.

"I'm pretty sure you're supposed to be wearing a bra, Allison," he told her.

"I know," she said. "I just think sometimes I don't really need to. I don't have such big boobies."

"Well, there are other reasons for wearing one, you know," he said as he noticed she had thrown her shoulders back, and it became readily apparent that she was again not wearing a bra. She blushed and nodded. "You should wear a bra. Starting tomorrow," he said, making a mental note that if he ever needed some glass cut, he knew where to go. "Did anything else happen?" he asked.

Allison shook her head. "I was afraid he might try to… you know. I got scared because I heard that it hurts the first time a girl… you know. So, I freaked out and ran away. Now, I don't know if he will like me anymore."

"I see," said Mr. Payne. "I think you did the right thing, Allison. Sometimes, young boys don't always care about how the girl feels; they want to make a score and brag to their friends. That's why you should make sure that the first time you… make love with someone, that you are with someone who cares enough about you that they won't hurt you."

Allison thought about it for a moment. "You care about me, don't you, Mr. Payne?" she asked.

"Of course I do," said Mr. Payne.

"You wouldn't hurt me, would you?"

"No, I would never want to hurt you, Allison," he said.

"Mr. Payne, I think I want you to…" she said something softly, which he wasn't sure if he heard correctly.

"I'm sorry, I didn't quite hear you," he said. "You want me to…?"

"Have sex with me," she blurted.

"Oh, I see. For a minute there, I thought you said you wanted me to make love to you," he replied.

"That too," she said. "You've had sex with lots of girls, haven't you? Some of the girls here at school."

What a loaded question. While he certainly had the opportunity and appeared to have a magnetism with many of the girls he taught, he didn't want to cross the line. Fortunately, he taught an advanced class, mainly attended by seniors, so he had opportunities because there were a lot of students who were 'victims' of a lousy teacher years ago. As long as it was safe, sane, and consensual, he figured, why not? "I suppose I've had my share," he said.

"Have you had sex with any of the girls I know?" she asked.

"I don't think a gentleman should talk about who he has been with. It should be between the girl and him," he said. He had always thought discretion was the better part of valor, not to mention staying employed, staying out of gossip columns, and staying out of the crosshairs of the hashtag MeToo movement. Or did you say *Pound MeToo?* Either way, it's the same thing.

"So, you wouldn't tell anybody if you had sex with me?" she asked.

"No," he said. "Not if you don't want me to."

"And you would do it so you won't hurt me?"

"It might hurt a little, but I'll try my best."

"How can you do that?"

"Well, you just have to go slow," he said. "It usually takes a lot of kissing and a lot of touching." He walked over to the door and locked it. "Then you need to relax and make sure you are ready."

"So, we start by kissing?" she asked. "I would like it if you would kiss me."

He kissed her lips, embracing her and kissing her ever more passionately. He asked her to open her blouse. She did it, and he looked at her for a long time. *This girl really needs to be wearing a bra,* he thought. *Starting tomorrow.*

"Do you like my titties?"

He smiled and said, "You have beautiful breasts, Allison."

Allison smiled. *Breasts. She has beautiful breasts.* She liked the way that sounded when he said it.

"You also have a cute belly button," he said as he began to kiss her on her body, running down her chest to her beautiful tummy. He spent time kissing the area around her navel, running the tip of his tongue into it and pressing into her with it as he pulled her blouse over her shoulders and off her body.

The feelings of a woman were beginning to stir deep within Allison. While these feelings were incompatible with her strict upbringing, she wanted to experience them with the depth of maturity she felt ready to explore. She felt like she wanted to offer him her body. She raised her arms and wrapped them around her head, expanding her rib cage, pulling her belly taut, and causing her ~~boobies titties~~ breasts to thrust forward and stand out in all their fullness.

He told her that he wanted to touch her legs. He slipped his hands under her skirt so he could feel her thighs, then worked his way up to the waistband of her panties and pulled them down. "There is a way I can touch you that will make you feel so good. Would you like me to do that?" he asked.

"Yes, please, Mr. Payne," Allison said.

Mr. Payne ran his finger along her sex and pressed it against the bud of flesh near the top of the opening and moved it in tiny circles over the sensitive area, and she started to moan. "Oh, that feels so good, Mr. Payne," she said breathlessly. After a while, she said, "Is there anything I can do to make you feel that good?"

"If you want to," Mr. Payne said, "you can use your mouth... down here." He then loosened his pants and let his male member out so she could see it.

"Oh, I've heard of that," she gasped. "You want me to do that?"

"If you want to."

"You might have to show me, but I want to," she said.

He guided her to her knees and let his cock point to her lips. He closed his eyes and waited for her to take it in. Soon, though, he felt an odd sensation. He looked down, and what he saw made him roll his eyes and shake his head. "Ahh, sweetheart, you don't actually have to blow on it; that is just an expression," he told her.

"Oh, really? I just assumed - "

"It goes in your mouth, honey."

"Are you sure?"

"Yes, absolutely."

"Oh. Thank you, Mr. Payne. You're such a good teacher," she told him.

It didn't take Allison long to get the hang of it. He believed with a little coaching and enough lube, this girl could suck a golf ball through a garden hose. He felt a powerful load about to come through, and he wanted to prepare her. "I'm going to come now," he said, "don't worry, it's okay to swallow it if you want to." Allison was reassured by his heads-up, and soon she was feeling her mouth fill with the salty liquid, and she swallowed it all, moaning with delight and the satisfaction of knowing she had done that for him.

With the intensity of the climax he experienced, Mr. Payne knew it would take him some time to regroup. "The problem we have now," he said, "is that we will probably have to start over with the foreplay so I can get recharged."

Allison understood. "I think I missed the part where that's a problem."

Mr. Payne smiled. "I see what you mean," he said.

After he collected himself, Mr. Payne asked Allison if she was ready to remove her skirt. She nodded, then took it off, and stood in front of him completely naked. "Do you think I'm pretty?" she asked him. He gave her a reassuring nod.

He stood behind her and reached his hands around the front of her body, caressing every inch of her. Now, it was time. He picked her up, set her down on his desk, and gently pushed her down so she was flat on her back on the desk. He stood between her legs and began to enter her. So slowly, just enough to make sure she wouldn't feel any discomfort, and she could let him know to wait or advance. "How does it feel?" He asked her.

"It feels good so far," she said. "Can we go slow?"

"Of course," he replied. "Take your time and let me know when to go further." A moment later, he asked her, "Can you tell me what is happening here in terms of biology?"

Allison thought about it. "The male is inserting the penis into the female's vagina," she said.

"That's right. And what is that called?" he asked her.

"Sexual intercourse," she said softly.

"Can you tell me another word for that?" he asked.

"Coitus?" she said.

"That's one. Can you think of any others?"

"Copulating," she answered.

"Very good. You have been paying attention. Give me one more," he said.

"Fucking," she replied with a nervous giggle. "We're fucking."

Fucking. He liked the sound of that when she said it. "We're getting there. Just let me know when you are ready for me to finish coming into you," he said.

"Almost," she said breathlessly. "Oh, keep fucking me, Mr. Payne. I want you to fuck me," she said as she propped herself up on her elbows so she could look down between her legs at his engorged penis as it worked its way into her vagina. She was suddenly less concerned about any potential pain than she was about her desire to have his fat cock inside her. She took a deep breath, then looked him in the eyes and nodded. "Fuck me," she urged. He advanced a little farther, and she shuddered. "Oh, fuck," she gasped.

"Was that it? Did it hurt much?" he asked.

After the initial jolt, she started to relax and said it was okay. Soon, she began to feel the urge to go harder. "Oh, please, Mr. Payne, fuck me. Fuck me. FUCK ME!!!" she urged him. "Oh, yes, oh, yes, OH YESSSSS. FUCK ME! FUCK ME! FUCK ME!!!!!!!"

After he had ~~fucked copulated with~~ made love to her, Allison felt uneasy. "I said a lot of really naughty words, didn't I, Mr. Payne?"

"Technically, you said one really naughty word a whole lot of times," he corrected her.

"Yeah. I should probably have my mouth washed out with soap," she said.

"You should be spanked, young lady," he told her, "But I'll let it go this time."

"No, I don't think you can," she said, "I should be punished. How else will I learn? You don't want me to turn out to be a dirty little slut, do you?"

"No, I don't. I like my little sluts to be clean and wholesome," he replied.

"Then you have no choice. You must spank me," she said as she bent herself over his knee and offered him her bare butt. "I'm ready for my spanking."

He spanked her hard on her ass till she started to cry softly. After he was finished, he cradled her in his arms. "I hope you've learned your lesson," he said.

"If I ever forget, I know where to come for a refresher," she said, then sprawled out on her back and spread her legs wide. "Now, how about giving me another good hard fuck?"

***

Over the next few days, Mr. Payne noticed Allison appeared to be more relaxed and content. He watched her in class and caught her eye, and she gave him a knowing wink and a thumbs up. He smiled back at her, understanding it to mean things must have worked out for Allison and her boyfriend.

However, a couple of days later, Allison stayed behind after class was out, and when everyone else had gone, she walked over to her teacher. "Oh, Mr. Payne, I need your help," she pleaded.

"Is everything okay, Allison?" he said. "It appears things are going well with your boyfriend."

"Oh, yes, they have been going fine. But last night, he said…" she paused. "He told me next time he wants to fuck me in the ass! What am I supposed to do, Mr. Payne?"

There was a long pause, after which Mr. Payne said, "Lock the door, Allison."

To be continued…

I liked how this one turned out, and since Sophia enjoyed the previous story I had done, I figured I might as well send it on to her. It would be one more item to add to the mix.

CHAPTER 9

"Never give a sucker an even break."
– W. C. Fields

The following Wednesday, I waited for Alice to contact me. Since she had stood me up last week, I figured she would be doubly conscientious about getting in touch with me this time around. The appointed time arrived and passed. Still no call. I waited. And waited. And waited some more. What else can I do? If she didn't start the meeting, I didn't have a way to connect with her. As luck would have it, Roberta decided this would be a good day to have me help her put up a makeshift water feature out on the lawn. At least it gave me a way to work out my frustration.

Later that afternoon, Alice sent me an email. She had been setting up a new laptop, and her calendar from the old one didn't make the trip over. At least, that was the version of events she put out there. She said if we could meet next week, she would tack on an extra hour at no charge. How can I beat a deal like that? There's not much I could do but agree.

***

Stu Pidasso and I were playing a round of golf one afternoon. He had expressed an interest in learning the game, and I was willing to give him some pointers. It was a way for me to get out and play with someone other than Todd since he is only around a couple of months a year, and I don't know too many other people who play. Stu was in the mood to talk about the great science vs. creation debate. The fact that I was not held little meaning for him. He is of the opinion and belief that you must take every word in the Bible as the literal truth. Therefore, the world was made in six literal days, and everything in it was set in place fully formed because it says so in black and white. I have tried to argue with him reasonably, but the problem with this approach is you can't reason with someone who did not use reason to arrive at their beliefs.

To these people, if accepted scientific fact doesn't fall in line with their narrative, the science is always suspect, whether it be geology, physics, astronomy, or what have you. I tried to appeal to him on the basis that astronomical distances are, well, astronomical. There are stars and galaxies that are, at a minimum, millions of light years away from us, and there-fore, the speed of light being what it is, light from those objects must have traveled millions of years for us to be able to see them. Oh, not so fast, he would say. Maybe the speed of light was different then. I have found it difficult to win an argument with an intelligent person, but it is downright impossible to win an argument with an idiot. You can make the most logical case possible, but if it doesn't line up with the narrative, they go into the most outlandish mental gymnastics to shoot holes in it. His fallback argument is always, 'Well, God can do anything he wants to.' Unfortunately, that won't cut it with anyone who has a three-digit IQ. So, I knew another track was in order.

I asked him if he believed the words of the gospel. "Of course," he said.

"So, when it says Jesus went about doing good, it is the truth, right?" I asked.

"I would say so," Stu replied.

"In fact, it says if all the good deeds He did were written, the world could not contain the books. Is that the literal truth?" I asked. "Or is it possible the writer of this passage is engaging in hyperbole? You know, an exaggeration to drive home a point."

"Not sure what you are getting at," Stu said.

"It says the things that were written were written so you would know what He did, right?"

"Yes," Stu replied.

"But not everything was written, or by its own definition, it wouldn't have been possible. So, more things were done than were recorded in the gospel. Dr. John Daniel once said the Bible contains all the truth you need, but it doesn't contain all the truth there is. Can you agree?"

"I suppose so if Dr. Daniel said it," he responded.

"Of course," I said with an eye roll. "So, as far as the creation account goes, maybe there was more to it than was recorded. Think about it." The look on Stu's face was like the gates are down, the lights are flashing, but the train ain't coming.

I knew it would only make him more determined to shoot holes in my case, but I figured it would take him until sometime in the distant future to accomplish it. I was hoping my attempt at illustrating the process of critical thinking would make an impression, but it remains to be seen. I was honestly so frustrated with him that I was ready to give him a nine-iron across the teeth, but it would be a shame to ruin a perfectly good golf club.

***

Our cat, Valentino, had a habit of wanting to go out to the backyard every morning when I got up. This morning, he didn't show up to the door like he usually does. I remember he came in last night and sat with me downstairs till I was ready to go to bed. I went down and checked and found him still lying in the chair. He felt warm and not at all energetic. I told Roberta we should probably take him to the vet to have him checked out.

After most of the day at the vet's office, the tests came back, and they said he had pancreatitis. It may be operable, but the prognosis was not good. They kept him overnight for observation, and we went home, not knowing what the outcome would be.

The next day, the vet reported Tino had taken a turn for the worse, and it didn't look good. We decided the best thing would be to put him down. It was a shock, as it happened so suddenly, and Tino was not such an old cat. We were going to miss him.

***

The following week, I emailed Alice on Tuesday evening to confirm we were still on for tomorrow, right? Right? Of course, she said. I went to bed with visions of horny happenings and conversations dancing in my head. For whatever reason, I picked up my phone and glanced at the emails. There was a new one from Alice that started, "Oh, gosh, I'm terribly sorry…" Are you kidding me? I'm thinking. What now? She went on to say her media team had notified her they needed to do a photo shoot the next day, and there was no way she was going to be able to work around it. She said we would have to figure out a new meeting time. This is getting ridiculous, I thought. How much more of this am I going to have to put up with? I felt as powerless as I ever have. I had put out what I considered significant dollars and was getting a giant run-around. I sent her a message stating I felt she owed me something that might involve large object insertion when we finally did get together. After I hit send, I immediately regretted it. I knew people at her level had a different way of viewing time and obligations and I was probably lucky she even acknowledged my existence. I knew I had to find a way to smooth things over.

I had some work-related projects I needed to concentrate on for a couple of weeks. It felt good to have the situation with Alice off my mind for a bit. Once my calendar cleared, I got back in touch with her, and after apologizing profusely, I asked what we could do to schedule a time to meet. She suggested a time, and I decided to make it work. I had sent her the schoolgirl story and thought we might talk about acting out something like that scenario. She thought it sounded like fun. She also had a Slave Leia outfit that was one of her favorite things to wear, so I suggested we start with her in that outfit. I had to find a location away from the house to meet with her, so I found a place where I could set up a mobile hotspot on my phone. At the appointed time, I sat and waited, and, unbelievably, she sent me a call. I answered, and there she was, in the flesh, as it were. At least as close as I was going to get any time soon. She was decked out as Slave Leia, and she looked good. We talked for a while, and I started by apologizing again for my relatively unsophisticated remarks about her inability to meet last time. She said she understood completely, and she was not easily offended. I could already see she was a better person than I was. After she had displayed her wares in the skimpy slave girl outfit, I asked if she had a chance to look at the schoolgirl story I sent her. She said she had and said it looked like a fun idea and wanted to discuss my ideas for acting it out. Unfortunately, about that time, the hotspot connection started getting flakey, and we got cut off. We were able to get it established again, but it wasn't the best, so we decided rather than go through the frustration of trying to act out a scene, we could pick it up later. She was going to be on her next tour at the brothel in another week, and we can try again. I figured it was about the best we were able to do.

***

When I next met with Sophia, she looked unusually hot. She was wearing a tight blue top and a skirt that showed a lot of leg, and I couldn't help but wonder if it was somehow for my benefit.

"I liked the schoolgirl story you sent me—good catch on making her over 18. I can't wait to see where it goes from there," Sophia said.

"What do you mean?" I wanted to know.

"You said it would be continued," she stated.

"Oh, well, I doubt I will ever actually do anything more with it. It was just a way to bail out on it," was my reply.

"I definitely think you should develop it. You appear to have uncovered a latent talent here. These stories might be the start of something big," she said.

"You mean to publish them?" I asked, somewhat in shock.

"Why not?" she asked.

"That would be problematic," I stated. "I mean, I would burn every bridge in my world if I did that. Most of the people in my tribe would be shocked to find out I know some of the words I use in those stories, let alone the situations I put them in. Hell, I have even had women I have had sex with tell me they weren't aware I knew some of the words I used, and this was while I was having sex with them. How lame is that?"

"Well, I don't notice you being particularly profane or vulgar when we talk like this," Sophia mentioned.

"Yeah, I try to restrict any explicit language to my stories. I don't usually go there in real life except under extreme duress," I said.

"Besides, the people I know firmly believe women in the sex worker or provider realm who are there of their own volition and aren't coerced, groomed, or trafficked into it simply don't exist," I continued. "So, for those reasons, I don't see how I could have my name attached to those stories if they ever got published."

"That's what pen names are for," Sophia said. "Have you ever considered using one?"

"Not really," I said. "I've never felt the need. There's no sex in my memoirs; they're about my real life."

"Why not try using something like Alexander or maybe Xander," she suggested.

"Yeah, use the back end of my name. I know at least one person who would think that is appropriate. Now I need to come up with a last name."

"Do you? A lot of people use one name," she stated.

"I'll think about it," I said.

Sophia brought up a sensitive topic. "I think I see where we are headed with these conversations. You stated that you wanted to figure out if your feelings and attitudes are normal. We can certainly explore those questions. But it might take some time," she said. "And time, as they say in my business, is money."

I knew what she was getting at. Maybe that explained why she was showing some leg. "Right, and the big issue I have is money leaves a trail. I don't have a problem with paying your price, but I need to figure out a way to keep it discreet." I figured I was living close to the edge with what I had sent Alice not long ago.

"I have some thoughts on that," Sophia said. "You see, I am working on a graduate degree in psychology. I think you would fit nicely as a case study in my thesis. If you're down with the idea, I could see my way clear to writing off most of the cost on a pro bono basis, so to speak."

"Hmmm, sort of like tit for tat?" I asked. "Then here's hoping I have an adequate supply of tat for you." Sophia sat stone-faced, staring into the webcam for several seconds until it started to get awkward. Finally, I made a show of jotting down a note: "No sense of humor," I said as I pretended to write.

"I'm sorry, did you say something funny?" she asked.

"Apparently not," I said.

The slightest hint of a crooked smile flashed across Sophia's face for an instant, and she resumed the expression which I started to think of as 'the look,' so I moved on. "Are we talking about abnormal psychology, then?"

"Oh, don't flatter yourself, you're not that fucked up," she shot back.

"It's comforting to hear you say so. What are you thinking?"

"My thesis is on how things in early development affect people later in life," she explained.

"So, are you going to name a syndrome after me?" I asked. "Like the Xander disorder?"

"Cute. If it comes to that, I'm sure I can think of something suitably arcane."

"Arcane," I mused. "You are the second professional person who has managed to work that word into a conversation with me."

"It refers to something obscure, puzzling, or understood by few," Sophia explained.

"Yeah, that fits me to a T," I said. Then it hit me. "Alright, there's my pen name: Xander Arcane. I think I can work with it."

"Sounds good," she said. "Now go write a story by Mr. Arcane."

"Any requests?" I asked.

"Perhaps something related to your early experiences in dealing with imagery from your dad's collection of, what did you call them, 'men's adventure magazines?' I have been curious about exploring those situations. I think it would be an interesting springboard from which to spin a tale. You can pull out all the stops, and we can delve into it in a big way."

PART 2 // CONNECTION

CHAPTER 10

"Fifty Shades of Grey **is only romantic because the guy's a billionaire. If he was living in a trailer, it'd be a** *Criminal Minds* **episode."**
– Jill Shalvis

Once again, I had a blank screen in front of me. Still, it wasn't daunting at all. I don't experience the kind of writer's block that I sometimes feel trying to write my blog. In these sessions spent creating something for Sophia, Alice, or Diane, the words flow from my fingertips. It's like a shot of adrenaline to my creativity.

Sophia had given me a challenge with this project: writing under a new identity and having the freedom to express thoughts I am uneasy with. I decided it was an excellent opportunity to establish how I came to feel about what I do in these matters and explain how influences from my formative years shaped how I see the whole spectrum of power exchange and dominance.

I thought about the materials my dad had hidden away in his workshop when I was a kid. They weren't hard to find. Dad probably wasn't that concerned about me seeing them. As long as I put them back where I found them, I figured I was safe. Most were just run-of-the-mill cheesecake pictures and the venerable Playboy magazines like I had seen among my brother Randy's belongings when I visited his house. It's all pretty tame by today's standards. But others were grittier. These were the 'sweats,' magazines on pulp paper with vivid four-color artwork on the covers. They depicted scenes straight out of the fever swamp of depravity. It was enough to get my juices flowing. I started to imagine myself as the man with the helpless damsel in distress in his evil clutches. For a kid who lives life being afraid of his own shadow, it provided a much-needed and wanted sense of escape from the dreary reality of my life.

As I looked through these magazines from time to time, I noticed that some of the women in these drawings appeared repeatedly. It was as if they used the same model in different scenarios. It got me thinking there must be a process where women pose for these pictures and willingly put themselves in these compromising positions, and they must be okay with it, or they wouldn't be doing them. That in itself was stimulating.

This is my chance to let everything come together and not hold back. If it is too much for some people, too bad.

Bound and Determined
By Xander Arcane

Alicia made her way to the building directory and searched for the name of the man she had come to see. She quickly found it:

OLIVER KLOZHOFF .... Suite 269.

She saw the way to reach it and headed in that direction. Alicia had met this man the previous week at a party she attended with a friend. The party, referred to as a munch by enthusiasts of the BDSM community, was a gathering of those interested in exploring the world of fetish, kink, or other aspects of sexuality that some might consider out of the mainstream. Her friend was curious about this, and Alicia saw an opportunity to learn something but also had an ulterior motive. While there, she engaged in a conversation with this man who had a mysterious air about him, and for some reason, she felt drawn to him, though he did not appear to be someone with whom she would ever consider a relationship. He had asked her to join him for a private get-together. Now she was here, feeling apprehensive. She took a deep breath and went inside.

As she entered the foyer, her phone beeped with a text message which read:

Walk through the door and make your way to the bathroom. Await instructions.

OK.

She was startled because she didn't remember giving him her number. She took a deep breath and followed the instructions. Once there, she found a hanger with a small bag over the hook. Another beep:

Take off all your clothes, place them in the bag, and go to the room next door.

OK.

OK, indeed, she thought. Now, she was curious, so she did as she was instructed and, after carefully opening the door and peeking inside to ensure this was not some sort of surprise party, stepped inside. She found it to be a bedroom and laid out on the bed was an outfit consisting of a pair of tiny white shorts and a skimpy crop top. Another message came: Put the clothes on and go out into the main room.

OK?

She put on the clothes and checked herself in the mirror, deciding that she was presentable in certain situations.

The room was dark, with a single light in the corner. In front of the light, she could make out the silhouette of a man seated in a chair. He beckoned her to step closer. He took a cursory evaluation of her appearance. "You look nice," he said.

"Thank you," she replied. She felt a bit awkward and wanted to break the ice, so she made an attempt at small talk. "You remind me of someone. The person on those commercials, they call him 'the most interesting man in the world.'"

He laughed out loud. "You flatter me. But I would never presume to claim such a title. Although I think I can make a strong case for being one of the more intriguing guys around."

Alicia giggled. His open manner and self-deprecating humor put her at ease, even though she was showing more skin than she would ever think to for someone this early in their acquaintance.

"I would like to know you better," Oliver said, inviting her to sit down. "However, I fear you may have no idea what it might entail. What do you know about our little community?"

"I know what the letters stand for, not much else," she replied. "My friend wanted to go to the munch and asked me to go along to keep an eye on her. After I spoke with you, she appeared to be having a good time, so I left."

"So, you were there for moral support. Nothing else there interested you?"

"I didn't fully understand," was all she said in reply.

"BDSM is a big tent, if you will. The uninitiated tend to treat B&D and S&M as two separate entities," he said. "What many do not realize is that there is a third aspect. If you combine the DS, or D/s as many prefer it, you come to the space I occupy, the realm of the dominant and submissive.

"The sadist is not complicated," Oliver continued. "Such a person seeks gratification through punishing a victim. At the risk of sounding arrogant, I believe the dominant is more nuanced. He must be able to read people, to know what motivates them, what stimulates them, what frightens them," he said. "Unlike the sadist, I am not motivated by inflicting pain. Rather, it is the suspense created in the mind of the submissive over what *might* happen that I wish to explore. Fear of the unknown is what I find fascinating, and its effect on the helpless victim.

"You see, I believe that people are drawn to those things which fall outside their mundane, everyday experiences. Would you like me to tell you what I believe I know about you from the brief time we have been acquainted?"

"Please do," Alicia replied.

"I would venture to guess that in your daily life, you are involved in the management of a large company. This company might be engaged in product distribution, in creating advertising campaigns, or in software engineering. Whatever you do, because you are a woman, you have been made to feel you need to work twice as hard to be considered half as good as a man doing the same job, correct?" She nodded. "However, deep down, you believe you are more competent and capable than any man you know. But how do you exert that capability? You do it by intimidating those under you to feel that you hold ultimate power over them and their livelihoods. This leaves you feeling guilty and unsure of how you can get away with wielding such power. You wonder what it would feel like to surrender to another and perhaps even assuage your guilt by being put in your proper place." Alicia was shocked to realize he had read her like an open book.

"It is really not a stretch to come up with that. It is a common phenomenon," he said. "I believe the same thing occurs when men who are high-powered executives or world leaders engage the services of a dominatrix. It is a search for balance.

"My situation is the opposite," Oliver went on. "Growing up, I was the youngest in my family, and so I felt I was under everyone's thumb. I wondered what it would be like to dominate others and be able to get away with it. As a youth, I discovered stories in magazines that were aimed at men who were lonely, frustrated, or otherwise disaffected by societal norms. These magazines featured artwork that invariably depicted a fetching young lady as a scantily clad damsel in distress, often awaiting her fate at the hands of some menacing scoundrel. These were lurid tales filled with such depravity and hedonistic excess that it would freeze your soul if the events described in them were to be encountered in real life, or so it seemed to an impressionable adolescent."

He continued, "So, because of my background, I was shy and withdrawn. Most people mistook this for my being cold and aloof. I lived my life vicariously through movies and the aforementioned magazines, which were the graphic novels of their day, I suppose, and they stimulated my fertile imagination. However, for most of my life, I have run with a staunchly conservative crowd. It has been difficult for my predilection to find expression without fear of judgment or condemnation, though I believe my 'kink,' if you will, is closer to the mainstream than most care to admit."

Alicia was pleasantly surprised at his candor and self-disclosure. It helped her to understand where he was coming from and the motivation behind his interests. She had always had a heart for those who struggled to find acceptance due to a lack of understanding. Perhaps this is the reason she felt drawn to him.

"Here is what I propose," Oliver continued. "I am intent upon imposing my will on you and, in the doing of it, to give you the most intense pleasure of your life. If I fail to do so, you are free to go, no harm, no foul. If I do, you will remain here for as long as I would like you to. Do you agree?"

Alicia was amused by his cocky assurance of his abilities, but she knew something he did not. So, feeling there was no possibility he would be able to fulfill his boast, she nodded in agreement.

The conversation turned to such practical matters as safe words, personal boundaries, and consent. That being established, Oliver felt they were ready to get underway. He asked her to stand up so he could get a better look at her. "Where then to begin?" he mused. "Hmmm... Your top. Remove it."

"No," Alicia responded.

"No?" Oliver drew a breath and rose to advance on the spot where Alicia stood. "Yeah!" he said, betraying a hint of an accent from his German heritage. Alicia looked startled, and he suspected the fact he held a considerable height and weight advantage over her might be unduly intimidating, so he decided to dial it back for now. He softened his manner and spoke thoughtfully. "I see two things that need clarification. First, you must learn to distinguish between requests and commands. That should be simple enough since I do not make requests. Second, you must answer the question, why are you here?"

She looked down and thought for a moment, and stammered, "I... I was curious. I wanted to find out – "

"No!" he said, stopping her abruptly. "That is incorrect. You are here for one thing, and one thing only, and that is to provide me with amusement. Since we are both adults here, I believe we can stipulate that, at some point, that comes down to sex. Now, have I said anything that surprises, shocks, or offends you?"

"No," Alicia said.

"Then, since you are new to all this, I will overlook a transgression on this one occasion, but I will say this in a calm and even-tempered manner just once more. Take. Off. Your. Top!"

His icy tone made Alicia shudder, so she felt it would be best to do as she was told. She removed the flimsy top and lowered it to her side, standing there with naked breasts, and felt his eyes bore into her. He reached out his hand but only to motion with his fingers for her to hand him the garment. He took it from her and stood there, expressionless, staring. Finally, after an awkward interval, he shrugged and said, "Not bad." He pointed to a spot on the floor near the center of the room. "Stand there," he commanded.

Her eyes had adjusted to the subdued light in the large room, and she saw him stride purposefully to his chair like a captain in command on the bridge of his ship. He sat there staring at her, looking up and down her body. She began to squirm. "You appear to be unsure of what to do with your hands," he observed. "You want to cover yourself with them. Does it make you feel self-conscious when I direct my gaze at your breasts?"

"Yes."

"Good," he said. After a few more minutes of intense gazing, he said, "Look above your head." She looked up and saw a pair of metal cuffs at the end of a large chain hanging from a hook in the ceiling. "Reach up and take those cuffs and clasp them securely about your wrists," he ordered her. Alicia could not believe he would expect that she would willingly do any such thing, but with the squint and the pursed lips he showed at her hesitation, she realized it would be unwise to arouse his anger. So, reaching up and placing the cuffs around her wrists, she heard them close and knew she was now at his mercy.

He chuckled under his breath. "You are very compliant," he said. "I like that in a woman.

"I have such interesting plans for you," he said as he moved to a cabinet and opened the door. From it, he pulled something that she could only see appeared to be several long strands attached to a handle. He flicked it, and it made a loud cracking noise, and she realized it was some sort of a whip.

Alicia was now becoming apprehensive about what was going to happen to her. "Are you going to whip me?" she asked.

Oliver's response was, "Only if you make it necessary. I hope for your sake you will choose not to."

"What must I do?" she asked.

I decided this would be a good place to leave things hanging. I can come back to it later.

CHAPTER 11

"It is one thing to mortify curiosity, another to conquer it."
– Robert Louis Stevenson in *The Strange Case of Dr. Jekyll and Mr. Hyde*.

After a brief respite, I was ready to dive back into the story. I had left our heroine in dire straits, chained in place, and confronted with a presumably heterosexual Dom wannabe with unknown intent. I could hold that thought indefinitely, but I knew it would get boring in a hurry, so I needed to come up with some context. I picked up where Oliver was making Alicia's situation clear to her:

Oliver allowed his gaze to scan up and down the bound form of the nearly nude young lady. "For the most part, you must simply follow instructions. Let me explain to you some of what will be demanded of you. From now on, you will only speak in response to my direct questions. When you do, you will address me as sir. If, for any reason, you need to say something to me, you must first say, 'Sir, may I please speak?' Do you understand?"

"Yes, sir."

"That's good," he said. "This is a test of obedience. If I tell you to jump, I will expect you to ask how high on the way up. If I order you to suck my cock dry, you will savor every drop. If I command you to offer me your ass to fuck, you will moan with ecstasy as I am doing it. If these conditions are not to your liking, I can only tell you that it is going to suck to be you for the foreseeable future." He draped the flogger around her neck, and it hung next to her body. She recoiled at the sensation of the rough leather against her bare skin but, at the same time, was grateful it rested over her nipples, effectively obscuring them from view.

He returned to the chair and continued to gaze at her helpless form. He was feeling stimulated at the thought of how vulnerable she appeared, bound and clad in only a pair of short shorts. It was one of his favorite methods of exerting dominance over a woman. He continued to stare at her for many minutes, enjoying the feeling of power.

"Sir, may I please speak?" she said after a long while.

"Yes, you may," he responded.

"Sir, I have to pee."

"I wondered how long that would take," he said, then sat silently.

"Well, will you let me down so I can go to the bathroom?"

"No," he said. "That is not how this works."

"So, I'm supposed to just piss my pants?" she shot back.

Oliver rose to his feet and advanced toward Alicia with a stern expression. "No. Under no circumstances are you to do so. If you do, I will make you wish you had not." He took a strand of the whip between his fingers and flicked it over her nipple.

"Then what?"

"Then what...?"

"Then what, sir?"

"Better," he said, again moving toward the cabinet. "It's quite simple." He reached inside and pulled out a plastic bucket. "You see, you have only to ask me, in a nice way, to remove your remaining garments. Then, you can use this," he said as he placed the bucket near her feet.

"With you standing there watching me," she snarled. "Sir!"

"Actually, I'll be sitting over there. It tends to splash all over, and I don't actively participate in 'water sports,' though I do like to watch."

"I wouldn't give you the satisfaction."

"You disappoint me," he said. "Well, I'm going to let you think about it for a while." He returned to the cabinet, took out an hourglass, and set it on the table in front of her. He turned it over so the end filled with sand began to trickle down slowly. "I have other matters to attend to for the moment. I'll be back by the time the sand runs out. At that time, I will expect to find you in a more cooperative frame of mind." He exited the room and left her standing there.

As she stood there with growing discomfort, both from the stress of being stretched from the chains holding her in place and also from the pressure of desperately needing to urinate, a thought occurred to her. She had been standing there in his presence, very nearly naked, for an hour or more, and he had yet to touch her. She began to wonder if he wasn't attracted to her. Although he had told her she looked nice when he first saw her, all he would say was "not bad" when he first laid eyes on her bare tits. What was she to make of this? She tried to convince herself that she didn't care, but she knew she was a hell of a lot better than 'not bad.' At least it was a distraction from the urge to relieve herself. She seriously considered wetting her pants despite the warning not to, but when she felt the rough leather of the flogger he had left draped around her neck, she suddenly shuddered at the thought of him swinging it in anger at her and the effect it might have on her delicate skin. At some level of awareness, she knew that he knew that she knew that he was thinking about it and realized it was all a part of the gigantic mind-fuck happening here.

After what seemed like an eternity, Oliver entered the room, as promised, just before the last grain of sand passed through the upper section of the glass. "I trust you have had time for a little attitude adjustment. Are you ready to follow my instructions?"

Realizing she simply had no choice, Alicia said, "Fine, I'll give you a show."

Sensing some resentment, he told her, "Alright, but since you kept me waiting, there is a new requirement. In addition to asking to have your pants removed, I would like a kiss."

"Oh, fuck off!" she shot back instinctively.

He pulled back, put his hands on his hips, and shook his head. "Fine," he said as he turned the hourglass over again. "Suit yourself," he said as he stormed out and slammed the door behind him.

"NO!" Alicia screamed. "Please, no! Oh, please come back!" she started to sob uncontrollably at the prospect of another hour of waiting for his return. A feeling of despair overwhelmed her as she fought to hold the contents of her bladder, which by now felt like it might explode. "Oh, fuck!" she cried.

This time, he returned long before the sand ran out and not a minute too soon. Perhaps he could show mercy after all. She looked at him through tear-filled eyes with a pleading look on her face. He said he was going to kiss her, after which she should ask him to let her pee in the bucket. She nodded, and he kissed her. Nothing that would induce fireworks, he lightly touched his lips to hers and waited. She uttered a close approximation of the words he wanted to hear, so he nodded and undid the button on her shorts and unzipped them. Slipping his hands inside the shorts, he slowly slid them down, making sure to feel her legs all the way down to the floor. Kneeling, he pulled them from beneath her feet and placed the bucket under her. "Wait until I tell you," he said. He moved to his chair and, sitting down in it, he swiveled it to face a water cooler standing to one side. He started to dispense water slowly into a large tumbler, and as he did, the transparent bottle atop the device bubbled and gurgled as the tinkling sound of liquid slowly filled the container below. Alicia could only turn her face and bury it in her arm to avoid the torture of seeing the waterworks show, which was so obviously staged for her benefit. She had no idea what this man did for a living but decided that if it did not have something to do with interrogating prisoners, he had wasted his life. Turning once again to face her, he took a long sip from the container and said, "Begin," and she let loose the pressure that had been building for hours. When it was over, he smiled and said, "Now that wasn't so bad, was it?"

She averted her eyes, feeling humiliated and used. "I guess not. Sir."

"You have done well. I think you have earned some pampering. I would like to give you a bath." He took her chin in his fingertips and looked into her eyes. "Would you like that?"

"Yes, sir." She welcomed the prospect of being released from her bonds and able to sprawl out in a luxurious bath.

He moved the urine-filled bucket to the corner of the room, after which he took the flogger from around her neck and set it aside. He brought out a small metal tub and placed it next to her feet. "Step inside," he said. Seriously? He was going to bathe her in this position. Par for the course, it occurred to her. So, she did it, curious as to how he intended to give her a bath even while she was chained in place. It soon became apparent when he produced a large pitcher filled with warm water and poured it out on her chest, over her shoulders, and down her back, running down the length of her body. He took a sponge, slathered it with body wash, and rubbed it up and down her entire body, starting with her neck, around her shoulders, and along her back. Dipping the sponge in the water again, he dabbed it over her breasts and her perfect belly before moving to the more intimate areas. Finally, he washed the length of her lovely legs, admiring the perfection of this exquisite female form. After caring for every inch of her body in this way, he got some fresh, clear water and poured it over her to rinse the soap off. He had her step out of the tub, wrapped her in a fluffy towel, and patted her dry. As he removed the towel and left her standing there, slightly damp and completely naked, the evaporating water caused her to cool off and shiver uncontrollably. He smiled as her nipples became rock-hard and stood at attention. This was his motivation all along; he knew it, and she knew it.

"I'm sure you have many questions," he said. "You may ask three."

"Are you going to kill me?"

"No."

"What do you want from me?"

He stood up and walked to stand next to her, placing his palm flat on her tummy. "I want your baby," he said.

She gasped, "My – but I'm not pregnant!"

"No," he said. "Not yet."

"So, you're going to rape me?"

"That is a rather harsh word. I prefer to think of it as giving you a wholesome, good old-fashioned fuck," he said with a bit of a twinkle in his eye. He gazed at her intently. "Do you like to fuck?"

"I don't know. I mean, I've never... with a man," she said, averting her eyes.

"I see. So, you like girls then?"

"Yes."

"And men... not so much?" he quizzed her.

"I wouldn't say that sir. Men are just... harder."

"Yes, that is the way it works," he deadpanned.

"That's not what I meant."

He chuckled. "I know. No, I get it, really, I do," he assured her.

Suddenly, the realization hit him. "So, this girlfriend of yours at the party. She really is your girlfriend?"

"No. I mean, I want her to be, but she doesn't know I feel that way," Alicia said. "I went with her to the party because I knew she was looking for sex. I thought I might get her to notice me. But she went off with some men, and I didn't know where she was. I got mad and left. And I don't know what happened to her. No one has seen her since."

"And you're worried about her," he said.

"Yes," Alicia responded. "I was supposed to be looking out for her, and I fucked up. And now she's probably dead."

"I wouldn't worry too much about it," he told her. "I know most everyone who was there. They are a pretty harmless bunch, with one notable exception." There was no discernible response from Alicia. "That was a little joke," he said.

"Sorry, I was concerned that the woman I love might be dead," Alicia replied.

"Perhaps I can be of some assistance in finding this person. What is her name?"

"Zoey," she told him.

"Someone must have noticed her," he said. "I can ask around and see what I can learn. Would you like me to do that?"

"Yes, please, sir, would you?" Alicia pleaded.

"It depends. What would you be willing to do if I could put your mind at ease about Zoey?"

"Oh, I would do anything, sir."

"Really? Anything?" he teased.

"Anything," Alicia repeated.

"Now, I should caution you that anything," he said, as he placed his palm on her tummy and moved up her torso, "could mean pretty much… anything." He grabbed her breast and squeezed hard, causing her to yelp before he continued, slowly moving the hand all the way down "…up to and including…" he ran his finger along the groove of her moist cunt "… anything." He began to move his finger in circles over her clit. Alicia started to weaken and surrender herself to the sensations that were overcoming her body. Her breathing became quick and shallow. Oliver started to work his finger up inside her but noticed something in her reaction. He began to think perhaps she was for real. "Are you quite certain that you are up for absolutely anything?"

"Anything," was her breathless reply.

But rather than penetrate her with his finger, he withdrew it. Alicia was bewildered and frustrated as she was beginning to feel things she never felt before. "You don't have to stop," she said.

"Yes, I do. You are not ready," he said.

"You should consider yourself fortunate," he went on. "You might have ended up with any man at that party. Or any woman, for that matter. I know for a fact the vast majority of those in attendance would regard you as little more than a collection of body parts. Very attractive body parts, I grant you, but just something to be consumed. But I perceive that you have a keen mind. That is something else I like in a woman. There are many things I appreciate about what women have to offer beyond the obvious. A pretty face… a shapely body… soft skin… tender lips." He kissed her deeply, after which he picked her up by her thighs and pulled her opening next to the bulge in his pants. She was hanging there by her wrists, entirely under his control, but he set her feet back down on the floor. He stood gazing at her with lust in his eyes.

"You are turning out to be a bit of a project. You see, in order to build a new structure, you often need to tear down the old one. I suggest you use that keen mind of yours to come to terms with your new reality. If you open your mind to the possibilities, you may find what you are looking for. Now, you think about that for a while." He turned to leave, but not before setting the pee bucket close to her, at least in the sense that if she stretched her leg all the way out and flexed her foot just right, she could snag the handle with her toe and pull it close enough to use it.

An indeterminate amount of time passed as Alicia continued to hang there, drifting in and out of consciousness. She heard the door open and waited to see what twisted thing he had in store for her this time. She didn't bother to look up; she knew she was being ogled, but she was too worn out to care. "Please take me down," she pleaded.

A soft, familiar voice replied, "That's what I'm here for."

Alicia looked up and could not believe her eyes. "Zoey! What are you doing here?"

"I've been here all week," she said. Alicia was confused. Zoey stood there in regalia that looked like something out of an Arabian sheik's harem.

Zoey produced a key and reached up to unlock the shackles that held Alicia in place. Alicia nearly collapsed into Zoey's arms. "I need to lie down," she said.

I decided I needed a break. I also needed to come up with a plan for this Zoey character. I can see possibilities for her beyond the specific reason she would be there in a role-play scenario at a brothel. I wondered what other situations I might put her in. This scenario was taking on a life of its own. I started to wonder if it was something I needed to be concerned about.

CHAPTER 12

**"Let's celebrate by enjoying a pleasant evening at the theater."
– Abraham Lincoln (Okay, I made that one up to see if you
were paying attention).**

I had an unusually long writing session this evening. I went to bed and
started to scroll through Y'allScreen videos when Roberta came into the
bedroom. "Would you be open to some snuggle time?" she asked.

"Sure," I told her. It was unusual for her to ask about this lately,
but when she did, it was at the strangest times. She disrobed down to her
lingerie and got under the covers.

"I miss doing this," she said. "I like to feel close to you."

"Me too," I said. It was true; we seldom take the time to simply be
close anymore. But now it felt good. I'm not sure if it was the fact that I was
feeling stimulated by the story I was working on or the fact that I couldn't
remember the last time Roberta and I had sex. But it turned out that by
morning, tonight would be that time.

***

It was time to get back to work on this story. I decided to go to R&R so I
could find a quiet corner and work undisturbed. As I tried to get my head
into writing, I thought about Roberta and the good, well, okay, great sex
we had last night. Such interludes were few and far between these days. I
wish that I could have a little bit of a hint about when they might occur
so I would be ready. I wondered if it might be caused by the stimulation I
felt from this scenario I was crafting. I wondered what would happen if I
showed Roberta these stories. I decided I should already know.

I realized I had been stalling. There was somewhere this was headed, and it was a place so dark it started to frighten me. Certainly, if it were in a published book, it would necessitate a warning about explicit language and strong sexual content. I wasn't sure how I was going to get there and even less sure how I was going to get out of it. In any event, it was time to put Zoey to work.

Bound and Determined continued

"We can go in there," said Zoey, leading Alicia to the bedroom where she had changed into her sexy clothes a short while ago. After Zoey helped her freshen up, they sat on the bed. Alicia had to take in Zoey's appearance in the over-the-top sexualized costume she was almost wearing.

"You look… nice," Alicia commented.

"Thanks. It's the required uniform here," Zoey said.

"Zoey, I love you," Alicia blurted out, not knowing where the courage to utter the words came from.

"Well, I love you too. I mean, you're my friend. I'm glad I was able to help you," Zoey responded.

"No, I mean, I really love you. What I'm trying to say is I'm in love with you," Alicia continued. Well, there, she had said it. Now, she waited for Zoey's response.

"What are you talking about?" Zoey asked. "You mean…?"

"I mean, I want to be with you. The only reason I went to that stupid party with you was so you would pay attention to me. But you ran off, and I couldn't find you."

"I had no idea. That's not really my scene," Zoey said.

"Will you let me kiss you? Just once," Alicia pleaded.

"Just once," Zoey said.

Alicia leaned toward her and softly kissed Zoey's lips for the first, and she feared possibly the last time. Afterward, Zoey looked bewildered, but she realized that Alicia might have made her job easier. "That was nice," Zoey said in an even voice.

"That's all? 'Nice'?" Alicia quizzed. "I think it could be a lot more than nice. Don't you want to kiss me?"

Zoey nodded and said, "Yes, I think I do." With that, Zoey embraced her and kissed her deeply, pushing her back on the bed till Alicia was flat on her back. Now Alicia felt she was getting somewhere. She gave in to Zoey's advances. Zoey took Alicia's hand and clasped a cuff around her wrist. Alicia was startled but amused at the turn of events. Then, her other wrist was clasped to another chain at the opposite corner near the head of the bed. Zoey stood up and looked down at Alicia with her arms spread out above her head. Zoey took another pair of shackles and placed them around her ankles, spreading them wide.

Alicia was feeling playful and said to Zoey, "You don't need these with me."

"Probably not, but there is someone here who might," Zoey said with a sober expression.

Alicia was suddenly horrified. "You're putting me here for him?" she gasped. "How could you?"

"That was my task. He commanded. I obeyed," Zoey replied.

"Obeyed?" Alicia asked. "What do you think you are, his slave? Since when does he own you?"

"Since I gave myself to him. He gives me what I need," Zoey replied as she turned to leave.

Alicia panicked. "Wait, you can't leave me here. You know what he's going to do to me. Please, I need you!" Alicia begged.

"Need me?" Zoey asked.

"I need you to love me. I need you to make love to me. If I'm going to be raped, I need my body warmed up. Please love me," Alicia pleaded, her eyes filling with tears.

Zoey was conflicted. Sure, Alicia was her friend, and she cared about her, but she didn't feel anything of a sexual nature for her. But she felt responsible for her current situation, so she felt she needed to give her any comfort she could.

"What can I do?" Zoey asked.

"Kiss me. Kiss me and touch me all over my body," Alicia told her. Zoey got close to her, kissed her lips, and put her hand on her belly. "Feel my breasts," Alicia urged her, "Kiss me all down my body."

Zoey started to fondle Alicia's breasts and ran gentle kisses down her torso, making her way down to her navel. There, she lingered for a while, pressing her tongue into her belly. She found herself starting to enjoy the feeling of the helpless girl under her control and increased the intensity of the kisses on her abdomen.

Alicia gasped, then urged her, "Lower, please... PLEASE!" she begged. With that, Zoey moved her face between Alicia's thighs and began to nibble and suck at her pussy. She was starting to move the tip of her tongue over her clit, and Alicia felt herself build up to a breathless climax.

Suddenly, there was a noise as the door burst open, and Oliver stood in the doorway. "Zoey! What are you doing?" he demanded.

Zoey stammered and tried to explain, but he silenced her. "You are way out of line. I never gave you permission to touch her like that. Go to our room and wait for me to return. I will deal with you later."

"Yes, master," Zoey said and left the room.

"She calls you master?" Alicia said incredulously.

"As will you eventually if I deem you worthy," Oliver said.

"I am no man's slave, and I am no man's whore!" she said defiantly.

"Is that a fact?" Oliver said, laughing. "Now, let's apply some critical thinking to that statement, shall we? First, you're a woman, so, practically by definition, you're a whore. And, in your current situation, chained naked to the bed, unable to move without someone to release you, about to be taken by a man who holds the power of life and death over you..."

with his finger, he traced a checkmark over her navel. "Slave," he said with a sneer on his lips.

He looked at Alicia's naked body spread-eagled on the bed before him. "Allow me to finish what she began." Oliver removed his shirt and lay down next to her and began to run his hands over her body and suckle her nipples and finger her clit, all the delicious things he had anticipated doing ever since he first laid eyes on her. Alicia did her best to resist any possibility of deriving pleasure from this experience, and he sensed it. "I think you will find that I can do anything with your body that she can do and so much more," he told the helpless girl before him.

Alicia glared at him. "That's right; you can rape me."

"You keep using that word. I do not think it means what you think it means," he replied. He wasn't sure if she picked up on the obscure cultural reference, but regardless, she was not amused.

Alicia stared up at the ceiling. "Just get it over with," she said numbly.

"My dear, it isn't a matter of 'getting it over with.' You see, after I rape you, as you insist on putting it, I am going to rape you again. And again, and again, and again. I am going to fuck you until your ears leak, you little bitch." He finished undressing and joined her on the bed.

"Oh, please don't," Alicia pleaded, her body stiffening in anticipation.

Oliver positioned himself over her. "Oh, one more thing. If this is truly your first time, you may experience some slight discomfort. There is no getting around it," he said, pushing the tip of his engorged cock at her opening, "it is just a cold, hard fact of life. So, we might as well 'get it over with.'"

With that, he thrust the full length of himself into her. She winced at the sensation. *Slight discomfort my ass*, she thought. It hurt like a son of a bitch, and the son of a bitch kept coming. Alicia began howling hysterically, "OH, IT HURTS! STOP IT! OH FUCK! OH FUCK! TAKE IT OUT!" she shrieked, "TAKE IT OUT!!"

"Make up your mind, girl. Do you want me to fuck, or do you want me to take it out?" he teased.

"TAKE IT OUT, YOU FUCKER!" she screamed at the top of her lungs.

"Let me assure you I have no intention of taking it out anytime soon. The more you struggle and cry out, the longer I can keep this up. So, by all means, knock yourself out," He taunted.

Alicia gradually went limp, her hysterical crying giving way to quiet sobbing. Oliver was fixated with pleasuring himself on her, and, with a final series of thrusts, he filled her with his hot cum. After he had finished with her, he looked her in the eyes. "Not bad," he taunted as he rolled off her. Alicia lay there in shock over the brutality of the sexual assault she had endured. He reached up and unlocked one handcuff and the corresponding leg iron. She turned over on her side and trembled quietly as she continued to whimper and cry at the thought of all she had lost. Her virginity, her faith in the basic decency of humanity, her hopes for a life with Zoey. All gone forever.

Oliver knew that this was a crucial time in the process. He could only hope that she was as strong as he thought she was. He gently touched her shoulder to calm her, but she was oblivious to his presence. He stroked her hair with his fingers and placed his hand lightly on her shoulder. "What can I do?" he asked.

"Just kill me," she sobbed.

"I already told you I'm not going to do that," he said.

"Why not?" she said weakly. "Why should I live? You said it yourself, I'm nothing but a sex slave and a whore."

"It's nice work if you can get it," he remarked.

"Fuck. You." She said in a calm and even-tempered manner.

"You always say the sweetest things," he said, smiling as he kissed the back of her neck.

"You're an ass," she told him.

He took on a more serious demeanor. "I try to not be," he said. "I know that was intense," he whispered in her ear, "I didn't want to hurt you, but it was the only way."

"Tear down the old so you can build the new? Well, you got it done," she said.

He slipped an arm underneath her from behind, gathered her body close to him, and held her. "Try to get some sleep. We can talk later."

At some point, she woke up, still wrapped in his warm embrace. She turned and said, "What are you doing?"

"Watching you sleep. You are so beautiful. I hope you are feeling better."

"A little," she said.

"It gets better. You'll see," he said.

"Prove it. My ears are still dry, so I suppose you'll be fucking me some more."

"Not at this time," he said, his voice barely above a whisper. "Right now, I want to make love to you. Is it okay if I do that?"

Alicia looked over her shoulder. "Is that a request?"

"Yes," Oliver replied, "it is."

She met his gaze. "Then yes. Okay."

He started by kissing her. He kissed her lips passionately and deeply. Alicia reciprocated as best she could with half her limbs bound. He kissed her breasts, kissed her belly, kissed her inner thighs. Finally, he turned his attention to her pussy. He kissed her pussy; he licked her pussy; he sucked her pussy. After ascertaining that she was ready, willing, and eager, then and only then did he gently insert the full length of his manhood into her pussy and returned to kissing her lips as they made love, mad, passionate love, deep into the night, until at last, he let the warm liquid flow into her body. He looked her in the eyes. "Fantastic," he said.

"Likewise," she replied. As Alicia drifted off into a blissful sleep nestled in his arms, she almost forgot how much she yearned for Zoey. Almost.

I was in a cold sweat as I concluded this phase of the story, but I knew there was more to come.

CHAPTER 13

"The perfect is the enemy of the good."
– Voltaire

I was getting close to wrapping up the bondage story. At this point, I wanted to delve into these characters on a more human level. What were they looking for, and how were they going to get it? From my earlier experience with BDSM scenarios, which I admit are shockingly limited, it was an exercise in power exchange and the full realization that it was the submissive who held all the power, meaning this person was the one who could bring the proceedings to a screeching halt simply by uttering one word. But now I wanted to explore what made these people tick. What came next would set the stage for my next session with Sophia.

Bound and Determined Conclusion

When Alicia woke up, all of the restraints had been removed. Oliver was sitting in a chair by the bed, reading from an iPad. "Rough night?" he asked as he offered her a large mug of coffee.

"It had its moments," Alicia said as she accepted it, trying to focus.

Oliver pressed a button on the arm of his chair, and a few minutes later, someone wearing the required uniform brought in a serving cart with breakfast for the two of them. Alicia was struck by how casually elegant Oliver looked, barefoot in a pair of relaxed-fit jeans and a cotton shirt with the sleeves rolled halfway up his forearms, while she was sitting there in, well, in her nakedness. "Am I ever going to wear clothes again?" she asked.

"I don't really see the need," he replied.

"Not even the 'required uniform?'"

Oliver smiled. "There may be times it would be appropriate. How much do you know about belly dance?"

"I have moves you would no doubt find enticing."

"An amusing notion. I will keep that in mind."

"So, where's Zoey?" Alicia asked.

"Oh, she's hanging out around here somewhere."

"I take it that means you've dealt with her."

A faint smile crossed his face. "Like you, Zoey is a work in progress," he stated.

"Could have fooled me."

"She's eager to please, but she has a way of testing her boundaries. I must say, I was impressed at the way you persuaded her to give comfort in your time of need. It is possible you have awakened something in her that she didn't know was there."

"I seem to have that effect on people," Alicia said.

Oliver leaned toward Alicia and spoke with mock earnestness. "You must vow to use this power only for good and never for evil," he intoned.

"Where's the fun in that?" Alicia scoffed.

"You're right, that's just crazy talk," he said. "Forget I brought it up.

"Quite honestly, I thought I may have to squelch this budding relationship of yours, but I have had cause to reconsider," he continued. "For one thing, I will confess I found your interaction with Zoey to be highly entertaining. But moreover, it is simply not in my make-up to stand in the way of your happiness, to say nothing of true love."

The corner of Alicia's mouth curled up in a wry smile. "So, you're saying there's a chance?" she said.

Oliver smiled. "My dear, in this place, the possibilities are limitless."

"I'll keep that in mind," Alicia replied.

"Breakfast was delicious, thank you."

"You're welcome."

"I would ask to use the bucket again, but it was pretty full the last time I saw it."

"Yes, it was thoroughly disgusting," he said. "I must remember to call the people with hazmat suits to come and dispose of it."

"Did I mention you're an ass?" she shot back.

"Believe me, that is a widely held opinion," he said with a mischievous grin.

"I can't imagine why," Alicia replied, in a voice dripping with sarcasm.

"I'm told everyone is entitled to 15 minutes of something. You may have 15 minutes alone in the bathroom," he told her.

"Thank you."

After she had freshened up, she believed there was still more time available. She decided to make a request of her own. Returning to the bedroom, she asked Oliver, "Sir, may I please take a shower?"

"Of course," he said.

"Will you take a shower with me?" she asked. Oliver was wary. Was she up to something? He decided he had better keep his guard up.

"Why?"

"I want to go down on you in the shower," she said.

"Well, now, that is a sharp pivot from crying rape to asking me to fuck your mouth," he responded.

"Well, we did make love, after all."

"True," Oliver said. "That we did."

"So, join me," Alicia said as she reached up and wrapped her arms around his neck to kiss him. Then she whispered in his ear, "You can stick it anywhere."

This page has been blocked
by the League of Decency.
We apologize for the inconvenience.

"Not bad," Alicia said with a grin after they had their fun in the shower and were drying each other off. Alicia asked if they were going back to bed.

"No, you are going back to the dungeon," Oliver told her. Her face fell, and she was about to say something, but he said, "But not like before. I have something a little different in store for you today."

He took her by the hand and led her, still in the nude, to the place she dreaded. Along the back wall stood a St. Andrew's cross. It looked imposing and large next to her petite body. He placed her with her back to the wooden structure and told her to raise her hands. She did as she was told, and he put the restraints around her wrists. Then, it was time to spread her legs. They were bound to the lower part of the frame, and she stood there, her naked body available to him. He gazed lovingly at her for a long time, and she began to enjoy the feeling of being desired.

"I must say I was surprised when you asked me to shower with you earlier," he said. "I decided either you were up to something, or you were under the influence of Stockholm Syndrome."

"Stockholm Syndrome? What's that?"

"That's where someone who has been abducted or held hostage begins to develop feelings for their captor. In extreme cases, they may even become sympathetic to that person's cause," he explained.

"And what is your 'cause'?"

"Well, at this particular moment, it has something to do with stretching your pussy in one way or another," he said dryly.

"Perhaps that is a cause I could come to embrace."

"I'm glad to see you are coming around to my way of thinking," Oliver said, hungrily eying her gorgeous body as it was displayed before him. He moved to press his advantage, anticipating the feel of her skin and the taste of her lips. Suddenly, her face contorted in a look of extreme pain.

"Ouch, oh shit. YELLOW, YELLOW!" she cried out.

"What is it?" Oliver asked.

"Leg cramp. My left leg, it has a cramp. Owww!" she shrieked.

Oliver immediately removed the strap holding her left leg and let it relax. "Do you need to come down?"

"No, I'm okay, just give me a minute," Alicia assured him.

Oliver took her leg in his hands and massaged the calf to relax the muscle. "Are you sure?" he asked. "We can take a break."

"No, I'm fine; we can continue," she said. He was impressed. He redid the restraint and looked into her eyes to make sure it was okay to proceed. "I'm good," she said.

"Compliant as always," he winked.

"I know you like that about me," she said.

"My girl," he smiled. He stepped back and looked at the device she was bound to. "Are you aware of the fact that in the ancient past, people could be nailed to devices like this as a means of execution?" he asked. "Believe me, cramps were the least of their problems. The whole idea was to inflict the maximum amount of pain, humiliation, and suffering and to serve as a warning to others."

"You wouldn't nail me to this, would you?" Alicia asked.

"No, but I wouldn't put it past me to nail you on it," he quipped.

"You're a sick fuck," she said with a slight smile.

"Yes, and you love me for it," he said with a wink.

"I think maybe I do, sir," she said, looking down as she bit her lip.

He shook his head and chuckled. "Stockholm Syndrome, for sure. Or maybe you're a sick fuck too."

"Would this be something else you like in a woman?"

"Most assuredly," he said. "Is there anything in particular you like in a man?"

"I like that you know about so many different things," she replied.

"Oh, I could go on and on," he said. "For example, did you know that the word 'fuck' supposedly came from the Puritans who were looking for a way to avoid offensive words?"

"No kidding?" she said.

"At least according to folklore. In those days, when it was still believed that public shaming could be an effective deterrent to bad behavior, people would be locked in stocks in the public square if they committed crimes. If they had stolen something, a sign would be put next to them that said 'THIEF.' But for adultery, well, this was too strong a word, so they decided to spell out 'FOR UNLAWFUL CARNAL KNOWLEDGE.' At some point, maybe because it was so prevalent that people were getting writer's cramp, it was shortened to 'F.U.C.K.'"

"You have an impressive array of knowledge, sir," she said.

"Oh, yeah, tell that to the people at *JEOPARDY!*" he responded. "I never could get on that show. Though, to be fair, I suppose 'Kinky Fuckery' was never one of the standard categories in that game."

Alicia snorted abruptly. "How do you expect me to role-play the frightened victim if you keep making me laugh?"

"Deal with it," he replied.

He then produced what appeared to be two small clips joined by a light chain.

"What are those?" she asked.

"Nipple clamps."

"What do they do?"

"Clamp nipples," he said. She shot him an annoyed glance, and he said, "Well, you did ask."

"Fair enough," she responded as he attached the clamps.

"Does that hurt?"

"Not particularly."

"How about now?" he asked as he grabbed the chain between them and jerked them away, making her wince. That told him all he needed to know. "Ooh, sensitive. I like -"

"Like that in a woman, yes, I know," she said, rolling her eyes as she finished his sentence.

He feigned exasperation with her. "How do you expect me to role-play the dominant overlord if you continue to mock me?" he quizzed.

"Deal with it," she smirked.

"Oh, I intend to, my dear," he said. He reattached the clamps and turned his attention to the rest of her body stretched across the rack. He slowly, gently caressed her inner thighs, her belly, her breasts, from time to time tugging on the chain that connected the clamps gripping her nipples.

Now, he had her right where he wanted her. She was totally under his control. He kissed her deeply on the mouth, then on her face and neck, moving down her body, kissing and licking every inch. He now turned his attention to the area between her legs.

"Your body is made for pleasure, both giving and receiving. I think it is time for you to be on the receiving end. Do you remember what I did before with my fingers here?" he asked, slipping his finger inside her. She nodded. "Do you want me to finish what I began?" Again, she nodded.

He found the area that made her moan with ecstasy. He turned his hand over and flexed his fingers in the tell-tale 'come hither' motion of an accomplished g-spot massager and continued to press harder and harder until she was writhing and gyrating as much as her restraints would allow. Now, he was indeed pressing his advantage and showed no sign of stopping. Finally, she experienced the physical release, which she had been denied repeatedly over the past day. She let loose and convulsed into violent spasms of pleasure. Oliver realized that as a result of giving her this intense pleasure, he had made her squirt. Finally, a water sport he could embrace.

"That was fucking incredible," she said. "Will you do it again?"

He licked his lips and nodded. "And again, and again, and again." She now believed she could fully embrace his cause.

By the time the agains were approaching the double-digit range, it was abundantly clear that Oliver knew his way around a woman's body. Alicia was delighted to be the beneficiary of such knowledge. After bouts of having her pussy stretched in every way imaginable and interacting with clips, crops, and floggers just because, she was nearing the limit of her endurance. Finally, exhausted, her head slumped forward, and her limp form hung from the cross, the rhythmic motion of her heaving belly the only evidence she was still alive. Had she not been fastened securely to the sturdy wooden beams the entire time, she would long since have been a quivering heap on the floor. Oliver surveyed his handiwork and lifted her chin to get her attention. He kissed her lightly and told her to get some rest since he had a special treat lined up for her. She could only imagine what pain or pleasure awaited her. In his world, the two were narrowly separated.

After a while, he returned and released her from the restraints which held her against the elegant device. He embraced her gently and asked if she could stand. She said she believed she could. So, he stood behind her and continued to hold her in an embrace. She stood calmly and took it in. He allowed his hands to roam over the front of her body, fondling and caressing her breasts and her abdomen, his two favorite parts of her body, though not necessarily in that order. He visualized a scenario where she would be his own personal belly dancer. She certainly has the belly for it. He thought of the outfit he instructed Zoey to wear for him not so long ago. Suddenly, he remembered.

"I almost forgot, I promised you a treat," he said. "Come."

He took her by the hand and led her to the bedroom. Once there, Alicia saw a sight that nearly made her heart stop: The naked form of Zoey spread-eagled on the bed, bound in the same chains that Alicia herself had been held in not long ago. "I thought I would return the favor," Oliver said. "If you surrender control to me, I will return what I see fit," he told her. He motioned his arm over the bound form of the girl stretched out before them and said to Alicia, "You may indulge yourself." He set the hourglass on the table by the bed and sat down in the corner. Alicia knew what it meant and realized she would have to work fast. She lay down beside Zoey and kissed her on the lips, then gazed into her eyes. Zoey looked at her.

"Alicia, I'm so sorry," Zoey said. "Please forgive me."

"Of course, I forgive you," Alicia said, "I told you I love you."

With that, she turned her attention to Zoey's body, which, for all intents and purposes, belonged to her now. She could not believe her good fortune. She had now been given the thing she had longed for since the first time she laid eyes on this woman. She knew she now had Zoey's undivided attention, and she intended to make the most of it. After several minutes of touching, kissing, and licking the incredible body of this woman, she heard a noise coming from the corner of the room and looked up. Oliver had taken the hourglass and turned it on its side. He leaned toward Alicia and whispered in her ear, "Every now and then, you just want time to stand still. I understand." After patting Alicia's butt, he left the room.

After an unknown length of time, Alicia and Zoey were basking in their mutual afterglows. They drifted in and out of sleep, Alicia resting her head on Zoey's breast. Zoey looked toward the head of the bed and rattled her chains. She smiled at Alicia and said, "Hey, you don't need these with me anymore."

"I know," said Alicia, "but there is someone here who might." With that, Oliver appeared, standing over them. Alicia got out of bed, reached up, wrapped her arms around Oliver's neck, and kissed him. "Favor returned. She's all warmed up for you," she said, glancing down at Zoey, who looked up apprehensively.

"I'm going to take a bath," Alicia said. She nodded her head toward the helpless woman on the bed and said to Oliver, "I want you to fuck that little bitch till her ears leak," and disappeared into the bathroom.

"Well," said Oliver as he advanced on Zoey, "I guess I have my instructions."

And they all lived happily ever after.

THE END

Well, there it was, for better or worse. I had poured my heart and soul into this scenario, and it came together in a surprisingly short period of time. Maybe the fact that these ideas had percolated in my mind for so long was part of the reason they flowed so effortlessly. Or maybe I have a talent for writing narrative fiction for the sickeningly depraved. In any event, I was curious to find out what Sophia would think of it.

CHAPTER 14

"Love is the delusion that one woman differs from another."
– H. L. Mencken

After we had gotten over the shock of losing Tino, we decided to look for a new cat. Once again, we visited the animal shelter and found a young male cat that was nearing the end of the time he could stay there, meaning, you know what. He looked a lot like Mittens, so we figured he was the cat for us. We named him Loki, after the Norse god of mischief and playfulness. It suited him. Loki is the sixth cat Roberta and I have had in the time we have been together. I could tell he was a catastrophe looking for a place to happen.

***

Sophia and I decided to have regular meetings on Monday evenings. Roberta was usually occupied with her friends for their weekly get-togethers at that time, so it provided some consistency. For this first session, Sophia was keen to delve into the epic saga I wrote for her.

"I wasn't expecting a novel," she said.

"I only spent a couple of days on it," I offered.

"Legend has it Robert Louis Stevenson wrote the first draft of Dr. Jekyll and Mr. Hyde in three days," she replied.

"He had a different motivation," I said. "His wife was sick, and he was broke."

"What was your motivation?" she wanted to know.

"I'm a little fucked up, remember?" I stated.

"Of course, I almost forgot," she said. "So, the character of Oliver in this story, is that how you see yourself?" she asked.

"Yeah, he is a version of what I would aspire to be if I had the means and the opportunity. The character of Craven Moorehead in the other story is closer to the real me, all full of insecurities, regrets, and repressed longings."

"I liked the way you opened up to Alicia in the beginning with the discussion of how you were drawn to the lifestyle," she said. "It was a good icebreaker to set up the situation."

"Yes, I think I would want to have such a conversation with anyone before embarking on a journey like that," I said.

"It gets pretty intense in places," she continued. "There is one part where Alicia is chained to the bed and assaulted. What is that about?"

"Consensual non-consent," I told her. "Like play-acting a rape fantasy." Sophia squinted at me ever so slightly. "She could have used the safe word at any time," I told her.

"Of course," Sophia said.

"You don't believe it?" I asked, sensing some skepticism on her part.

"I neither believe nor disbelieve," she said. "Just checking. What is it they say? Your kink is not my kink, and that's okay?"

"Something like that," I said. "I don't think I'm over the top in reality. I'm not much into flogging or anything that would leave a mark. It is more about eroticizing the suspense of the situation. In general, I have some pretty specific guidelines for what works for me."

"Which are?" Sophia asked.

"Enthusiastically consenting adult members of the extreme opposite gender," I replied. "Considering the influences I had early on, it's probably to be expected. Who can say what I might have gravitated toward if Dad had been into child porn, butch bikers, or even farm animals, which were readily available where we were. Does that have any bearing on your theories about early developmental influences?" I asked.

"Possibly, I think it would be worth exploring," she said.

I didn't think we needed to get into the whole nature vs. nurture debate right now, but I was open to revisiting it.

"And Zoey," Sophia said. "Where does she fit into the scheme of things?"

"Something I heard Alice talk about in one of her videos," I said. "She mentioned if a provider is being restrained in any way, there needs to be another person there to supervise for safety and protection—kind of a wise and necessary precaution. So, I figured if I were ever to have a session like that, money would be no object. So, I would include the other person in the scenario. And given what I know about Alice's sexuality, I didn't think she would mind."

"Right," Sophia mused. "Well, your kink is not my kink."

"Yeah, you mentioned something about that a while back," I said.

"What would it take for money to be no object in a situation like this?" Sophia wanted to know.

"Good question," I pondered. "Aside from becoming suddenly single, I suppose if I won the lottery or found out I have six months to live—any or all of the above—I'm pretty sure at least two of those things would have to happen simultaneously."

"What was the part about the page blocked by the 'league of decency?'" she asked.

"I wanted to leave something to the imagination."

"Your wife isn't down with these types of scenarios?" she asked.

"Not remotely," I said. "When I tried to explain how I got into the mode of getting curious about these settings in looking at my dad's magazine collection, she suggested it was the reason my parents' marriage sucked. She has apparently convinced herself Dad had coerced Mom into going along with it, and it turned her off so much she didn't want to have anything to do with him. I think the chances are more likely that Mom being asexual caused Dad to feel left to his own devices, and that was what came of it. I have often thought he could be into worse things which might have cogitated in my brain. Roberta doesn't appear to be able or willing to see it that way."

"Do you see any possibility of getting her to see it your way?"

"I've thought about it; I'm not sure it's a hill to die on," I said. "Still think I'm not that fucked up?"

"I've seen worse," she replied.

"Good to hear," I said.

***

I had to make considerable accommodations to my activities for the evening Alice and I tried to connect and continue the schoolgirl scenario. It was an evening when I knew Roberta would be at Eileen's house doing their usual church lady activities. To throw me a curveball, the hookup gods decided to have Eileen invite us over for dinner, which meant I would have to come up with a brilliant excuse to duck out immediately afterward so I could get online with a solid connection.

Eileen and her hubby moved here from New York years ago, and they are both staunch Yankees fans. The previous weekend, the Rockies had made the trip to New York and swept a series against their beloved team. I'm not sure who among us was more shocked. In any case, I could gloat just enough so they were not sorry to see me leave.

I made it to a place where I figured I would have some expectation of privacy and waited. Almost instantly, I got an email that said the internet at the brothel was down and cell service was spotty at best. She said they were working on it and would keep me up to date. I'm sure it occurred to me to wonder, if the internet was down, how was she getting an email out with lousy phone service? I was hoping against hope at this point. As time dragged on, it was becoming apparent it wasn't going to happen this time either. The next day, I sent her an email and asked if there was a way we could chat on the phone. She said, of course, she would love to; let's try for next week. This was becoming the default fallback plan.

***

I got an email from Todd. I hadn't heard from him in a while, and I figured we would catch up when he made his annual pilgrimage to the farm this summer. He said he had broken his arm and was taking it easy for a while. He would let me know what he planned about coming to see us later.

My current conflict with Roberta made me think about Todd's situation. Truth be told, I wouldn't be surprised if Todd would be a lot happier were he not married to his wife. She was always a bit too aristocratic for my comfort level, like she considered herself better than anyone in this family. It probably extended to Todd as well. My suspicions in this area were all but confirmed once when I was visiting Todd and offered to make margaritas. It turned out he was out of tequila, and he told me I could just use vodka. This told me he was either clueless or desperate. Something else I noticed was his dog was becoming a bit hefty. I mean, if the dog were a foot taller, he would be square. Todd said he had gotten into the habit of giving the dog a treat when he had 'happy hour,' and now he expects a treat whenever Todd fixed himself a drink. It probably should have occurred to me that if your dog is morbidly obese, it might be a sign you have a drinking problem. In any event, I understood what was happening, and the track record for marriages in this family was not the best.

***

It was time for another 'Devil's Advocate' post. I wanted to do one on how religion objectifies women. And so, I did:

How Religion Objectifies Women

There are few areas where women are more objectified than in religion. Even the act of instructing them to dress appropriately can be a form of objectification if it focuses undue attention on their appearance. Plus, the many ways they are viewed as property, and they must be submissive to their husbands further the patriarchal worldview of a culture of objectification. Some commentators debate whether women should be seen in public wearing a bikini. Please. Get real, folks. That ship has sailed, and it ain't coming back.

There is the whole discussion about 'marrying and giving in marriage,' which is part of the jargon that religious personnel toss around without fully understanding what it means. In one of the Lutheran congregations we attended at one time, the pastors were a husband-and-wife team, and the wife was a real piece of work. She had a burr up her butt about anything which might remotely sound like the woman in a relationship being treated as other than an equal partner, which I'm down with, but when it has to be stressed to this extent, it defeats the purpose. Incidentally, this duo ended up getting a divorce while they were serving in the church. But not judging. Just saying.

Christianity doesn't have a corner on the market when it comes to objectifying women. Islam teaches that men can end up in a blissful afterlife in the company of 70 virgins if they slaughter enough infidels. I'm thinking maybe Solomon has a better deal with his 700 wives and 300 concubines. Still, some men use his example and, to this day, assert the Bible teaches that a man is entitled to more than one wife.

I suppose it can be debated where the line is drawn as to lust. Men are, by nature, drawn to women in most cases. It was once considered a problem for that not to be the case. So where does natural attraction end and lust begin? I'm not sure there is a pat definition. Those who want to err on the side of caution will probably say don't look.

On the topic of sexuality, we are so repressed and judgmental about it compared to some countries. There are places in the world where nudism isn't seen as a big deal, and in some large cities, women are able to walk the streets topless. It made me think of a movie I saw once where the main character observed that if people could be conditioned to believe it is morally necessary to wear gloves and earmuffs, then we would all want to stick our fingers in each other's ears. Which is to say, whatever you tell people they can't have, that is the thing they want. Perhaps it serves to contribute to the mystique.

Then there is a thing they call the 'Billy Graham rule,' which is where a man in a position of power and authority finds it advisable not to be in a situation where he is alone with a woman who is not his wife. This includes, but is not limited to, elevators, automobiles, meeting rooms, etc. This would be a wise and prudent course of action due to the undeniable fact certain men can have their reputations ruined by the mere appearance of an inappropriate get-together. Surprisingly, though, many women have complained that such constraints can actually hurt their own chances of advancement if men are afraid to meet with them. You just can't please some people.

***

Next week, Alice doesn't show up again. I got an email saying she left the ranch early and asked if I could give her a call. I called the number she sent, but she was in a bad reception area, and I couldn't get through. I was beginning to wonder about how many times this had happened. I had to admit that at least she got in touch to let me know what was up. Still, it was becoming something between a comedy of errors and a joke, the butt of which was me.

CHAPTER 15

"Good judgment is the result of experience, and experience is the result of bad judgment."
– Mark Twain

A few days later, Alice emailed me to say she had a fender bender when she got home and was out of it for a few days. She asked if we could text each other directly so we could stay in touch. We started chatting over text messages. I told her I was going to have some free time later in the week and maybe we could schedule something then. During our text exchange, I mentioned it appeared as though the universe was conspiring against us getting together, although I believed there were worse things I could be doing than chatting with her or even seeing her naked, for that matter. She said it did appear to be odd that we had such a hard time connecting, though I had to admit it was essentially my fault due to the fact that I had to be extremely careful so I didn't get observed in a video call with a sex worker.

I was feeling good about the fact we had been able to connect, however briefly, and were beginning to communicate. I was inspired to revisit the story of Allison, the schoolgirl. I left the story hanging and didn't have a plan to follow through on the continuation, but since I had visited with Alice, I thought I would take a shot at wrapping it up. The resulting story went like this:

Payne and Pleasure Part 2
By Xander Arcane

Allison locked the door and turned to face her teacher. "Do you want me to take off my clothes?" she asked.

Mr. Payne nodded. "I would like that very much," he replied. He held the hope in the back of his mind that he would someday see her naked again. She has a lovely body.

Allison confidently undressed herself, and then it was his turn. She watched appreciatively as he joined her in complete nakedness. For an older man, he took quite good care of his body, something many of Allison's friends had noticed and commented on.

He guided her to the edge of the desk and told her to lean forward and rest her forearms on it. "Just relax, and don't be tense," he instructed her. "I'll go slow, like before, okay?"

Allison looked over her shoulder at him and nodded. She had complete faith in him that he would do his best not to make it hurt. She thought back to when he took her virginity only a few days earlier and how patient and gentle he was with her. She knew it would be the same now.

After putting on a condom and applying some extra lube which he kept on hand for just such an occasion, he gently separated her butt cheeks and placed the tip of his engorged penis on the tight hole. He began to push forward, ever so slowly, until the head of his cock disappeared into her sphincter. She had buried her face in her hands and was doing her best to stay calm. As he felt her relax and prepare for his next advance, he softly stroked her back and shoulders, then reached around and touched her belly and thighs, all the while continuing his steady advance. He leaned down and whispered in her ear, "Is it alright?" She nodded, and he gave one more firm but gentle thrust until his organ had penetrated to the maximum depth he felt she could accept, and he continued to rock his body along with hers. After a while, he began to slowly move in and out as she started to groan. Before long, the groans turned to moans as she began to let go and accept this new sensation. He could sense her growing willingness to give in, and the excitement overwhelmed his senses, and his orgasm exploded inside her. Sensing it, Allison went limp from the exhilaration in her body and collapsed on the desktop.

Mr. Payne took Allison in his arms and caressed her gently. "How did that feel?" he inquired.

Allison shuddered and tried to come up with the words to describe it. "Very intense," she said. "It could take some getting used to." She looked into his eyes, then buried her face in his chest and began to cry softly. "Mr. Payne, will you make love to me again? I mean, like, the regular way?" There was a pleading look in her eyes as tears streamed down her pretty face.

Mr. Payne nodded. "Yes, but not here. I would like you to come to my house."

"How can I do that?" she asked. "Don't I need to be back in my room by curfew?"

"There are ways around that," he replied. "I have some pull with the headmistress. And by pull, I mean leverage. It involves some pictures I have of her with a Siberian Husky." By now, he knew that when you have his reputation for being a serial schoolgirl fucker, whether deserved or not, it is good to have as many people as possible in your back pocket.

***

Once they arrived at his house, he invited her to make herself at home. "Would you like some dinner?" he asked.

She threw her arms around his neck and kissed him full on the mouth. "After," she said in a throaty whisper.

"Well, now, you are one horny little slut, aren't you?"

"I'm pretty sure you told me once you like that in a woman."

"I may have mentioned it in passing," he said.

"I think I would remember. After all, I haven't been a woman all that long. But I guess I don't need to tell you that," she said with a wink.

As he led her to the bedroom, Allison noticed a door that appeared to be sturdier than others she had observed. "What's in there?" she wanted to know.

"It's just a, um… rec room," was all he would say.

"You mean with, like, a pool table?"

"Not exactly."

"What then?"

"Party supplies."

"Like what?" Now, she was becoming curious.

"The usual," he said. "Chips, dips, chains, whips. Nothing you would be interested in."

Allison would have begged to differ, but he continued to lead the way to the master suite as she looked back in wonder at the mysterious door.

"I think it would be good to start by taking a shower," he suggested.

"You mean together?"

"Would you like to take a shower together?"

"Oh, fuck YES!" she responded.

They eagerly undressed each other and headed straight to the shower. It was a large tile shower with a built-in seat that Allison could stand on and bring herself up to a level where they could see eye to eye. It also served to make it less of a reach for him to bend down to suckle her breasts, run hot kisses down her body, and focus on her adorable belly button, attacking it with his tongue and lips. Once they had slathered each other with body wash, they hugged and kissed like sex-starved forbidden fruit addicts who were married but not to each other. Allison stood on the floor of the shower, bent her body forward, and urged him to stick it in somewhere, anywhere.

After their lust-fueled fuck-fest was over, they toweled each other dry, and he led her to the bed. He pulled the covers back and gestured for her to climb in, joining her right after. He embraced her, and they cuddled for a time. "This is the part where we make love," he whispered in her ear. And so they did. For a while, they lay there enjoying each other's presence. They kissed, they gazed, they caressed, each feeling the other's warm body and anticipating what was to come. He wanted her to feel loved like she had never been loved before. They climaxed as one, and the look in her eyes told him she indeed felt the love.

As they recovered their senses, Mr. Payne resisted the urge to ask Allison how their lovemaking compared to the times she was with her boyfriend. It turned out he didn't need to. She wanted to talk about it. "This is so much better," she said. It appeared to him she wanted to cry.

"What do you mean?"

"With him, it's always so rushed and hurried. He just sticks it in and humps away, and it's over before I know it. I think you're right; boys his age really don't care how a girl feels. It's all about what he can take from me. Like what he wants to do to me next time." Her eyes filled with tears. "I'm not sure I could handle that with him."

Mr. Payne brushed her cheek with his fingers to wipe away the tears. "You shouldn't ever feel like you have to do anything you don't want to do," he told her.

"It's so different with you," she said. "He fucks. You make love. I can tell the difference." She knew she was going to have to make a choice, and soon.

"All the girls I know have boyfriends," she continued. "I felt like I needed one, too, or I wouldn't fit in. I don't know if it's worth it, even if he can go all night."

"Well, you won't get that from me. I'm not 18 anymore," he told her.

"I'm barely 18," she replied.

"I'm aware of that. But what I'm saying is, I'm at a place where I need to focus on quality, not quantity."

Allison began to kiss him with all the passion she could muster. "If it's quality lovemaking you want, you've got it," she said. She covered his body with hot kisses until his cock stood straight at attention. She climbed on and lowered herself onto it, straddling him and making her whole body available to him: her thighs, her belly, her chest, shoulders, and back, all there for his eyes and hands to devour. She leaned forward so she could drag her boobs over his chest, then thrust a nipple into his mouth and pressed it in as if offering to feed him her whole breast in one mouthful. Soon, she began to convulse with a screaming orgasm that made the walls shake. She collapsed on top of him and lay there quivering. "Best fuck ever," she gasped. Mr. Payne was not in a position to argue with her.

They lay there in a semi-conscious state for a long time. "What do you think the odds are that we could end up together?" she asked him.

He thought for a moment. "I imagine the smart money would put it roughly equivalent to Donald Trump's chances of getting elected as emperor of Mexico. But then, stranger things have happened."

"What do you see in me?" she wanted to know. "I'm only a silly schoolgirl. I didn't even know how to give a blowjob until you clued me in."

He smiled at the memory of it. "You're a quick study. I do believe you could suck the chrome off a trailer hitch if you put your mind to it."

"Is that anything like sucking a golf ball through a garden hose?"

He explained, "There are subtle variations in the respective skill sets, but the outcomes are similar."

"I'm up for giving you one of those outcomes," she said.

"You cannot be serious," he responded. "I've been inside of you four times already today, which is more than I do in a typical month these days. There is no way I can go again right now," he stated emphatically.

"What are you talking about?" she wanted to know.

"The simple truth is men of a certain age often need help getting and staying hard. So, I recently sought out help in this area, but it didn't go quite the way I expected. I went to see a medical professional to get some treatment. I thought he was going to give me a prescription for Cialis, but when he handed me the slip, all it said was, 'See Alice.' I said, 'What's this?'"

He said, "That's the treatment plan; it's 100% guaranteed, never fails."

Allison looked bewildered. "So, who the fuck is Alice?" she asked.

"I don't know, probably just some whore," was Mr. Payne's response. "Anyway, until I get all of this figured out, I can't make any promises that I can be as functional as you might hope for. In any event, you can expect it to be at least an hour before I can come close to being up for another go."

Allison was having none of it. "I think maybe you haven't been with the right woman. I'll bet if I wrap my lips around that bad boy, I can have you filling my mouth with hot cum in less than 10 minutes."

"No possible way," he said.

"Then bet me."

"What's the bet?"

"The winner says do, the loser does."

"You're on," he replied.

Her mouth latched on to his sexual organ, and it got invigorated almost instantly. Mr. Payne was not a big porn watcher, but he imagined from what he had been told that Allison had all the tools at her disposal. His praise of her cock sucking prowess was not misplaced. With minutes to spare, she had him gushing like a Texas wildcat oil well.

"You're welcome," she said. "Now pay up, loser."

"Fine, what's your pleasure?" Mr. Payne asked.

"I would like you to show me around your rec room," came her reply. "Right after dinner."

Seven years later...

Allison was still settling into her new position as headmistress here at Switchback Academy. The opportunity came when the previous headmistress suddenly left and ran off with the drummer in a Three Dog Night tribute band. No one knew what the lady was thinking, but Allison seized the chance and became the youngest headmistress in the history of headmistresses. And to think that her newfound confidence and assertiveness all started with a visit to Mr. Payne's rec room.

This morning, Allison was returning from an important staff meeting when she stopped by the faculty lounge to get a fresh cup of coffee. While she was there, she happened to glance over at the TV and saw a news bulletin that included a picture of someone she recognized. It was her old boyfriend from before she and Mr. Payne officially became lovers. Curious, she turned up the volume to hear what the story was about. Her jaw dropped when she heard the reporter say that he had been apprehended and charged in the recent failed assassination attempt on Emperor Donald Trump of Mexico. *Wow,* she thought. *What are the odds?*

But Allison had other matters to attend to this morning. She called Mr. Payne into her office to give him some news. "The administrative staff met this morning to discuss the state of affairs with the girls at the school," she started to explain. "I'm sure I don't have to tell you things have gotten completely out of hand. It was pointed out to me that they appear to do fine until they take Advanced Biology class, and that's when about half of them turn out to be dirty little sluts. Do you have any thoughts on that?" she asked, tapping her fingers on the desk.

"Wow, what are the odds?" he mused. Allison continued to tap her fingers, and Mr. Payne got the message that she was neither amused nor satisfied with his response. "Look, we both know that a lot of these girls could benefit from a good spanking," he told her. "But if their parents expressly tell us we are not to do it, my hands are tied. What do you expect in those cases?"

"I see what you mean," she said. "But we have to do something, so there is now a zero-tolerance policy with regard to sex on campus," she told him. "I thought I had better tell you myself."

"Well, I hope I have enough pull with the headmistress to get those restrictions relaxed a little," he replied.

"Oh, don't worry, you're 'grandfathered' in," she told him.

Ouch, that's cold, he thought to himself.

"But only in this office," she continued with a stern look on her face.

Oh, well, perhaps that will do, he thought, *considering how good she looks in leather.*

THE END

I liked the way I wrapped up the story, and it appeared to come to me out of nowhere. I hoped Alice would pick up on how I worked her directly into the story through her alter-ego, Allison.

After I sent the story off to Alice, I figured I might as well send it to Sophia also since she mentioned she was curious as to how it would end. I was interested to see what she would have to say about it.

CHAPTER 16

"Strong minds discuss ideas, average minds discuss events, weak minds discuss people."
– Socrates

I finally meet Diane face to face. She has a hungry look in her eyes. It is obviously a no-bra day. I walk up to her, and we embrace and start kissing. I spin her around so I am standing behind her, pull up her tank top, and wrap my arms around her bare-breasted body. They feel so soft and supple as I cup them in my hands and gently squeeze them and flick her hard nipples. I lift her chin so she is looking up at me as I continue manhandling her. She raised her lips to meet mine in a lusty kiss as I run my hand down her belly. I momentarily break off the kiss and tell her, "I'm not sure we should be doing this."

"I know, that's what makes it so much fun," she says. "That's what forbidden fruit is all about." I can't argue with that, so I continue letting my hands roam. I slide one hand down her belly and slip it inside her shorts and feel her bush and run my finger over her clit as she moans and becomes wet. Soon, she is panting, and I know we are close to a hot, heavy pound sesh.

"Why don't you drop to your knees and suck my cock?" I say to her.

"As you wish," she responds. She kneels and undoes my pants and lowers them so she can wrap her lips around my swollen member. As she takes it in and works her magic, my imagination runs wild...

"OH, MY GOD! ALEX!" Roberta yells from the kitchen. "Get in here; you need to see this." Fantasy buzz-kill. *Oh well, later, Diane.* I go and see what Roberta needs.

"Look what the cat brought in," she said.

Our cat Ginger had brought a bird into the house. Not just any bird; it was a live owl. A very young owl, as it turned out. She brought it in and set it down on the floor, and it was flapping its wings and staggering around. I figured it needed to be taken outside. Roberta said it might be injured, which was true. But first, it needed to go out. I was able to chase it out the door, and it went out and limped along on the lawn.

"The vet's office will take birds like this and patch them up, then release them back to the wild," Roberta told me. It was simply a matter of getting it over there. I asked Roberta to try to find a small box, and I would go out and collect the bird and run it over there. While she was looking for a box, I went out to find the owl. I could see the bird had made its way to our neighbor's house and hid in a corner under a shrub, looking for cover. I knocked on their door to let them know I was going to reach under the bush and grab the owl, and when she came to the door, her miniature poodle came tearing out the door and immediately went under the shrub to catch the bird. I was able to get the bird away from the dog and put it in the box Roberta had found. The poor bird mostly needed to get out of our neighborhood.

When I got to the veterinarian's office to drop off the owl, I spoke to the receptionist. She said they could take a look at the bird and see if they could help it. While I was there, an elderly lady was exiting a treatment room and was obviously upset. The receptionist said this lady had been coming here for years with her dog, and today, she had to have the dog put to sleep. She told me she was concerned about this lady as the dog was all she had, and without it, she might not want to go on. It's sad, but this is the way it happens a lot of the time. People who had a pet who needed them suddenly didn't have a reason to continue living.

I thought about the times we had lost a pet. In addition to Mittens and Tino, we had a cat named Gabrielle that was left in our care by a friend of Roberta's who moved away and didn't want to put the cat through the stress of relocating, so she asked if we could take care of her. We had her for several years until the cat got old, and one day, she wandered off when the first snowfall of winter came. She had gone outside, and we saw her paw prints in the snow on the doorstep, but we never found out what happened to her. Another 'foster cat,' Mitzy, we got in pretty much the same way. She also aged out and had to be put to sleep after apparently having a stroke. We found her on the floor of the closet one morning, unresponsive. It is never pleasant, but it is one of those things that all pet owners eventually deal with. In our case, we usually cushioned the blow by getting a new cat after a certain length of time had passed. I wondered, at what point do you realize it is time to put it behind you and acknowledge you probably won't outlive another pet, and what will happen to it?

***

On the way home from the vet, I stopped at R&R. I saw a car drive up, one that caught my eye. It was a Corvette Stingray from the mid-seventies. I had always had an appreciation for this car, as I started to notice them when I was in high school. It was in the days of the Apollo era, and all the astronauts drove them. General Motors made a special deal with them; since the astronauts couldn't do product endorsements, they made it possible for them to lease cars at dealer invoice. The astronauts could have leased any GM car they wanted, but for some reason, the one they all wanted was the Corvette. Who could have imagined?

I watched the car pull up, and who should have stepped out of it but Sue Nami and her partner, a Black man with whom I hadn't gotten acquainted yet, but now I had a reason. I loved to talk about Corvettes; the C3 model he drove was my specialty. I can tell most of the different model years' subtle differences. I enjoy chatting about it. It is one of the few things, other than cats, about which I can carry on an extended conversation.

Sue and her friend came in and sat down at a table. I walked over and said hi to Sue, then addressed her friend. "Nice ride," I said. "Is that a seventy-five?"

"Seventy-six," he replied.

137

"Okay, I probably would have had to look inside at the steering wheel to figure that out," I responded. The seventy-six 'Vette is famous for using the same steering wheel as the Chevy Vega.

"Yeah, I switched that one out for one from a Camaro," he said.

"Clever," I responded. "I'm Alex Anderson," I said.

"Arnold," he replied. "Arnold Schwartz."

I froze. They both looked like they were waiting for me to say something. No way. If ever there was a time when silence was golden, now is the time. "Nice to meet you," I said.

***

When Alice and I first started communicating over text messaging, I hinted there was a thing called sexting that she might want to try. "Is there now?" she said. "I'm not familiar with it. Explain, please," she texted with a winking kissy face. She sent me a picture of her in her schoolgirl uniform. We scheduled a phone call for later in the week.

When the time came, she actually texted me and asked if I would be interested in doing our call over Skype. She said it was the least she could do after all the snafus we have had. I said sure, and we talked for close to an hour. It was a fun visit, nothing terribly risqué; I did mention I had watched her stream earlier today, where she talked about the great 'spit or swallow' debate. She said it wasn't really a thing at the brothel since the rule is condoms must be used for everything. "Wow, even for oral?" I asked.

"Yup, even that," Alice replied.

"Gosh, I can't really get my head around that," I said. "But then, I guess that would be your job, wouldn't it?"

Alice got the same look I have noticed I get from Sophia when I say something off the wall like this. "I've been told I'm very good at my job," she winked.

"All I can do is take your word for it at this point," I told her. I went on to talk about how that is a bit of a change from my one and only visit to one of the Nevada brothels, which had happened decades ago. "That's way too long," she said. "We need to get you out here."

Yeah, good luck with that, I thought. Then, out loud, I said, "Sounds like fun."

***

At our next meeting, Sophia asked if I had given any more thought to compiling and publishing my short stories. I had sent her the continuation of the schoolgirl story, and she appeared to think a collection of erotic short stories could be marketable. Now that I have a pen name that provided me with cover, I was at least willing to consider making the attempt. I thought about how I would present it to my editor. She would most likely think they are self-indulgent shit.

I am still somewhat hesitant, knowing it would not be well received by people in my circle of friends and family. But honestly, what do they have to say about it? They haven't exactly been supportive of my self-published books. I have given away far more of those than I have sold. Of course, they will read them as long as they don't have to spend a dime on them, and heaven forbid they should recommend them to their friends and relatives. It gives the lie to the scriptural admonitions that the laborer is worthy of their hire, or what good does it do to tell someone to be blessed if you are not going to be part of the blessing, you know, by actually giving financial support? I mean, for all the monetary contributions I have given to various churches over the years, I have never gotten so much as a 'Pentecostal handshake' in return. (Google it). To me, it's called putting your money where your mouth is.

"I'm reasonably sure Roberta would have objections to these stories I have been writing," I said. "People in her realm are so put off by discussions of sexuality. It's like people in the church have to suppress all notions of it. They can't even see movies or shows if that is part of it."

"Go on," Sophia said.

"I once knew a real zealot who made a point of boasting about the fact he wouldn't go to an R-rated movie, presumably because someone might flash a nipple or a butt crack. At the same time, he said he loves to watch a good shoot-em-up; the more blood, and gore, the better. That's insane."

"How so?" Sophia asked.

"I struggle to see how two consenting adults hooking up is worse than seeing people indiscriminately murdered. Yet things like rebellious kids or people who lie and cheat and steal are all over the entertainment landscape. These are necessary plot points unless you are like my wife, who only wants to watch shows where they all live happily before, during, and ever after.

"Honestly, my friends and family, or maybe I should say my acquaintances and relatives, don't actually buy my books anyway, so what they don't know won't hurt them," I said.

"I wonder if I ask too much out of life," I said. "Am I wrong to want something that other people appear to be able to get without having to move Heaven and Earth, or at least make a federal case out of it?

"In any event, I am a couple of fries short of a happy meal to put out a volume of erotica. I will need to get more stories put together. In the meantime, I can work out how to rationalize the outcome," I told her. She appeared to be willing to accept that and move on to the topic of the day.

"What can you tell me about your formative years and how you came to your beliefs and attitudes?" Sophia asked.

"I was raised with traditional values and a spiritual mindset," I told her. "Growing up among Scandinavian Lutherans, I developed the typical stoicism and reserve about my personal beliefs. We tend to play it close to the vest. When I met my wife, she was active in a Pentecostal church, which is night and day different from what I had ever experienced. I was intrigued enough that I was willing to check it out, and I ended up joining her church after we were married. Over the years, we moved on and tried different churches. We eventually got back to various flavors of Lutheranism, of which there are many.

"Mom was indeed a religious woman. Not that she wasn't fun-loving and friendly. It's just that she wouldn't say shit if she had a mouthful. And if I ever thought to, she would open up a can of whoop-ass on me. I'm not sure how it went with my brothers; they were so much older than I am I couldn't imagine what their lives were like growing up. It was like we were from different eras.

"Another factor in my outlook on life is the fact I was hitting puberty during the height of the sexual revolution, which began in the late sixties. This was a time when attitudes about traditional gender roles were being challenged, and it became incorrect to cling to a lot of old-fashioned beliefs. It was common to hear activists talking about how being a man was nothing to be proud of, and sayings like 'A woman needs a man like a fish needs a bicycle' were all over the media. I understood the root of the conflict as I observed old-style thinking in action. My mom always adopted the traditional mode of identifying as 'Mrs. – my dad's full name,' and I never quite understood how someone could not feel diminished doing this. I guess you could say in that regard, I was woke before woke was a thing.

"In any event, I heard a lot about how terrible Dad was, with his appetite for pornography and other issues, but there was never any talk of Mom's contribution to the situation. Over the years, I had developed a theory about it, but you already know my thoughts on that subject," I went on.

"Still, Roberta holds Mom blameless in that situation; she prefers to believe it was all Dad's fault. I feel like that extends to me in the way everything I do is a problem in our relationship. I think of the song by Meatloaf called Two Out of Three Ain't Bad. The refrain goes, 'I want you, I need you, but there ain't no way I'm ever gonna love you.' That's how I feel about Roberta, but switch the words love and want," I said. Sophia appeared shaken when I said this. "Is it terrible of me to feel that way?"

"What do you think Roberta would say if you asked her?" Sophia asked.

"Good talk, Sophia," I said.

***

Roberta had been withdrawn most of the day, more so than was usual for her. Finally, she asked if we could talk about something. "Are you paying someone for sexual favors?" she asked.

"Why would you think that?" I asked back.

"I found evidence of a significant payment to someone named Alice Modicum in your emails," she said.

I was stunned. I had no idea she would have a reason to be rummaging through my email, but I thought I had stashed that where it wouldn't be apparent. Still, I could see that there was no point in trying to deny it. The best course of action was to confront it and set the record straight. "Yeah, okay, fine. I did make a payment to her, but it was only to talk to me about the things you won't address."

"Well, who is she?" Roberta demanded.

"She is a sex worker in Nevada," I started to explain. "Or, in terms you would understand, a prostitute." There, I said it.

"How could you do that?" Roberta asked.

"Because you won't engage with me at a level I want to explore. I need to feel that there is someone, somewhere, who will talk about the things that interest me." I'm not sure my explanation even convinced me, and it sure as hell didn't convince Roberta.

One thing is certain: it will be dicey going forward.

CHAPTER 17

"Great spirits have always encountered violent opposition from mediocre minds."
– Albert Einstein

I was in fight-or-flight mode over Roberta's latest development. I decided I should let Sophia know about it, so I gave her a quick phone call. "Roberta found out about my arrangement with Alice. She is treating it like a potential crisis situation. Not that I would probably blame her," I said.

"Do you think she will escalate it? Think about breaking up?" Sophia asked.

"I don't know. I remember hearing someone say that when a man meets with a divorce lawyer, the first question he needs to consider is, 'Was the screwing you got worth the screwing you're about to get?'" I didn't want to think about that.

"Keep me apprised of the situation. We can discuss it more at our next meeting," Sophia said.

***

The next afternoon, I had a meeting scheduled with Alice. My current situation with Roberta made that iffy, but Roberta decided to spend the afternoon with Eileen. I could only imagine what they would be talking about.

I watched Alice's live stream on Y'allScreen that morning, and she mentioned it was hot where she was, and her air conditioner was acting up. I didn't think much of it at the time, but it turned out to be a harbinger of what was to come for the day. Shortly before our scheduled time, she sent me a text saying she had workers there fixing her swamp cooler on the roof, and there was an excessive amount of noise, so it was not likely we would be able to conduct a meeting. Wow, what a shock. We texted back and forth most of the afternoon, as she had nothing better to do with all the banging on the roof; she could at least text. I asked if she was convinced that we were operating under some kind of a doomed curse. She said she was beginning to see it but suggested maybe it is a message that we need to arrange an actual get-together. I couldn't imagine any way the logistics for such an event could be realistically accomplished. I mean, the way things have been going, it could turn out like if Apollo 13 got hijacked by D. B. Cooper and had its reentry blown into the Mount St. Helens eruption. But bless her heart; she appears to think it could happen. Well, if this is what makes her happy, who was I to squelch it? I asked her if it had ever taken this much time to do three hours of Skype calls, and she admitted it was definitely a first for her. It all but confirmed to me that there were cosmic forces at work.

***

At our next session, Sophia asked me to explore my family life and how having stepkids affected it.

"I had never been married when I met Roberta," I stated. "I was in my early 30s and was starting to think I didn't relish the idea of growing old alone. She was a widow with two boys in middle school, Freddie and Jason. Freddie was the older of the two and was a bit off, to say the least. I suppose an armchair psychologist would describe him as a low-functioning sociopath, but I thought of him as the evil of two lessers. As for Jason, he and I appeared to hit it off all right early on. However, he fell in with a crowd of friends who didn't have his best interests at heart.

"At one point, Jason got a job as a dishwasher at a local restaurant and kept it for a couple of years. Shortly after he turned 16, he decided it was our duty as parents to provide him with a car. He talked Roberta into going shopping with him, and before they knew it, they came home with a car and a contract to purchase. Long story short, they were obligated to buy the car, and the only way it was going to happen was for Roberta and me to cosign the loan. Wouldn't you know? Within days of this happening, and without letting us know right away, he managed to get himself fired from the job he had had for two years or more. I guess having to work to pay an obligation wasn't as much fun as getting to spend every dime you took in on cigarettes and dope. On the drive home one evening, he got the car pointed into the sun, couldn't see the vehicle in front of him, and rear-ended it. His car, or I guess I should say, my car, didn't fare too well. Of course, we also made the mistake of assuming he would keep the insurance in force. The truth is, I was probably not a good fit for that family structure from day one. By the time I realized it, it was too late. I felt committed to the relationship, and I was going to make it work.

"I wasn't always good at dealing with the drama. Especially with Jason. Roberta and he would often get into heated discussions, and it stressed me out. One time, I felt Jason had crossed a line by not showing her the proper respect, and I thumped his melon. Roberta reacted badly to it, in a way I felt made me look bad. Not that I was proud of the way I handled it, but I figured I needed to get his attention. She didn't see it that way. The funny thing is, Jason handled it surprisingly well, and we ended up almost bonding over it. But, the result was I saw that Roberta and I had widely differing views on how to administer discipline. Hers relied mainly on starting a slow count to three when they acted out. She didn't realize her bluff had long since been called. In any event, she wasn't interested in having my help in parenting; she just wanted me to rubber-stamp her lousy parenting choices.

"One time, when Jason was transitioning out of a stint as a guest of the state, he got himself a place to live in Grand Junction, and I thought

I was rid of him. He came home over the holidays. Later, Roberta drove him home, and I figured it was the last I would see of him for a while. But when she got back, he was still with her, and she announced things weren't working out for him there, and he needed to come back and set up in our area. He said he would stay with us until he could get settled. It wasn't long after that he failed a pee test with his probation officer, and it was determined he would be under house arrest. In my house. Well, in my wife's house, too, but still, my house. Things came to a head when a police officer paid a visit to us to check out his accommodations. He had pretty much taken over the basement by then, and to say it resembled a pig pen would be an insult to pigs. To make matters worse, it somehow came out that we had some adult beverages in the house. The officer kindly pointed out that since Jason was under house arrest, we could not have alcohol on the premises. I lost it at that point. 'Now let me get this straight,' I said. 'For the privilege of housing this worthless ass-wipe, my rights are curtailed. What? Fuck that. He can go live with you. I did not sign on for this bullshit. I'm out of here.' So, I took off. Maybe if I were smart, I would have ended it then and there.

"In my mind, I feel like she has some profound mental health issues," I said.

"How so?" Sophia asked.

"Well, she is certainly passive-aggressive," I said. "Like, one of the biggest things is not ever being able to discuss an issue when something is clearly bothering her. It's as if I'm supposed to just know. And I recognize that because I know I do the same thing. And she complains when I don't go into detail with her when something is upsetting me. To me, it's the epic struggle between the pot and the kettle."

"So, you're saying you are passive-aggressive too?" Sophia asked.

"By that definition, I would have to say yes," I stated. "I mean, I recognize the telltale signs. It's bad enough when one person in a relationship is that way, but when two are, it's a recipe for Hell on Earth."

Sophia certainly had a way of drawing me out in a conversation so I could look at issues from a different perspective and work out some of my own conclusions. I was starting to think of her as a friend and a confidante, kind of like Diane but without the frequent booby flashing.

***

A few weeks passed, and I heard from Todd again. He said in the course of taking care of his broken arm, the doctors had done some tests and found he had a form of bone cancer called multiple myeloma. He said they told him it was treatable and shouldn't be too big a problem. I hoped he knew what he was talking about, but I felt uneasy. The truth is, anytime someone mentions cancer, it is a red flag. Mom had her battle with the disease, which went on for over 20 years. She appeared to have beaten it, but all of a sudden, it came back and settled in her liver. It was literally only weeks after we found out it came back that we lost her. It started me thinking about my own mortality.

I knew I needed to pay attention to my health and physical conditioning. I get down on myself often for not being in shape, but I rationalize that round is, after all, a shape. But I knew I needed to be more like the character in my stories, which, as an older man, still takes care not to let things get out of hand. After all, I reasoned, isn't it only fair if I expect the ladies that I want to keep company with to look good naked? Shouldn't I do the same? I wouldn't feel right about asking more of someone else than I can deliver myself.

***

I knew I would have to gain more of a following for potential readership of my stories if I ever decided to get serious about publishing them. I thought I should start a podcast where I could interview content providers in the sex-positive space. I wondered whether I could persuade Alice Modicum to be on the program, but I remembered all the hassles we had simply trying to connect for a virtual date and decided it wouldn't be worth the stress. Besides, she would most likely want a four-figure cash payment and a sperm sample to even think about it. On a whim, I got the idea to mention it to Diane Marie, and much to my surprise, she was enthusiastic about the idea. So, I scheduled her to be my first guest.

***

I set up another meeting time with Alice. I would need to come up with a way to connect offsite since Roberta was hosting the meeting of her group, and it would not be possible to do my thing in the same space. Once again, I set up at an undisclosed location and waited for Alice to call. And waited. And waited. Seriously, you must be kidding. It was like a bad situation that I didn't appear to be capable of, nor willing to accept the fact that it wasn't meant to be. Finally, she gets in touch via text message. The situation this time is her horse got loose, and she had to try to wrangle it back into the barn. The thought occurred to me it could be highly entertaining to watch as this 4'8" young lady tries to entice a horse to go where she needed it to go, but I had other thoughts on my mind. Another wrinkle in the epic saga with Alice, with which I was getting more than a little frustrated.

CHAPTER 18

**"After a time, you may find that 'having' is not so pleasing a thing after all as 'wanting.' It is not logical, but it is often true."
– Spock**

I was still feeling jittery about Roberta's precarious situation. Fortunately, my big podcast was coming up, so I could take my mind off it for a while.

My debut podcast

In order to make a splash with the podcast, I knew I would need to launch it in a big way. In my mind, I had already scored a significant coup by arranging for Diane Marie to be my first guest. Diane might dispute it, but I considered her to be nothing short of an A-list celebrity in this space. I figured I should go all out and do a live stream with video in a studio setting. We would be doing this over a Zoom meeting with all the bells and whistles. I made a point of letting my blog subscribers know when it would go live so I could get the maximum exposure.

The podcast begins, and I introduced Diane. "Thank you for being on the program," I said.

"Yes, it's an honor and a privilege," Diane replied.

"Well, it's an honor and a privilege for me."

"That's what I meant," she said.

"Oh, of course, so it is."

Moving on. "You have a significant following on various social media platforms. Without being specific, does that translate to much in the way of revenue?"

"Oh, yes," she said. "It took time to cultivate and develop a following, but I would venture to guess that I make an income comparable to that of a software engineer or an accountant. In fact, there is something of an inside joke among some of us that when asked, we say we are accountants, which has a way of putting an end to any more questions."

"Well, I would certainly like to know your secret to growing your platform," I said, as I had been struggling with my blog and book sites for quite some time.

"It helps if you have something people are interested in," Diane replied.

"Yes, I suppose it does," I said. "I have a question which I'm sure is on the minds of many people who might be listening to this program. It has to do with the stigma about sites like Just Our Intimacy, or should I say JOI?"

"Yes, everyone knows what JOI stands for," Diane replied.

"Of course. But a lot of people think poorly of the individuals who browse such sites. Some say it is strictly for pathetic misfits or involuntary celibates who can't spend time with naked women any other way. What do you say to them?"

"Oh, that's true, absolutely. Yes, I agree one hundred percent," Diane said.

"Huh?" I sputtered.

"Let's face it, if not for all the limp-dick losers who come to my site hoping I'll lift my shirt and show my boobs, I'd be making retail wages. But I'm sure I don't have to tell you that," she said.

Wait, what? I fully expected Diane to refute my assertion. How am I supposed to react to this? Now, I was dogpaddling. I tried to imagine how I would come out of this tailspin. I thought if I had a sponsor, now would be a good time to cut to a commercial. Before long, Diane started to giggle.

"Come on, Xander, I'm just yanking your chain," Diane laughed. "Where's that sense of humor I have come to know and love?" she teased.

"Oh, yeah, I knew what you were doing," I said.

Diane launched into a defense of her followers. "The truth is the vast majority of the men who visit my site are successful, intelligent, articulate individuals who simply struggle with a lack of ability to express sexual intimacy. That's why they come to me. I create a safe space for them to indulge their fantasies."

While Diane was articulating her position on the quality of men who subscribe to her site, I had cut my audio and video and was breathing into a paper bag in a desperate attempt to restart my cardio-pulmonary system before I would have to speak again.

After Diane stated her case, I continued. "What about the whole area of the content providers and how they are viewed? Does that give you any grief?" I asked.

"No doubt, there are preconceived notions people have about us. That's where the accountant cover story comes in handy," Diane said. "I don't feel anyone has the right to judge me or anyone who runs a business on this site. In fact, I really feel that this is my calling, to help people who are lonely and isolated know someone cares."

"Wow," I interjected. "I think that would probably be a tough sell to folks from my tribe, but I understand where you are coming from, and I am all for you in your efforts."

"Much appreciated," Diane replied.

"Does it create any problems in your personal life? You are married, correct?" I asked.

"Yes, happily married," Diane said. "My husband is supportive of my work and proud of me. He understands I have boundaries and it is a business. He has been accommodating and supportive."

"Wow!" I said. "It must be nice to have someone like him in your life who doesn't regard any sexual discussions you might have with others as an existential threat. I know my wife would have my guts for garters if she knew I was even talking to you. Fortunately, she probably doesn't know the difference between a podcast and an air raid warning."

"Sounds like she could use some counseling," Diane suggested.

"You have no idea," I said. "Anyway, you have certainly added a much-needed ray of sunshine in my life at times," I told her. "I have come to think of you as the definitive MILF. In fact, if you think about it, definitive MILF and Diane Marie both start with DM. Maybe you could come up with a tie-in for your brand."

"That's silly," Diane responded; however, she appeared to reconsider. "Wait. Gosh, come to think of it, I kind of like it."

"Sure, well, feel free to use it. It's a gift from me to you," I told her. "Of course, I'll want a percentage of all the Definitive MILF merch you sell on your site since it was my idea, after all."

"That's fair," Diane said. "I'm sure we can work something out."

"Great, I'll have my people call your people," I said. "Anyway, I have to tell you, I have long been a fan of your site, where you start each day with a little bit of fantasy exploration. It adds some much-appreciated stimulation at the start of the day."

"I'm glad you think so," Diane said.

"I remember one of the first situations I saw you talk about," I went on. "It was shortly after I came over to your site. I found you on Y'allScreen doing one of your trademark 'Bra or No Bra' videos. In that one, you had on this sexy golf outfit, and you played it up to the hilt. One day, in your morning talk, you referenced the video and started to embark on a fantasy where you were at a golf course and showed up to play as a single. The guy in the pro shop decided to pair you up with another golfer, and you said it turned out to be someone who was a follower on your site. Do you remember that?" I asked.

"Yes, I think I recall that one," Diane stated.

"Well, I remember coming up with a fantasy situation of my own related to that. If you are up for a little adventure, I could start us off, and we could go back and forth acting out a fantasy encounter," I suggested.

"Hey, yeah, go for it," Diane said. "I'm up for anything!"

"Are you now?" I teased.

"Try me," Diane said.

"Okay, here we go," I said. "The pro shop guy hands me a key to the cart and tells me he put me together with a lady playing as a single. I don't think much of it, then I see you. You are standing there in a short skirt and a form-fitting knit polo shirt, and it is readily apparent you are not wearing a bra. That's okay, I figure. Then I take a closer look at you. 'Holy fuck,'

I think. 'I know her.' This has been my fantasy for a while now: meeting you and spending some time one-on-one. I have no idea if you know that I am one of your followers, but it doesn't matter. I help you load your clubs onto the cart, and we head out. As we move to the first tee, I can see guys looking at us, and I wonder if they are aware of who you are. I mean, anyone would notice you in your short skirt and the polo top you have on. We start our round, and we play a few holes, flirting with each other; you are just so sexy. As we drive along the course, you make sure I get a good look at those thighs you are showing off.

"After a while, the sun is high in the sky, and it is a hot day. You pull your shirt up and tie a little knot in the front. I notice as you stand there with your belly showing in that barely legal short skirt. You have a pretty good idea what it is doing to me to see you standing there showing that much skin, but you play it coy, acting like you have good sense. I am thoroughly distracted as I hit my tee shot, and it slices off into the trees. Now we will have to go in there and look for it. Okay, your turn," I said as I handed it off to Diane.

"Okay," she said as she picked up the story. "We are walking around back in the thick growth of trees; no one could possibly see that we are back here. We look around for your ball, and as we do, I turn to face your direction. I take a step and stub my toe on a tree root and fall straight towards you," she said. "Back to you."

I felt the need to interject a comment here. "Now, if this were one of your morning fantasy adventures, this would be the point at which you would say, 'Tomorrow, we'll pick it up from here,'" I said. "You would milk this situation for a whole week. But since this is my only chance to have you here, we need to wrap it up and make it happen here since I may not get another chance. Incidentally, that is the story of my sex life up to now."

"Sorry to hear that," Diane said.

"It is what it is," I said as I resumed. "You fall toward me, and I manage to catch you before you hit the ground. You look up at me, and I can tell you are grateful for me keeping you from falling to the ground. I look into your eyes and say, 'Do you like to fuck?'

"'Yes, I do, but not with you,' you say to me."

"Wait, whoa," Diane said. "Run that by me again?"

"Oh, yeah, that is real life creeping in for a minute there. In fantasy land, you lick your lips and say, 'Mmm, I thought you'd never ask.'

"I take you in my arms and plant a kiss on your lips, and you melt against me. I turn you around so your back is to me, and I lift your shirt and cup your bare breasts in my hands, fondling and feeling them as you push yourself back against me… Okay, your turn," I tell her.

"I'm tilting my head back to take your kiss," Diane continues. "I love the feel of your strong hands on my naked breasts as you squeeze them and flick my nipples the way you know I like. I feel your hands slide down my belly and slip down inside my skirt and panties. I'm so wet and I love the feel of your strong hands on my pussy, my clit. I want you inside me, now!"

I'm getting into this now. "I throw you down on the ground, on your back, I slip your panties off, and you lie there, writhing and panting like the bitch in heat we both know you are. I open my pants to let my rock-hard cock out and press it against your opening. I push it inside, and you moan and gush with the blatant lust of a wanton whore. As we fuck on the ground, our grunts ring out as we cum together in a lust-fueled fuck fest. We collapse in each other's arms and gradually regain our senses."

"That was hot," Diane says.

"Thanks for noticing," I say. "As we put ourselves back together, we came out onto the fairway and noticed that several groups had played through while we were there in the trees. Hopefully, no one will have any idea that we have been back there having sex the whole time."

I continue, "We head back to the tee, realizing the futility of trying to find my ball. As we get back to the tee box, about a dozen guys are standing there. It turns out, these are also followers of yours on JOI. They saw us head off and decided to follow along. You appear to be glad to see them.

You ask if we all should go back into the trees and look for balls. WTF, I figure.

"We go back in there and discuss how we will spend our time here. It is readily apparent that it will take a long time if we do you one at a time, so we decide to pair up and fuck you on both ends."

"Wait, are you talking about a spit roast?" Diane asked.

"Oh, well, I mean, one of us does you from behind, and another does it orally. I usually call that fucking on both ends," I told her.

"I prefer the term 'spit roast,'" she said.

"Whatever," I said. "Anyway, you are only too happy to oblige us as we spend the next several minutes fucking you on both ends."

"Spit roast, you mean," Diane interjected.

"Whatever," I say. "But even that is slow going, so we decide to get in groups of threes and make you airtight."

"Whoa, wait," Diane said. "Airtight?"

"Google it," I told her.

"Doing it…" she said. "Oh, my!" she gasped. "So, it's double penetration with oral added on."

"That's one way to describe it," I said. "What are you thinking?"

"Hmmm, your kink is not my kink," she said.

"Fair enough. So, back to fucking you on both ends then?"

"Spit roast," she said.

"Okay, fine. Have it your way," I responded.

"I always do."

"I know that about you, Diane."

"Because I can," she winked.

"Anyway, after we have all been serviced, we come out of the trees, and it is getting dark. That's okay, as we guys figure that we have all gotten in at least nine holes. We decide to head back to the clubhouse to plan tomorrow's outing."

"Whoa, that got my juices flowing," Diane said. "I might need to take a cold shower."

"Go right ahead," I said. "I'm sure we would all like to watch."

"Be careful what you wish for," Diane teased. "It wouldn't be the first time I took a shower in a live stream. But those are usually the hot and steamy variety. I'm doing a stream of my own tomorrow; I might as well start it off being naked in the shower for all to see."

"That I have to see," I said.

"I'll be watching for you," Diane said.

"Well, I want to thank you for being my guest today, Diane. After the way you got me going at the beginning, I was thinking this might be the first, and possibly last, episode of this podcast."

"It was fun, you did great, and I can't wait to see more," Diane said.

"Right, all I need to do is go through this all over again with someone I don't know nearly as well as I do you. What could possibly go wrong?" I concluded. "You are a class act, Diane, and I look forward to enjoying your content and possibly even having you back here for another round."

Diane truly is a class act. It was readily apparent from our session that she is pretty much everything I am not. She is fun, smart, successful, sexually uninhibited, and happily married. In addition, she has built her life on her own terms. Yeah, everything I am not.

CHAPTER 19

"When you come to a fork in the road, take it."
– Yogi Berra

One afternoon, I was at the R&R coffee shop working on my blog. I was still walking on eggshells at home over the discovery Roberta had made. I had to try to put it out of my mind. I couldn't decide whether to try to write something or browse Y'allScreen videos. About that time, Sue Nami walked over carrying a stack of books and sat down at the table next to me. I could see the books she was looking through mainly had to do with obtaining professional certifications in various tech disciplines involving the Internet and some on social media marketing. It occurred to me I didn't know a lot about her other than her political leanings and the fact that her boyfriend is a Black man. "What kind of work do you do, Sue?" I asked.

"I'm an accountant," she responded.

Whoa. I froze. Given what I had learned from my recent interview with Diane, I wondered if there was more to it. I decided to delve into it. "So, I imagine you are well-versed in the double-entry system, then?" I quizzed.

She sat there stirring her coffee, squinted at me, and furrowed her brow. "That's usually how it's done," she said.

"No doubt you produce air-tight financial statements," I pressed on. "You could have clients from all around the world."

"What are you talking about?" she asked with an annoyed expression. "I work for the CPA firm in the Venture Center in LoDo. What did you think I was saying?"

"Oh, right. I know them," I said. So, she is an accountant. "I didn't mean to question your veracity," I said.

"I lost that a long time ago," Sue replied.

It was beginning to look like she was messing with me. I decided it would be best to change the subject. "So, tell me something," I said. "Your boyfriend. His name's not really Arnold Schwartz, is it?"

"No," she replied. "It's Bjorn Sorenson."

I must have looked dazed. "Funny, he doesn't look Swedish," I said.

"Norwegian," she stated.

"Ah, that explains it."

"Yeah, he just tells everybody the other name so he doesn't have to listen to insensitive, racist comments like that," Sue said, with what appeared to be a bit of a smirk.

Now, I was sure she was messing with me. I nodded. "Good talk, Sue," I said as I walked away.

"Later," she said.

***

I begin to wonder if Roberta and I are headed for a divorce. It appeared I was entering the FAFO phase of things, as in fuck around and find out. The thing is, I never wanted to be that guy. When I married Roberta, I figured it was settled and I was committed to her, and I would be done with the hassles of dating. And I certainly had no interest in having an affair, despite how things might look. I wasn't prepared for how things could spin out of control the way they have.

At this point, I didn't know if I was more worried Roberta would file for divorce or worried that she wouldn't. The reality is the only reason we are still together is because two can live as cheaply as one. The harsher truth is if we split up, neither one of us would have a pot to piss in. In any event, only fans of absurdist fiction would call what we have a marriage at this point.

Sophia came to our next meeting in a string bikini. "Sorry, hope you don't mind," she said. "It's hot as hell, and my AC is out."

"Yeah, there's a lot of that going around," I observed.

"How are things progressing with the situation at home with your wife?" Sophia asked.

"Well, I guess I have been worried about what it would look like in our social connections if the marriage didn't work out," I said. "I never thought I would have an affair, even though technically, I haven't. I mean, where do you draw the line for cheating?"

Sophia thought for a moment. "Certainly, before things get physical. It can be harder to say about the emotional aspect. It might be a gray area."

"There are zero shades of gray with Roberta," I observed. "And she has a way of taking things to heart and making it all about her," I continued. "I just hate the thought of failure."

Sophia asked what I meant.

"I know a lot of people who appear to go through the motions of life because they are afraid of what people will think of them. Other people are like, I don't know, all sail and no anchor. I could never get comfortable being like that. I don't want to be like a frightened child who is afraid to do things for fear God will get me for it."

"Do you believe God is vindictive like that?" Sophia asked. "It can be a limiting factor for sure if you let it be."

"I sometimes feel like this marriage is a punishment from God for something I did before we even started seeing each other," I said.

"What did you do?" she asked.

"I enjoyed myself," I said. "There was a woman I met at a conference we attended. It turned out she lived close to me, so we started seeing each other. It was a whirlwind romance. You might remember a story that came out some time ago called '9 ½ Weeks.' That was about how long it lasted.

Her name was Virginia; she was a few years older than I am, and I got hooked on her big time. Things escalated quickly, and I think I got a bit too needy and let it show. Apparently, she got spooked and broke it off. Looking back on it, I think I was only there to validate her attractiveness in her mind, and once it was accomplished, there was no longer a need for me to be around. I was devastated, and I remember not ever wanting to feel like that again. I remembered I had met Roberta a few weeks earlier, so I gave her a call. I needed someone to talk to. I think she was open to any relationship with someone who wasn't only after 'one thing,' so we hit it off. It wasn't long before we were talking about getting married. She had two kids, and as much as I didn't want to have kids, I figured beggars can't be choosers, so I went ahead."

"And it didn't work out as well as you would have hoped?" Sophia asked.

"I hate to think of it as a rebound situation, but it is essentially the fact of the matter. If I hadn't gotten tangled up in that earlier relationship, I might not have started seeing Roberta and wouldn't have ended up making both of us miserable. Sad, isn't it?"

Sophia appeared to understand what I meant. At least I could sense a realization from what I had told her some time ago.

"I would have to say I consider my experience as a stepparent to be the biggest failure of my life up to now," I continued. "I certainly haven't done anyone any favors by getting involved in their lives.

"Roberta and I are both repressed and inhibited. She deals with it by clinging to religion; I deal with it through my stories in an attempt to come to terms with the feelings and gain control over them. All I am looking for is a partner who looks good naked and thinks it's okay for a man to be a man.

"Statistics say the divorce rate is about the same inside or outside of religious circles, about 50 percent. So, what is the difference? I'm convinced sex has never brought me anything but misery and grief. Now, to top it off,

I have been put through so much of a hit to my self-esteem over it that I can't function.

"They say if you take sex and fun out of a marriage, what you are left with is a business deal. I might as well be at a brothel. At least there, fun and sex are on the table. Well, maybe not literally on the table. But then, I guess it could be. I don't know." Sophia executed a perfectly coordinated jaw drop and eye roll. It occurred to me I preferred her belly rolls to her eye rolls. But I figured if I mentioned it, all it would get me was an icy glare. I would have to discuss it with her at some point, even at the risk of getting 'the look.'

"Have you ever considered the possibility that you are depressed?" Sophia asked.

"You mean in the sense of not being gay? Maybe that explains it," I said.

"Can you be serious for once?" she snapped. Now I am getting the look accompanied by some fingers tapping on the desk, so I decided I should stymie the attitude a bit.

"Sure, what are you thinking?" I asked.

"I have suspected it for a while, but I didn't know how to bring it up. But now my suspicions are all but confirmed. I am not qualified to make a diagnosis, but in my opinion, you are suffering from clinical depression. I would like for you to seek out a professional who can confirm the diagnosis and try to settle on some kind of treatment."

I had never seriously considered something like that, but it made sense. Sure, I was a bit sad and moody a lot of the time, but I kept it at bay with my sense of humor. But I also had to account for the sleeplessness and other issues. I couldn't ignore the possibility.

I also noticed I had been drinking more than usual lately. Not that it was any wonder, with Roberta's mental state being what it was, I was under considerable stress. I will admit there were times when I messaged Alice while I had a little of the captain in me and said things I probably wouldn't have otherwise.

When I finally got to see Todd, he told me about his struggles with his broken arm and his cancer diagnosis. I asked if the two were related. He said they were.

"One day, I was sitting in a chair and grabbed the armrests to get up, and my upper arm snapped in two. They said that is usually the way it happens. Some people experience a broken leg when the bone snaps as they are standing on it. Anyway, they are watching it, and I'm getting regular treatments. They are hopeful we caught it in time."

He went on to explain that the doctors were not crazy about the idea of him coming here for his annual visit, but he really wanted to. He made arrangements with a doctor in Denver to monitor his readings if necessary, but it was important to him to make the trip. I'm glad he did, as I always enjoyed having him here so I could catch up on old times.

Blaine and Jimmy had made the trip with Todd so they could keep a protective eye on him. As we were hanging out visiting, Jimmy had another question. "What's a MILF?" he asked.

I froze. "Well, it's ahh… why do you ask?" I said.

"I was on the Internet just now, and I saw this woman who was selling stuff; she said she was the definitive MILF. It didn't make sense," Jimmy said.

Wow, Diane doesn't waste time, I thought. She is definitely no slouch as a businesswoman.

"But why are you asking me?" I wanted to know. Jimmy waved his hand toward Blaine and Todd and rolled his eyes.

"Oh, right," I said. "Well, it means, uh, it stands for a Mother I'd Like… For unlawful carnal knowledge," I said.

"Oh," Jimmy said. At that moment, I could see the wheels turning in Jimmy's head. Suddenly, his eyes grew wide. "OH! Good talk, Alex." I couldn't help thinking Jimmy must lead a very sheltered life.

On the Fourth of July, a bunch of us gathered to have an old-time fireworks party like we had when I was a kid. In recent years, I have lost interest in such things, but the idea of being able to celebrate was a welcome relief from the problems going on currently. I recalled hearing the story of the fireworks party when Todd and his friend Don were goofing off, and they let a stray sparkler fall into the box of fireworks, and the whole thing went off all at once. I was too young to remember it. I do remember a specific time when I was around eight years old. It was the summer Todd turned 21, and he was standing there with a beer in one hand and a lit Roman candle in the other. Mom decided that was his way of declaring his independence. Just something silly and whimsical that brought back a fond memory. It was one of those rare times when the years melted away, and we were simply in the moment, reveling in a trip down memory lane.

CHAPTER 20

"Treat a lady like a whore, and a whore like a lady."
– Wilson Mizner

I thought more about compiling these stories into some kind of a volume. Since I had done about all I could with the schoolgirl scenario, I wondered where I could go from here. Not wanting to come up with a whole new story idea, it thought about doing something with the BDSM setup. I let my mind wander to the possibility that it would ever get made into a movie and what it might look like to audition an actress for the lead role in that story. I have to admit, the thought had some appeal.

The Audition
By Xander Arcane

The young actress made her way to the studio location where the casting director had told her to go. She had never tried out for a role like this, a story about a young woman exploring the darker side of her sexuality. She knew it would involve extensive nudity and sexually explicit content, which she had never done on screen before, but she couldn't get over the possibility this could be her big chance. She decided she would just have to cross that bridge when she came to it.

This would not be a typical audition. Due to the pandemic, certain restrictions were required, and so this audition was being conducted over a Zoom call. She found the room where the meeting was to take place and went inside. She saw a laptop computer on a table with a Zoom meeting already set up. There was a stool in the middle of the room, and hanging from a chain, a pair of cuffs. The laptop screen came to life, and the famous actor/director appeared on it and greeted her.

"Heywood Jablomie," he said. "Thank you for coming."

She wondered if this was the way he greeted everyone. Then she realized this was his name.

"And you are Miss…?" he continued.

"Woodstar," she responded. "Holly Woodstar."

"That has a nice ring to it," he said. "May I call you Holly?"

"Please," she replied.

"Great. You can call me sir," he said with a grin. "Kidding. Call me Heywood, please. Unfortunately, we have to go to these lengths to conduct our audition, but we will get by as best we can. I hope this isn't too uncomfortable for you."

"Well, I am kind of new to all of this, so I guess it doesn't make much difference," Holly said.

"Yes, I see you don't have many film credits listed," he said. "But this is actually a good thing. You see, we are looking for a new, fresh face to play this part. You might be just what we are looking for. It's possible you could be the next Dakota Johnson."

Holly perked up at the notion. "I would like a chance to see if it could happen," she said.

"That is why we're here," he responded. "We are still in talks to find the supporting female role. It appears to be a choice between Scarlett Johansson and Karen Gillen. I have even heard Hallie Berry has expressed some interest in it, though she is concerned there may not be enough explicit sex and nudity. It will likely come down to a choice over whom we have more leverage," he said with a twinkle in his eye.

Holly couldn't resist asking. "What about the male lead?"

"Now, that has been the subject of a lot of discussion around here," Heywood said. "We have talked about Kurt Russell, we've talked about Brad Pitt, and we've even talked about Leonardo DiCaprio. But it turns out they're all pussies, so I'm most likely going to end up doing it myself," he said.

He continued, "So, you are familiar with the scene we are going to do here today?" Holly nodded. "Alright then, are you ready to begin?" Another nod from Holly. "Are you nervous?" he asked.

Holly took a deep breath. "Sort of," she admitted.

"Oh, you'll do fine," Heywood said with a reassuring smile. "So, to begin with, suppose you show me your legs. Along with everything else," he said, his demeanor turning more ominous.

Holly gasped. "What? You want me to take off all my clothes?" she asked incredulously.

"Oh, I'm sorry," Heywood said. "I was under the impression you had glanced at the script. Because if you had, you would have noticed that this girl goes completely naked through almost the entire story."

"Well, yes, I know," Holly stammered. "But I thought today was... I don't know, a read-through or something?" she said, averting her eyes nervously.

"Well, whether it is or not," Heywood said, "the point is if you are going to work with me, you need to be ready for anything. And if you're not ready to show some skin, well, there are any number of eager young starlets out there who would jump at the chance to be where you are, and I mean that literally. What it boils down to," he continued, "is in the event that you are the lucky young lady who is selected to play this part, it means your tits and your ass are going to be carrying this movie, and I am on the hook for it, and I don't want any surprises."

He continued with an icy tone. "And in the spirit of that works both ways, I'm going to give you some information you need to know, which is I don't pull any punches with the sex in my movies. This means that while the film may not carry an NC-17 rating, it does not necessarily mean what the crew sees takes place on set might not be just that. In plainer language, the sex onscreen might not be of the simulated variety. Now, I need you to tell me if this is going to be a problem for you."

Holly had to stop and think. While she desperately wanted to be in this movie, she couldn't quite believe what he appeared to be saying the cost of it could be. She took a deep breath. "No, it won't be a problem," she stammered.

Heywood brought his palm up to his forehead and closed his eyes for a moment. Peering at Holly, he said, "Well, I can only hope you are more convincing when the cameras are rolling."

Holly averted her eyes, starting to feel as though this extraordinary opportunity was slipping from her grasp. Heywood tried to get the proceedings back on track. "Alright," he said, "show me what you've got." As Holly hesitatingly moved her hands toward the waistband of her skirt, Heywood became agitated. "That means get naked, you little bitch, and that's the last time I'm saying it nicely!"

Holly started to quiver as she slipped out of her skirt and stood there, waiting for his reaction. She was sure she would have to go further, but he did say at first he wanted to see her legs, so she paused. He took a polite inventory of her and said, "You have nice legs. I hope you aren't expecting a lifetime achievement award for that. Keep going."

She unbuttoned her blouse and took it off, standing there in lacey black lingerie. She had seldom felt more awkward, feeling his eyes take in her half-naked form. After a moment of gawking, he said, "You're real cute, honey, but honestly, I can see more in the Sports Illustrated Swimsuit Issue. Now let's get serious here, I don't have all damn day."

Holly's breath nearly caught in her throat as she reached around to unhook her bra. She held the 34C cups next to her and let them slip down to reveal a pair of breasts that could best be described as perky. He took in a deep breath and blew it out slowly, then said, "Have you ever thought about maybe getting a boob job?"

She wanted to disappear. *Were they that bad?* she thought to herself. "No," she said in a defensive voice.

"Well, don't," he said. "Because they're perfect." He chuckled softly. "Is that not what you were expecting me to say?"

"It's not," Holly said, her lip still quivering.

"What were you thinking I might say?"

"That they should be bigger," she said, almost sobbing.

"Interesting," he said, seeming unaware of how close Holly was to bursting into tears. "Why couldn't I have just as easily said they should be smaller?" he asked, narrowing his eyes as he quizzed her. "You are aware there are those who appreciate smaller breasts on girls or, well, women, right?" She nodded. "If you could choose," he continued, "would you rather your breasts were bigger or smaller?"

"I like them how they are," she said, showing her first sign of assertiveness since the audition began. Heywood took notice.

"Good answer," he said. "Don't touch them. Well, you can touch them," he said, making an exaggerated cupping motion with his hands over his own chest. "Just don't do anything with them; they're fine. Alright, continue," he said.

"Do I have to?" Holly pleaded at the thought of removing her panties.

"You're pissing me off, girl!" he exploded at her. "I am all done fucking around with you; now strip!"

She slipped the panties down and kicked them off to one side, standing there naked. She recognized the futility of attempting to cover herself and resisted the urge to do so. Heywood sat on the other end of their meeting and stared in silence for a minute, then two, then longer. Holly was unsure of what to do. She was beginning to think the screen might have frozen. Feeling like she had to do something, she decided to borrow a line from the character she was hoping to play. "Sir, may I please speak?" she said.

"Speak," Heywood said with a slight smile.

"Is there something you want me to do?" Holly asked.

"Yeah, I want you to grow some cunt hair so I can see if the carpet matches the drapes. I'll wait," he said. "I'm sorry, am I making you uncomfortable?" he asked.

"Yes," she said.

"Good," he replied. "Because I have a theory that anyone who can be made uncomfortable should be.

"Alright, turn around," he said, making a circular motion in the air with his finger.

Holly turned around, and he instructed her to lean forward, put her hands on the front of her legs, and look back over her shoulder at him. "You have a very beautiful ass, do you know that?" he asked. "Yes, I do believe I would very much like to fuck it. Alright, you can stand up." As she stood up and turned to face him again, he asked, "So how about that? Oh, let me guess, anal sex is something else that's not on your list of accomplishments, right?"

"I'm afraid so," she said.

"Now I wonder why that doesn't surprise me," he sneered. "That's okay; back-door virgins are my specialty," he said with a gleam in his eye. "So tell me," he went on. "Just how experienced are you? Sexually, I mean. And before you go off on a pound MeToo rant, I want you to know this is a perfectly legitimate question for someone at your end of the food chain; it's what's known as a bona fide occupational qualification; you can look it up. So, I'll put it another way. Are you a good fuck?"

Holly had just about all she was going to take. "Yes, I am a great fuck!" she stated emphatically.

"Is that a fact?" Heywood continued, unfazed. "I don't suppose you could provide some references to vouch for that."

"As many as you need," Holly snapped back.

"Really," he continued. "And would any of these references, by any chance, have a penis?"

"You're an ass!" she shot back.

"So I've been told," he said. "Alright, I think this has told me everything I need to know. I've got to say, the flesh does hang pretty well off your bones. I think we are ready to move on, but before we do, I need to come clean about something. I have just spent the last ten minutes or more being a total dick to you, and you need to know there was a reason for it. That is,

I need to know if you have the mental toughness it takes to play this part. There is some heavy shit here, and it is not for the squeamish," he went on. "I appreciate how difficult this is for you and the effort you are making. The fact is, this was a test, and you passed. So, that's my apology, and I just wanted to check in with you to make sure we are all good, no hard feelings. Because you are tough as nails, and you're sexy as hell. And I meant what I said about your breasts; don't forget it," he said.

Holly gave him a crooked smile. "And my ass?" she asked.

Heywood chuckled. "That too. Everything I said about your ass!" he grinned. "But especially your breasts. Don't ever let anybody tell you that you need to have work done on them. In your case, that would be a crime against nature. I mean it!" he said.

He continued, "Now before we get started, I wanted to get your take on a couple of things. There is a scene coming up, one we aren't going to do today, but, like I said, it is pretty heavy. I mean, there is no way to sugar-coat it, it's a rape. So, how do you feel about that?" he asked.

"I'm not sure I follow you," she said.

"Well, I mean, as a woman and as the person who is going to portray this, will it be uncomfortable for you?" he asked.

"It's part of the story," she said. "That is what we are here for."

"Okay, thank you," he said. "Do you believe this girl is a virgin, from the way she is written?" he asked.

"I hadn't thought about it much. I guess she could be?" Holly responded.

"Yes, maybe. Or maybe this is just her 'kink,' you know. Like maybe she is acting out her own 'rape fantasy,'" he conjectured. "We aren't given a lot about what they were discussing in the area of personal boundaries or what was being consented to. So, there is plenty left open to interpretation, and we will need to discuss those things. And I expect you to be involved in those discussions. I want to know what you are thinking about all this."

Holly felt like he was showing her a lot of respect as a full partner in this collaboration. She started feeling much more at ease after the way he had her rattled during the process of getting her naked.

"Now, if you could go ahead and cinch yourself up in those cuffs," he said, "we can begin. Now, as we go through this, there will be parts where I am going to be touching you, and when that is happening, I will describe how I am doing it and give you an opening to tell me how it's making you feel, okay?"

Holly nodded, reached up and placed the cuffs around her wrists, having to reach up and elongate her body in the process. "They put those cuffs a bit higher than I would have liked," Heywood said. "I need to clue them in. I have a feeling this story was written with someone like Alice Modicum in mind," he stated.

"Who the fuck is Alice Modicum?" Holly asked.

"Just some whore," Heywood responded. "No one you need to be concerned about. You look great," Heywood said. "Could you maybe arrange yourself in some various poses, like curving your body in different ways?"

Holly complied, knowing, in all probability, he liked compliance in a woman.

"That looks great," he said. "Would you mind turning around with your back to me and throwing your head back?"

She did it, and he liked what he saw. "Thanks," he said. "I just wanted another look at your butt." He said with a mischievous grin.

"Alright, let's get into this," he said. "We will start with the part right after he has bathed you. I will begin," he said. "I'm sure you have many questions..."

As the scene played out, he noticed Holly was arranging her body in some very erotic poses. She would stretch seductively and had a way of positioning herself with a supple S-curve to her elongated form. He was impressed with the way she appeared to be able to sense the light in the room and use it to cause the highlights and shadows to accentuate her body's curves and contours. Then Holly started to notice something unexpected. She was beginning to feel horny as hell. Something about the way she was stretched out and on display was causing her to feel hyper-stimulated. She wished she could get her hands free so she could reach between her legs.

After some time, he could barely stand it anymore. "It's probably a good thing we are not in the same room for this session," he said. "I don't know what you have been told about me, but I have never actually had sex with an actress when I was auditioning her. I never wanted to be that guy. But if I were there with you and had you like this, I don't think I could make such a claim much longer. You see, this is where I'm supposed to pick you up by your thighs and grind your pussy against the bulge in my pants. Only, there is no bulge in my pants. That's because my pants are around my ankles right now like they would be if I were there with you."

"Will you show me?" Holly asked breathlessly.

"There you go," he said as he stood up and pointed his rock-hard member at the camera.

"Fuck, I want that," she panted.

"You would love it for me to pick you up and pull you onto my shaft, and we could fuck each other's brains out. Would you like to have your brains fucked out by me?" he asked.

"Definitely," she said.

"That's good because I would love to have my brains fucked out by you," he responded. "This is what you planned. You wanted me to see you naked all along, didn't you?" he asked.

"That's for me to know and you to find out," she said.

"So, let's find out. I'm just two doors down from you. We can contin-ue this exploration face-to-face," he said.

"Are you serious?" Holly asked incredulously.

"As a heart attack," he replied.

"HA! You would have a heart attack if you got next to this naked body," she taunted.

"That's a chance I'm willing to take. I'll be there in a few seconds, and we can turn this into more of a 'hands-on' tryout," he said.

THE END

I decided I would send this story to Diane to see if she wanted to give me any feedback.

CHAPTER 21

"Always do sober what you said you'd do drunk. That will teach you to keep your mouth shut."
– Ernest Hemingway

Several months had passed since I last spoke to Todd. He would occasionally email me updates about his treatment program. They sometimes were concerned about the numbers, but overall, he appeared to be responding favorably to the regimen.

Roberta was seemingly coming to terms with my contact with Alice. At least it didn't appear to be a sticking point like it had been. I had told Alice I wanted to cool it for a while, but I did keep in touch. I still had nearly an hour of time left with her, and it went without saying there would be no cash refunds. But she kept it on her books and said we could take it up again later. Apparently, she has some knowledge of accounting practices.

***

I decided to send the audition story to Diane and see if it would spark interest there. I heard back from her not long after. Since we had connected over doing the podcast a while back, we had established enough of a rapport that we were comfortable meeting over a Skype call.

"Wow, I liked the story," Diane said. "I remember doing a webcam session with a man when I was still doing those, and he had me do a scenario much like that one."

"Sounds hot," I said. "What did you find appealing about it?"

"The way you were dominant with that woman and making her do as she was told," Diane said. "Even though I would probably have walked out on the situation before too much longer, I can see how you used your leverage to test her. It was sexy."

"One of the ideas I wanted to explore is being a total prick and feeling entitled to it - something I wouldn't be able to do in real life. But they say women like the bad boys. Do you agree?"

"I don't think so necessarily," Diane said. "I like good guys. Maybe a good guy with an edge, though."

Diane suggested we try a scenario in which she was the aggressor. She would come on to me and make me feel like an object of desire to try to bring me out of my shell. "How would that work?" I wanted to know.

Diane considered it for a moment and presented an idea: "I could be a photographer, and you could be my model for a calendar I'm working on."

I was skeptical. "I think it's been done. There was a guy who called himself Flabbio who did a calendar a while ago."

"I'm not having that," Diane stated. "You are a hunk."

"Oh, yeah, I'm a hunk of something," I said. "It rhymes with hard but starts with L."

"Oh, quit," Diane said. "Even my body isn't without its flaws, you know," she stated.

"I hadn't noticed," I said.

"Do you expect every woman to be a size zero supermodel on a swim-suit calendar?" she asked.

"No, in fact, I have seen a lot of women who could be thought of as 'pleasingly plump' that are really quite hot," I said. "What makes it work is their confidence in their appearance and how comfortable they are 'in their own skin,' as they say. As long as the skin doesn't sag so much around the middle, they wouldn't have to wear pants. Not naming names, but yeah."

"What would it take for you to be comfortable in your own skin?" Diane asked.

"Rum would help," I said. "But I do have to say I have always admired you for your willingness to show yourself naked on a daily basis. I'm sure it takes a lot of confidence."

Diane appeared to be thinking about something. "Is there any chance I could persuade you to send me a nude photo?" she asked.

"You mean of me?" I asked.

"No, of your cat," Diane said, somewhat exasperated. "Of course, you."

I was relieved to know Diane wasn't into kitty porn. "I can't get past feeling like that could result in any number of problems. It could fall into the wrong hands, and I could get blackmailed," I offered.

"You're letting your imagination get the best of you," Diane said. "You wouldn't have to show your face. I'll trust it's you," she teased.

"You mean, like, put a bag over my head?" I chuckled.

"Either that or crop it from the neck down. That way, it isn't easily traced back to you," she offered.

This was getting to be kind of cloak and dagger, but it appeared I was going to have to come up with something to humor her. "Okay, when I get off this call, I'll figure out a way to snap a selfie and send it to you. Is that satisfactory?" I asked.

"I'll be eagerly anticipating it," she said.

"Alright, well, I'll get back to you. Later," I said as I disconnected the call.

I wanted to get this over and done so I could move on with my life, so I wracked my brain trying to come up with a way to keep my promise to Diane and still maintain my dignity. Maybe I was making a mountain out of a molehill, but my experience with people's unfair judgments of me over the years didn't want to let go. After I arranged a place to pose where I knew the positioning would provide the necessary anonymity to maintain privacy, I tried to bring myself to snap the picture. Just one thing was missing. I looked around and saw just what I needed. With one small adjustment, I felt I could send Diane what she asked for. I wished I could see the look on her face when she saw my photo with the bag from a recently purchased bottle of rum strategically located. I added a caption, "Baby steps, darling."

***

To take our minds off our troubles, Roberta and I decided to plan a trip to Arizona for the winter, possibly in a rented RV, and try out the lifestyle. Then, we saw a good deal on a rental through Vrbo, so we decided to go that route.

On the way there, we decided to stay in kitchenette places as far as possible so we could do our own cooking and not be dependent on eating out more than necessary. Plus, since we had the cats with us, we needed to find places that allowed pets. As we headed out on the second day of the journey, we made some sandwiches to eat along the way. We headed down the road; things were quiet as usual. I tried to find a way to start a conversation, but it was an exercise in futility. Roberta always complains about how we never talk while we are traveling, but when I try to start a conversation, she sticks to one-word answers to my questions. Maybe it's her passive-aggressive way of getting to be right. By midday, we found a small town with some roadside picnic tables that we decided would be a good place to stop and have our lunch. After we had eaten and took a short walk to stretch our legs, we resumed our travels.

As we were driving down the interstate, we saw a Class A coach coming toward us in the distance. Suddenly, the coach swerved and jumped to the side of the road and landed in the ditch. We stopped to see if we could help. There was a couple inside who were a bit shaken up, to say the least. They were pulling a car behind the rig, and when it came to a stop, it had run the hitch through the grill of the vehicle, which evidently totaled it. We made sure they were okay and did what we could to get them out of the coach. The man, whose name is Larry, said he had lost steering control and the bus had jumped the ditch on its own. His wife, Brenda, was more than a little shaken; it appeared she had been hit on the head by a falling cabinet. Roberta offered to let her sit in our vehicle while they waited for help to arrive.

Larry tried to call his insurance company to let them know about the accident, but his phone couldn't get service, so I let him use mine. After a while, when it looked like they would be able to manage, we went on our way. It was an unusual adventure to start our trip and something we could think back on while we planned our own RV future. Emerson never mentioned anything like this coming up.

As we resumed our journey, Roberta remarked about how things worked out so we were in the exact time and place we needed to be to lend them a helping hand. If we hadn't stopped for a lunch break when we did, we never would have seen the accident and been in a position to help out. Of course, she credited divine providence with orchestrating events so they would work out just so. I rolled my eyes in private at the notion, but it was so like Roberta to hold such a belief that I figured things were normal.

Soon after we got underway again and headed for Arizona, I got a phone call. It was Todd's son Blaine. Todd had taken a turn for the worse, so he entered home hospice care, and he wasn't expected to last long. It was a shock. He appeared to be responding to his treatment, and things had been looking up. This news was devastating. I wondered if I should drop everything and run out to see him, but it didn't sound like there would be time. The next day, it turned out to be a fact. He was gone— that one hurt. Todd was the only member of the family, other than Mom, with whom I ever actually connected. I was looking forward to spending time with him when things settled down, and I had time to spend on my terms. But it wasn't meant to be.

I was thinking about how my life was going from bad to worse—the problems with Roberta, losing Todd, and just generally a bad time. We did Arizona, mostly going through the motions. During the pandemic, spring training took a hit, and now that it was behind us, things were getting back to normal. Unfortunately, my heart wasn't in it. Baseball was just one of many things that I used to enjoy but couldn't find a way to get interested anymore.

After being back home for a while, I was still coming to terms with the loss of my brother. I know I was probably more withdrawn and moodier than usual. Roberta was giving me space, but I could tell it was hard on her, too. Eventually, I found out Roberta had been seeing a counselor. I asked her about it, and she said she was at the point of leaving. She asked if I would go with her to her next session. From my experience with Roberta over the years, I knew she would only seek a counselor who approached it with a religious perspective. I wasn't sure I gave them much credibility, but this is what we got.

When it was my turn to address the counselor, I figured that since she had gotten the jump on me, I felt I needed to tell my side. "I'm the dirty, rotten scoundrel you've doubtless heard so much about," I said. "I just want to say I am aware that we have had our problems over the years, and I will own up to my part in them. I am curious to see if she is aware of her contribution to the situation."

I went on to assert that I do not have a sickness; I have a God-given sex drive that admittedly hasn't had the best of influences in its formative years. It was hindered by a mother who thought it should be squelched rather than encouraged, so it had to be kept private. That meant I could develop any thoughts and feelings I wanted since they wouldn't be exposed. What I need is someone to encourage me in knowing I am sought after and wanted and needed. And I am sure as hell not getting that from her.

The counselor asked what I thought of Roberta's feelings on sexuality. "She doesn't appear to have a problem with the sex, as long as it is on her terms," I said. "Which is strictly within the framework of the 'marriage bed.' I think people who say that with a straight face only add fuel to the fire of those who equate religion with mental illness." There, I got that jab in to establish I wasn't going to be a docile recipient of their mumbo jumbo.

I continued, "I'm not sure what my expectations of privacy are, but I believe my personal space has been infringed upon. She not only held onto this information for months, not wanting to confront the reality, but she went through my browser history and any and all of my curious searches. I shudder to think what conclusions she has drawn from that. She tends to believe the worst about me, so I can only imagine.

"I will admit I am not the easiest person to live with, but I would be willing to bet there are a lot of women out there who would gladly trade problems with you," I stated emphatically.

The counselor gives us some information to look over and exercises designed to help us connect. I'm not sure what good it will do at this point.

The truth is, Roberta was becoming increasingly, it appeared to me, bipolar about our situation. One day, she acted like everything was fine, and the next, she sounded like she was ready to call it quits. I was beginning to wish she would make up her mind. I was becoming more and more apprehensive about her mental health state. It was becoming apparent to me that the most merciful thing to do would be to put this sham of a marriage out of its misery.

CHAPTER 22

"Half the marriages end in divorce – and then there are the unhappy ones."
– Johnny Carson

At our next session with the counselor, Roberta is hesitant to go into any details until pressed. I feel that for what we are spending to be here, we need to tackle it.

I decided to steer the conversation back to the subject at hand. "I feel her lack of willingness to engage in discussions about sexually active adults shows a disturbing lack of maturity or ability to deal with real life. Forget watching porn together; she won't even watch a mainstream TV show where the male lead has a penchant for bed-hopping. If she is honestly so hung up about it, she needs to pull the holier-than-thou stick out of her ass and realize she is married to an adult male human and all that goes with it.

"Roberta has an expansive definition of pornography, to mean anything I see that she doesn't like, which is pretty much everything. Even the Sports Illustrated Swimsuit Issue has been a bone of contention between us. I get it, but I feel like I can view such things in the abstract, where she sees it as a personal affront."

I was getting on a roll and not one I was comfortable with. "At the risk of sounding like a real ass, I could go on and on about how she has let herself go with her appearance in the past few years, but I am well aware I don't have much room to talk myself.

"If anyone should be thinking about leaving, it's me." I ranted on. "Does she realize the blizzard of shit that I have been through for the privilege of being with her? She used to look through my emails and copy them to a file she saved to a disk she labeled 'evidence.' Now she wonders why I feel like our relationship is an adversarial one. No wonder I need a stiff drink almost every afternoon.

"In my mind," I continued, "it comes down to the problems we had with the kids. If she held them to the same standard she does me, then maybe between the two of them, they would be worth the powder it would take to blow one of them to hell.

"The next time you are at the point of leaving, please do so," I snapped. "Otherwise, the only chance I have for a life I would want to live is to outlive you. And if I have learned anything about divine providence from all of this, it's that this is not part of the master plan."

Roberta and the counselor sat in stunned silence. "There, I said what's on my mind; how do you like it?" I snapped.

I knew I exhibited an explosive decompression of epic proportions in the finest tradition of Clark W. Griswold and his raving meltdowns over the slings and arrows of outrageous vacation misfortune. I don't lose it often, but when I do, it is something you have to see to believe.

It was readily apparent to everyone there that the next person to speak needed to choose their words carefully. The counselor wisely suggested we all step back, evaluate our positions, and talk again when cooler heads could prevail.

After a while, we were able to sit down and have a rational discussion about it. I could tell I had hit a nerve with Roberta when I brought up my point about the kids. "You don't appear to have a healthy attitude about Freddie and Jason," she said.

"Thanks for noticing," I said. "Let me ask you something. How many 12-step programs has Jason been through over the years? I'm pretty sure there have been at least two."

"Sounds about right," Roberta said.

"I thought one of the steps in those programs involves going to the people who have been injured by your behaviors and making amends, or at least acknowledging the fact that you have done damage. Because if that's the case, I'm still waiting."

But getting back to the salient point, "Why don't you tell me exactly what I do that is so distasteful to you?"

"It's just the whole dominance thing. It doesn't feel right. Plus, you have all of these unrealistic fantasies."

"That's why they are called fantasies," I said. "You appear to be turned off by me being assertive. Some people want this so they can be removed from the responsibility of what is happening in those situations. The biggest issue I have with you is it appears like your sexuality is nonexistent. Plus, if you see sexuality in others, it pisses you off. How can I relate to this? It's not a healthy way to coexist.

"Since you have made it clear you are not open to acting out those scenarios, it is apparent to me that I can do one of two things. Either suppress those feelings and pretend they don't matter or seek it elsewhere. Some would say if I did the latter, you wouldn't have a complaint coming since you left me no alternative. Just like what happened with Dad when Mom didn't want to be with him." She was starting to see where this was headed. "If this is your position, then I don't need or want you in my life. Because of your attitude, I can only think I am repulsive to you. This doesn't work for me."

***

After I sat through our session with the counselor, I wasn't in the best of moods. Probably the last thing I needed was to sit and listen to Stu go on about how he and a friend of his had spent the morning going door to door trying to persuade poor lost sinners of their need to come to church, preferably his. I have been on the receiving end of such visits from zealots over the years. It always starts with them asking what church I go to. From there, no matter what church I say I go to, the response is always they used to go to that church before they found out everyone who goes to that church is being led down the road to perdition or some damn thing.

Stu's virtue signaling was getting old to me. I asked him, "Are you doing God's will, or are you doing your own will in God's name?"

"What's the difference?" Stu asked.

"Results," I stated. "You know, you would make a great church lady."

He got in a huff over it. "Well, I'm a Christian; what are you?" he snorted.

I had all I was going to take. "You are the farthest thing from a Christian there is," I stated. "A Christian is someone who believes Christ died for their sins, but you don't believe this since you think you can do it all on your own. You're nothing but a fucking poser. No one in their right mind would want to be like you. You're chasing people away who most need to hear the message with all your preaching to the choir."

I continued. "All I can do is be the best version of myself that is humanly possible and trust the grace of God to cover the rest. If that's not good enough for you, then you can go straight to hell, you self-righteous son of a motherfucker." I got up and left, bridge burned.

**

I had scheduled a meeting with Alice to wrap up our time together, which I had purchased literally months ago. Not that my heart was particularly in it just now. We talked and went through the motions of a hot BDSM session. I think I was more relieved to have it over with than turned on, but at this point, I was willing to take what I could get.

Alice said I should call the ranch and make arrangements for a visit. I told her I would think about it, but I didn't get to Vegas much anymore.

She said she only goes there on the tour dates she schedules far in advance. She usually is in the Denver area, where she has a small goat farm with a few horses.

WTF, I thought. I had no idea.

***

Blaine and Jimmy made a trip to the farm to gather up the rest of Todd's things and decide what to do with the place. Todd had left the farm to Blaine, and in all likelihood, he would continue to spend time there as it had been part of his life for as long as he could remember. I made a trip out there to meet them and see if there was anything of Todd's that I wanted. I was a bit surprised that Todd's wife had not come along, as Blaine said they wanted to invite Todd's friends who still lived in the area over for a brief gathering to celebrate his life. Still, I should have known she would skip it. Mom always wondered what Todd saw in her. The fact is, Mom typically evaluated women based on the standard 1 – 10 scale of attractiveness. She once said the lady was as homely as a mud fence. I translated it to rate, at best, a 3. That was probably being generous.

At the gathering of friends, many of whom Todd had known since his school days in the area, we reminisced about our fondest memories of him. When my turn came, I was prepared. "Even though I loved him dearly, I always thought he was a bit pretentious," I said. "He was very much into status symbols. In his day, it meant owning a Cadillac and playing golf, as this was simply what affluent White guys did. So, he liked to flaunt his fancy car, his country club membership, his trophy wife… well, as the song says, two out of three ain't bad." I thought Blaine was going to choke, trying not to laugh out loud at this remark. It probably came across as vindictive, but it was my way of applying some levity to mask my profound grief.

Part of my grief consisted of wondering if Todd was honestly happy in the life he chose. He was financially well-off, but only because he married money, and money never let him forget it. I doubt he ever got to enjoy much of it, other than the fact he had been able to purchase the farm to help Mom and Dad in their final years. But it gave him a place to escape to for a couple of months every year. For the most part, he was tighter than two coats of paint. He never bought a golf ball in his life; he would fish them out of water hazards he drove by. His version of the wealth of the wicked laid up for the just, no doubt. I wonder how much he took with him.

After everyone had left, I took a walk by myself. As I looked around, I felt that this might be the last time I would see the home I had growing up. Not that I would miss it a great deal; it felt like another time and place. I wasn't so close with Blaine. He was okay; he's just not part of my generation.

As I walked along the pasture, I stopped by the coulee, where there was a windbreaker fence Todd had built when I was a kid. It was one of the times I actually got to spend some time with him one summer. I stopped and gazed at the aging planks that sheltered an old well that had long since run dry. I saw Jimmy off by himself and went over to talk to him. He appeared to be taking the loss especially hard. I understood what he was going through. Other than Mom, Todd had been the only person in my family I could relate to. I wished I could have spent more time with him while I was younger, but he had other things to think about and do. I always thought the day would come when we would have all the time we needed to talk over the good old days, and I could find out about all the crazy things he did with Randy and Dean. But that isn't going to happen now.

Jimmy said he had a fondness for this place as a result of spending so much time here each summer. Blaine had made sure he had the opportunity to experience the place. But it wasn't going to be the same without Todd here to keep us all together. I knew the reality of that all too well. I thought about the last Fourth of July when we were together here and how magical it felt, like being transported to a time when life was simple and carefree. If only I had known at the time, it would be the last time I would ever see him.

As I drove home, I tried not to think about all the missed opportunities in life and what the future might hold. I had a sense of melancholy over thoughts about all those long-ago Christmas times and the summer days with gatherings of friends and family. I had so much going on; it was a bit overwhelming. As I drove, a song came on the radio. Barry Manilow was singing a song called *Memory*. The song spoke of smiling at the old days, and the time I knew what happiness was. Of my day in the sun and wanting the memory to live again.

I pulled over and cried. All alone in the moonlight.

PART 3 // ACCEPTANCE

CHAPTER 23

"My candle burns at both ends;
It will not last the night;
But ah, my foes, and oh, my friends –
It gives a lovely light!"
– Edna St. Vincent Millay

Most people would take it as incontrovertible that beautiful women possess the innate ability to cause intelligent men to commit acts of mind-boggling stupidity. I felt I had contributed more than my share toward proof of that concept in recent months, but I still wasn't finished.

Roberta and I had just been to a routine meeting with our retirement planner. Due to employment challenges and family issues over the years, our nest egg was anemic. We needed to beef up our portfolio. After our meeting, I decided to test the waters to see if she wanted to go shopping for an RV and plan for next winter's getaway to a warmer climate.

That's when she dropped the bombshell on me. "I've been doing a lot of thinking," she said. "I don't see you having any concern about our situation. At least not that you are willing to do anything to change. I need to spend some time alone and sort things out."

I went numb - not because she was leaving, but because she thought I didn't care to do anything. In all the years of our marriage, if there was a point of conflict, I felt I was always the one who had to change. Only in doing so was there any chance of maintaining an even keel and keeping the peace. I wanted to say I would hate to have her nerve in a tooth.

Roberta went to stay with a friend of hers, the one who had asked us to adopt her cat Mitzy years ago. She now had her own home and could have pets. Roberta decided to take Ginger with her and left Loki to stay with me. I could almost visualize a divorce proceeding where we battled over custody of the cats. They appeared to be the only things we cared about anymore.

I spent most of the day at home, my mental state somewhere between shock and relief. By evening, I needed to get out and do something, even if it was wrong. I ended up at the R&R. It was getting late, so I didn't want to have coffee. I walked up and down the aisles of bookshelves, trying to find something of interest. I was glad it was Stu's day off. I didn't want to bump into him now. I did, however, bump into Sue Nami. She was sitting in a chair in the corner by the self-help section. She was looking in almost as bad a shape as I was in. I decided to stop and chat with her to take my mind off my troubles. She appeared to be upset, with a vacant expression. I wondered what was going on. She told me her partner Arnold, or Bjorn or whatever the hell his name is, had taken off and moved in with another woman. This woman is a White lady, and it appeared to be a sore point with her. I told her about my situation. "Misery loves company?" I asked.

"It might love it more in a place where the drinks are more potent than they are here," she said. I figured, why not?

Since Sue had used the Gruber service to get here, she rode with me as we headed down Colfax Avenue in search of a quiet spot to drown our sorrows. I parked in a large lot and could see a couple of prospects. One was a place with live music called the Horn Pub. Sue mentioned it had some bad Yelp reviews, and we preferred a less raucous environment, so we opted to try out the new Eastern European-themed lounge called the Crimea River Room. We must have looked like a mismatched pair; Sue, a millennial Asian lady in a long-sleeved white blouse and black pants with matching pump shoes, looked like she might have just come from her job, her long, straight dark hair framing her face, and me, a Scandinavian boomer in jeans, a sweatshirt, and casual shoes, with hair and beard a bit rough around the edges.

We found a table in a quiet corner and started to chat. It's probably true that we each found the other to be an acquired taste, friendship-wise.

But I did enjoy the banter we had back and forth. Sue appeared to agree. "I like the talks we have at R&R," Sue said. "I admit I like giving you a bad time, but you are fun to talk to."

"Same here," I said. You probably wouldn't think we would get along. We kind of have different viewpoints on things, but I find I can be considerate of other opinions. It doesn't have to be like a war."

Sue frowned inexplicably. "Well, I guess I can appear to be a little slutty at times, but I don't think I'm that bad," she said.

Wait, what? I thought. "No, I said a *war*, you know, like a battle or a struggle," I said.

"Oh, I get it now," Sue said. "I know I can appear to be opinionated and headstrong, but I am willing to see the other side in an argument. It started for me when I read someone's blog post where they came out with a firm anti-abortion stance. I could see the person's point, but I couldn't resist leaving a comment that since the person was a man, he couldn't have a valid point of view. But when he responded to my comment with a personal story about how his own father had wanted him aborted, and if he had, we wouldn't be having that exchange, it made me think."

Holy crap, I thought. *She was the one who wrote that?* I didn't say it out loud, but it showed me what a small world it is.

"Do you want to tell me about what happened with old what's-his-name?" I asked, trying to steer the conversation to something more current.

"He's been seeing this woman for a few weeks. I suspected something was up, but I didn't want to face it. When we would make sex, it was like he was with someone else. When he let me know, it was devastating."

Make sex? I thought. I'm not sure if this was fractured English or if she really was having a conflation issue. "I can sympathize. I've got some similar issues. How do we deal with it?"

"Get drunk," she said.

"Not a bad idea," I concluded.

"I think he was upset because he found out I was running an online sex site, and he didn't like the fact," Sue continued. "A friend of his had found it and told him about it. After that, he moved on. I thought I did a better job of covering my tracks."

"I thought you said you work at the accounting firm," I said.

"I do," she replied. "As a receptionist. To make any real money, I have to get down and dirty on a webcam site. It's only now getting to where I can make a full-time business of it if I want to."

"So, you're on JOI?" I asked.

"JOI? You mean jerk-off instructions?" Sue asked.

"No, I mean the site called Just Our Intimacy," I replied. I thought everyone knew what JOI stands for.

"No, I'm on the other one. It's called Fair-Weather Buddies. It's not as well-known, but I still tell people the standard accounting story to throw them off."

Fair-Weather Buddies? I thought. *FWB? Like friends with benefits?* I was getting confused. I must say, Sue was full of surprises tonight. I started to feel more at ease with opening up about my personal problems. "I have a similar situation," I told her. "My wife found out I was engaging some ladies in conversations on JOI, and it caused big problems. We had other issues, but this brought it to a head. Still, I think if she isn't willing to discuss the things I want to try, she shouldn't be surprised if I seek it elsewhere."

"So, you have loveless marriage?" Sue asked.

"Well, not sure I would put it that way. Sexless for sure, though," I replied.

"Oh, right, I forgot, they're not the same thing," she said, rolling her eyes. "How's that working out?"

Crud, I thought. *She has me there.* I knew I would look pretty silly if I tried to mount my high horse and defend my soap box rant from a while back. "Good talk, Sue," I said ironically. She looked at me with what appeared to be a bit of a self-satisfied smirk, which was not at all unwarranted.

We sat and drank and talked for a while. Sue was knocking them back at an alarming rate. At some point, I switched to ginger ale since I was driving. Finally, I said, "It's getting late. Maybe it's time to call it a night. I can give you a ride home if you want."

Sue sat staring at the bottom of her empty glass and shook her head. "I don't want to go home," she said. "Can we go to your place?"

I couldn't think of a single good reason not to, aside from the undeniable fact that it would be totally fucking insane and might lead to a plethora of disastrous outcomes, any one of which could irrevocably turn my life into a festering pile of dog shit. "I suppose so," I said. *Wait, did I just say that? Why did I say that?* I thought. Could I have subconsciously been thinking about a line Tom Cruise said in the movie *Risky Business*; "Every now and then, you've just gotta say what the fuck?"

***

We got to my place, and Sue excused herself to the bathroom. I sat down on the sofa and tried to clear my head from the few drinks I had and the barrage of information that had been thrown out at me. Nothing could have prepared me for what happened next.

Sue came out of the bathroom wearing only her unbuttoned blouse and a pair of slinky red panties. She came to me as I sat on the sofa and straddled my lap on her knees. She wrapped her arms around my neck and planted a kiss on my lips that I thought might blow the soles off my shoes from the inside. She reached down and removed my hand from the back of her thigh and placed it on her breast, pressing against it. "Let's make sex," she said. She again met my lips in full-on suck-face mode, and I got lost in her passionate expression of wanton lust.

But I was lucid enough to know this was a bad idea, from the standpoint of safety, sanity, consent, and any number of abstract concepts. I disengaged my hand from her body, held her by her shoulders, and looked her in the eye. "I don't think that's a good idea, Sue," I said.

Sue straightened up, and the look on her face was one of total dev-astation. "You don't want to make sex to me?" she asked. "You don't like me?" She sat up and opened her blouse so I could see her tiny breasts and flat tummy. "Don't you think I'm pretty?" she asked, a tear running down her cheek. "Won't you... love me?"

"It's not that. You're beautiful and I do like you," I assured her. "I just think the timing isn't the best for this to be happening. We might regret it later." Sue broke down and sobbed, shaking as she buried her face in my chest. It appeared to come from the depths of despair, and she was letting it all out. I realized anything I did to further any sexual contact at this point would be taking advantage, and I did not want to do that. She cried for a while until I could tell she had either fallen asleep or passed out.

Once I was sure she wouldn't be waking up anytime soon, I turned her over and fastened a couple of buttons on her blouse so it would stay closed; I carried her to the bedroom and put her on the bed. I pulled the covers back, placed her in bed, and tucked her in. After grabbing a blanket and a pillow, I headed for the sofa. As I was sacked out on the couch, it occurred to me to wonder what Roberta might think if, for some reason, she opted to come back and retrieve something she needed. I calculated the odds of that happening to be long.

As I lay there, thinking about Sue sleeping in my bed, I couldn't help but wonder how I was able to handle it without at least wanting to get in there with her. It's obvious she has a banging body, with great skin stretched out over a pair of long, shapely legs, a trim, flat tummy, and two of the smallest breasts I have ever seen on a grown woman. Still, I found her sexy and alluring, no doubt due in large part to her attempt to go all FWB on me earlier. Still, I was able to resist. But I realized it wasn't mere resistance. Despite how excited I felt at Sue's advances, my natural response wasn't happening. I mean, I couldn't get it up to save my soul from hell. After all the grief I had taken from Roberta over the past few years about my proclivities, it seemed I was numb to the chance that occupied the next room. Talk about a pathetic misfit. I swear, if I fell into a barrel of tits, I would come out sucking my thumb. As I lay there wallowing in self-pity, my cat Loki jumped up on my chest and curled up in a little ball with his head tucked under my chin and started to purr. At least there was one source of unconditional love in my life.

In the morning, I woke up and discovered I had a condition I hadn't experienced in some time – morning wood. Once my thoughts turned to my situation, it soon went away. In any event, it was a relief as I was beginning to think the pilot light on that furnace had gone out for good. I went to the bedroom to check on Sue. I rapped on the door softly to see if she was awake. I got no response, so I cracked the door open and peeked inside. She was still sleeping it off; it looked like she hadn't moved. I went to the kitchen and put on a pot of coffee. Starting up my iPad, I began to go through my morning ritual of reading an assortment of online newspapers. After about an hour, Sue came out of the bedroom, having at least buttoned her blouse. She paused in the doorway, pointed back toward the bed, and looked at me quizzically. "Did we…?"

"Make sex?" I asked. "No." From her reaction, I couldn't tell whether she looked more puzzled or hurt. "Not because I didn't want to, in case you were wondering," I said.

She was holding her head and looking like she might get sick. "Help yourself to coffee," I said, pointing to the pot on the counter. "Sorry, I don't have any soy milk to put in it."

"That's fine. I need it strong and black," she said.

Like your men, was my knee-jerk thought. I caught myself before I actually said it, and I was feeling almost proud of myself that I didn't say it. I soon realized I shouldn't be. There is not now, nor has there ever been, nor will there ever be a corner of the multiverse where that would be a cool thing to say. As I got to thinking about fixing breakfast, a thought came to me. Sue checked off enough boxes on the left side of the political spectrum that I had to consider the odds that vegan could be among them. I estimated them to be better than average. That was a problem since I had grown up on a dairy farm, and my breakfast fare weighed heavily on eggs, milk, and cheese, with a side of bacon thrown in for good measure. "Not sure what looks good for breakfast," I said as I surveyed the contents of the refrigerator. Almost in desperation, I pulled out a jar and offered it to her. "Pickle?" I asked.

Sue's face appeared to turn almost as green as the contents of the jar I was holding, and she covered her mouth with her hand and made a dash for the bathroom. I guess she was a bit queasy from her hangover. I could hear her letting it all out, and I was glad I could help. While she was so occupied, by the grace of God, I found an avocado I remembered I had purchased with the intention of trying to whip up a new guacamole recipe but decided it could be put to better use at the moment. I mashed it up and fixed some whole wheat toast to spread it on. Sue soon reappeared, having finished getting dressed, since the bathroom was where she had left the majority of her clothes last night, or rather, earlier this morning. "You should probably eat something," I said, offering her the toast and some orange juice.

"Thanks," she said. After managing to keep it down, she commented, "It's not bacon and eggs, but it will do."

Crud, I thought. *I suck at reading people.* Then I calculated the odds that she was just messing with me, and I estimated them to be about even.

I asked Sue if she needed a ride home, and she said she had already sent for a ride-share. As she was about to leave, I took her hand and looked her in the eye. "You are very smart, very beautiful, and you deserve all the happiness this life has to offer," I told her. "I hope we're still friends."

She looked at me, and with a meek smile, she nodded and kissed my cheek. "No hard feelings," she said.

Thanks for reminding me, I thought. I took her chin in my hand and said, "Sometimes love isn't what you feel. It's what you do. Or don't do," I told her. She looked me in the eye and nodded, and I think she understood. But it made me think about my situation. Sue left, and that was it. Leave it to me to consign a beautiful, sexy woman to the friend zone.

CHAPTER 24

**"Second marriage is the triumph of hope over experience."
– Samuel Johnson**

After my night with Sue and all that had gone before, I felt like I needed to talk to someone. I considered Diane, but I knew she was unavailable. She said on her morning video yesterday that she would be on one of her quests to have a 'secret rendezvous' with her hubby, as they like to do from time to time when he is on the road for his work. It did my heart good to know somewhere in this world, a married person was sneaking away to have hot sex with the person they are married to—more power to them. Then there was Alice, but the meter had run out on our connection, and I wasn't about to open that can of worms again. Sophia was the only one left to turn to, so I sent a text to her. "Are you available? I need to talk," I said in the text.

"I can get on Zoom right now," she said. "Go ahead and fire up the meeting."

It was amazing how easy it is to reach Sophia compared to the issues I had trying to connect with Alice. Perhaps Sophia is on the approved list the universe set up for me.

Sophia could tell I was near a crisis. "What is bothering you?" she asked.

"I feel like I'm in an existential quandary," I said. "I have this morbid fear of missing out. But all my ships have sailed, and I didn't get on any of them. The hell of it is, there hasn't been a single successful marriage in my family. Todd is the only one who managed to stay married, and I wouldn't be surprised if he would have preferred to get away from his shrew of a wife. At least he stayed with it till the end. He is the only male member of my family who wasn't found on the floor of his bathroom. I gotta say, it's not looking good for me." Sophia shifted in her chair. "It wouldn't be hard to visualize a situation where Roberta ends up living in a downsized house, and I park an RV in an undisclosed location and live out my days as a monk hermit," I continued. "Which sounds pretty good to me right now. At least it's better than waiting till I'm dead to have a life."

"Have you thought about what I said earlier about seeking help with your depression?" Sophia asked.

"No, I've been too depressed lately," I said.

"I'm not kidding, Alex! Clinical depression is no laughing matter. It will kill you if you let it. That's its job. You need to talk to somebody. I'll make an appointment for you if I have to," she said.

"I'll get to it," I said. I'm not sure I convinced her. Or myself.

"It sounds like this experience was a catharsis," she said. "You can use it to spur your creativity. You've been saying you need to come up with one more story for the collection, and this might provide the impetus and the inspiration to do it. In fact, I have every confidence it will be the best one yet. See what you can come up with, and let me see it."

***

I knew Sophia was right. About a lot of things. Especially my worsening depression. I knew I couldn't put it off any longer. While it may have appeared to be a recent development, I realized it has been a pattern for most of my life. It probably explained the insomnia, the drinking, and my attempts to gloss over it with the aid of my wise-ass sense of humor. I decided I would see someone who could help.

She was also right about the writing. It was time to wrap up my story collection. But what to write about? My life was spinning out of control at this point. I wanted to find a way to settle my mind, to maybe think about something that would give me a sense of peace and calm. I tried to imagine a scenario of a life that would be, if not meaningful, at least enjoyable and free of interference from nosy friends and relatives. I knew it was time; I needed to bring my story collection to a proper conclusion. But what would it look like? I decided it would have to be a look into the future for a few years to see how the consequences of these choices could end up playing out. I thought about it and figured out a way to bring the collection full circle.

Resolutions

By Xander Arcane

'**WELCOME TO NEVADA,**' the sign said as he drove his small motor home down the highway. He had a destination in mind but no set time he had to be there. The RV he was driving had only been his for a few months. At one time, he and his wife had planned to spend their retirement years in a big coach-type home on wheels. But life is one of those things that happens while you are making other plans, and now he was on his own. He found the Class C Sunseeker was more than adequate for just himself.

A few miles inside the state line, he saw a car pulled over on the shoulder, and someone appeared to be working on changing a tire. As he got closer, he could tell it was a woman struggling with the lug wrench, trying to loosen the nuts but not having much luck. He pulled over and got out of his vehicle and thought he would offer to lend a hand. "Can I help you?" he asked.

The lady was wary as he approached but could tell from his manner and apparent age that he was likely not a threat. Just a Good Samaritan offering a helping hand. She stepped back from the flat tire and said, "Thanks. I would have called for help, but it's a cellular wasteland around here. They sure crank these nuts on tight at the tire shop." She was a young lady with a sturdy build and stylishly but casually dressed. She had on a large straw hat and oversized dark glasses. Her trim waist and ample breasts were adequately contained by the simple white blouse she wore, and her khaki short shorts made her legs look luscious. He hadn't seen legs like those since, well, some time ago.

He took the wrench and, with several firm twists, managed to get the nuts off and change the tire. "I'm lucky you came along. Where are you headed?" the lady asked.

"Pahrump," he said. "There's an RV resort there I can spend a couple of weeks in before I head on to Arizona for the winter."

"No kidding, I work in Pahrump," she said.

"What do you work at?" he wanted to know.

"Sex," she said.

He turned to face her. "Oh, right, they have those, what do you call them, brothels, or ranch-type places there. Gosh, I haven't been to one of those in ages."

Something in the way he said that triggered a memory fragment in the woman. She brought her hand up to her mouth and gasped as she recognized him. "Are you… Craven Moorehead?" she asked.

"For as long as I can remember," he replied. Then he took a closer look as she removed her sunglasses. He gasped, "It's you, Allie!" he said as he recognized the lady whom he had spent a memorable evening with years ago at the Midway Inn.

"Yes, you can see now," she said with a grin.

"How long have you been working at a 'ranch?'" he wanted to know.

"Since not long after that night when we almost… you know. I got some good advice from a friend. Turns out he knew what he was talking about."

"Would you like to get together, have a drink or something, catch up on old times?" he asked.

"Sure. Your place or mine?"

"These days, I take my place with me wherever I go," he said, waving his hand toward the RV. "I know the number of the campsite I reserved; do you want to follow me there?"

"Give me the number, and I'll catch up with you. I need to freshen up a bit."

"I'll be looking for you," he said as he gave her the campsite number. "Don't keep me waiting."

After he got parked and extended the slide-outs of his motorhome, he tidied up a bit while he waited for her to arrive. He decided that while he was waiting, he would unhitch his car from the tow trailer. The car he traveled with wasn't your typical run-around vehicle. He was driving a vintage Corvette Stingray from the mid-seventies, a white T-top coupe with saddle tan interior. As he brought it alongside the RV, Allie appeared. She had changed out of her blouse and shorts and was wearing a sundress, and it appeared to him not much, if anything else. "Please tell me that's not a mid-life crisis," she said.

"Oh, trust me, I'm hell and gone from a mid-life anything," he said. "This is the only car I've ever wanted, and I've wanted one since I was in high school. I figured it was now or never. This little two-seat gas hog has to be the least practical thing I ever bought, but it makes more sense than trying to take the motorhome to the convenience store for a jug of milk. Although a jug of milk and a loaf of bread is about all I can carry in there, maybe a carton of eggs if I get creative about stashing things," he grinned.

"I'll bet it set you back some," she said.

"Well, when they were new, they went for about a year's pay for someone with any kind of a decent job. Nowadays, to get a drivable one is probably about the same. So, even though it has been through its depreciation cycle, the cost is about even," he rationalized. "So, let me show you the rig."

He opened the door and helped her up the steps. She walked into the living area and looked around. "Cozy," she said.

"Yes, this is about right for one person."

Allie thought for a moment. "So… your wife isn't in the picture anymore?"

He shook his head and remained silent. Allie wasn't sure what to make of it. Had she passed away, or were they separated or divorced? He didn't appear to want to talk about it, and she didn't want to pry it out of him.

He opened the makeshift liquor cabinet tucked into the cabover area. "What can I fix for you?"

"I could go for a 'Quick Fuck' if you have what that takes," she said with a smile and a wink.

He cracked a smile and started to mix the ingredients for the requested beverage. "And to think I once accused you of not having a sense of humor."

"What makes you think I'm joking?" she responded, leaning forward on the counter to accentuate her cleavage in a suggestive manner, which was hard to miss.

"We'll see. All the same, I think I'll make mine an 'Old Fashioned,'" he said with a wink of his own as he reached for the bourbon and bitters. He invited her to have a seat at the dinette table, which was somewhat reminiscent of the table at Big Dick's, where they began their acquaintance.

"So, how have things been at the Midway Inn?" she wanted to know.

"Smokin' hot. At least until the fire department arrived, but by then, it was too late."

"It burned down?" she gasped.

"Yeah, not long after Big Dick sold the place to P.O."

"What caused the fire?"

"They were never able to prove anything, but the insurance inspector thought it was friction."

Allie had known this joker long enough to know she was being set up for a punch line. "Okay, I'll bite. What was rubbing?"

"A six-figure mortgage against a seven-figure insurance policy."

"Sounds like something P.O. would try to pull."

"That was the general consensus. Now, the place is a vacant field. They have a farmer's market there now. There is this one lady who set up a stand and sells artisanal pickles. People come from all over and line up to buy them. She does quite well for herself."

"She must have found an unmet need and fulfilled it," Allie said. "That's what I try to do."

She continued to look around the small living quarters. RVs don't provide a lot of room to display sentimental knick-knacks. She noticed a small picture frame, and at the top was a photo of an attractive lady with dark hair and a pleasant look about her. "Is this her?" Allie asked. He nodded. "And these?" she gestured to the remaining six photos in the frame. "Your kids?" she smiled as she referred to the cats occupying the remaining spots in the montage.

"You could say that," he said. "We were always cat people. They have a way of getting to you. But they have all gone over the rainbow bridge."

"What's that?"

"Sentimental BS," he said. "Something the veterinary-industrial complex likes to promote to keep people coming back for more. The story goes that when a beloved pet has to be put to sleep, they go to a place where they can run and play in perfect happiness, only lacking the companionship they had with the person who loved them in their forever home. In time, that person comes to find them, and they cross over that shimmering bridge to live out a blissful afterlife. So, basically just telling people what they want to hear." He gazed off into the distance and said, "Kind of like what religion does."

"Are you religious?" Allie asked.

"I have been, I suppose, because I lack the faith it requires to be an atheist," he said. "There has always been a spiritual component to me. Are you familiar with Mahatma Gandhi?" he asked. She nodded. "A reporter once asked him what he thought of western religion. He said, 'I like your Christ, but not your Christianity.' I know exactly what he was talking about. Most of the good Christians I have encountered appear to live by a code of ethics which is nothing more than a big, long list of dos and don'ts, mostly don'ts that they mostly do when they think no one is watching."

"So, you're saying they are all sinners?"

"As are we all."

"Especially people like me?" Allie asked.

"And what would that make me?" he responded. "I don't preach, and I don't judge. The former is above my weight class, and the latter is above my pay grade. I always figured if you are sincere in wanting to be forgiven of your sins, the first thing you need to do is sin." Allie smiled. "Think about it," he said. "If you read the Bible, God never forgave anyone who hadn't sinned. It could be thought to be an expectation. That tells me I'm no better or no worse than anyone else. I sleep pretty well at night, knowing that. It's just the religious-industrial complex that wants to try to keep people under their control and make themselves relevant."

"Sounds a bit cynical," Allie observed.

He nodded. "The more I know people, the more I like cats. But those days are over. It isn't easy having a cat in an RV. And I'm not sure I'm up to having to say goodbye to any more of them. I always made a point of being with them when we had to put one down, to give comfort in their final moments, and make one last connection."

"And did your wife get that?"

He sat and contemplated for a long moment, gazing out the window. "It wasn't quite as neat and tidy as all that. But we did come to an under-standing of sorts, and we resolved the majority of our issues," he said. Allie still wasn't sure exactly what he meant but decided she would take him at his word.

"So, is this the whole living quarters?"

"Pretty much, except for the bedroom in the back," he said.

"Want to show me?"

"I'll have to think about it," he responded. Seven-hundredths of a second later, he said, "Sure, why not?"

They went to the back, and he showed her the cozy sleeping area. "This is very nice," she said. She wrapped her arms around his neck and leaned forward so the sundress she was wearing allowed her breasts to come into view for him. She pulled him closer and kissed him. Then she stepped back and let her dress fall to the floor, revealing herself completely nude. "Is my body as good as you remember?" she asked.

Moorehead drew in a long, slow breath and let it out with a sigh. "Better," he said, gazing longingly at her.

"That's quite a compliment," she replied. "I remember how much you enjoyed coming to the club and watching me get naked."

"That I did. You always were my favorite."

"I also remember a time when I had you in my bedroom, and I let you get away. That won't happen this time," she said.

"What are you talking about?"

"What I'm talking about is, I'm not leaving here until either we've had mind-blowing sex on that bed, or you've tossed me out on my ass."

He met her gaze and shook his head. "You're not getting tossed out."

"That's good to hear," she said. "So… fair's fair. Get naked."

He undressed, and they embraced and kissed like long-lost lovers. She eased him backward onto the bed and surreptitiously conducted the requisite inspection. She began to kiss and touch him all over until she could see his member start to respond. She moved her face next to it and positioned the tip next to her lips. She opened her mouth to take it in, slowly and steadily pulling it in with her lips wrapped around it. As she let it out, he could see that a condom had magically appeared ready to go. He smiled, and she winked at him, then she straddled him as she drew him inside her. She rode him with increasing intensity, allowing him to take in the sight of her gorgeous body. She slowed down and leaned her body forward so her breasts came near his mouth. He reached up and took them in his hands and kissed and sucked them until she was moaning and writhing. He knew it was time. Just as he had taken ownership of their kiss long ago, he now felt it was time to take possession of her body, and she willingly offered it. He turned her over so she was on her back. He arched his back and started thrusting with a vigor he had not felt in years. They climaxed in a perfect storm of longing, lust, and affection, which left them both exhausted and eager for more.

"How was that?" she asked.

"Hard to say. If I didn't know better, I would think I had just been raped."

Allie held her hands out toward him with the heels together. "Want to slap the cuffs on me, haul me off to prison?" she teased.

He thought about it for a moment. "No, I'll let it slide this time. Although the thought of having you as my captive in handcuffs does have a certain appeal."

"I have some in my car. I could get them," she said.

"Maybe later. I'll keep it in mind," he said. As he removed the used condom, he said, "That was pretty slick, whatever you did there."

"Tricks of the trade," she responded. "Glad you appreciate it."

"Ahh, yeah. About that. What do I owe you?"

"What are you talking about?"

"You are professional, right?"

"You have been out of it for a while, haven't you? Nothing happens until I say we're good to go. You've had that coming for a long time," she responded.

"Really?" he said. "I seem to recall that I got what I asked for."

"That may be, but the interest on your investment has more than kept pace with inflation," she said.

"So it would appear," he replied.

"Call it a make good," she said. "I know you would have done it that night if you felt you could. I understood what you were about back then, but I wanted it too, and it took this long to make it happen. Besides, you came to my rescue out on the highway. So, chalk the rest up to rescue sex. Some say it's even better than make-up sex."

"You make things happen on your own terms, don't you?"

"You can't make it in this profession unless you do. I learned that from Alice Modicum," she said.

"Who is Alice Modicum?"

"A good friend of mine," Allie said. "She's a fellow sex worker, and she's a real force of nature. She took me under her wing when I was getting started out here. She called it being a 'big sister,' which is comical since she is almost a foot shorter than I am. Seriously, she's the best. You'd like her."

"I'd like to meet her," he replied.

"That could be arranged," she said.

Changing the subject, Allie asked, "Your name? Craven. Is that what you go by?"

He chuckled. "Not much of any way to make that warm and fuzzy. It belonged to some great-great grandparent way back when. In some circles, I used to go by Roger."

"Oh," she responded. "Your middle name?"

"No, more like a nickname I picked up in college. Some of the ladies there decided I was their go-to guy when they wanted a good rogering. I guess I was a lot more fun back in those days. Or people in general were. Plus, I didn't have a religious wife back then."

"You said you haven't been to a brothel in more years than you care to think about," Allie said. "Why not stop by the ranch? I could show you around. I think you'll find it's state of the art in the 'sex-industrial complex.' Who knows? You might even get to chain me up in the dungeon."

"Now you're talking," he said. "I just might do that."

"Great," Allie said. "Pick a time and come on over."

"How's tomorrow night at 8:00?" he asked.

"It's a date," she replied. "Ring the bell twice, and I'll know it's you."

They lay there for an hour or more, simply talking like before and enjoying each other's company. After a while, Allie said she needed to leave. "I'll find my way out," she said.

When he woke up the next morning, Roger wondered if it had all been a dream. The note he found stuck to his bathroom mirror confirmed it had not been:

"Don't keep me waiting! ♡ *A."*

That was as good a way as any to wrap things up, I thought. Still, I could see there was one more bit of unfinished business to be dealt with. I wondered if I was ready to let it go.

CHAPTER 25

"It ain't over till the fat lady sings."
– Sam Goldwyn, among others.

I still had another issue to resolve, and if I could deal with it, I figured I could move on and be done with it. In doing so, I would revisit a long-dormant memory and have a chance to heal some fresh wounds.

Resolutions continued

Roger took Allie's note and tucked it in a secure place where it would serve as a reminder of a special occasion that would live in his heart for as long as he did.

He was eagerly anticipating their upcoming date and brothel tour. Roger recalled the research he had done on meet-ups at these establishments. He decided a phone call was in order. A few minutes later, he had his financial planner, Robin Banks, on the line. "Hey, you old goat, where are you hiding out these days?" Robin asked.

"Nevada at the moment," Roger replied.

"Really, I hear it's hot there," Robin said.

"Yeah, but it's a dry heat. Hey, the reason I called is that I wanted to check on that little side fund I set up a while back, you know, the one I said should be earmarked for a 'special purpose.' How's it doing?"

"Well, let's have a look," Robin responded. "Looks great; it's close to seven figures. Six to be exact."

"I'm likely going to need to free up any five of them, you know, for one of those special purposes," Roger said.

"Oh, are you finally going to take that trip around the world?" Robin asked.

"You could say, uh, something like that. Yeah, we'll call it that," he said.

"Wait a minute, where are you? Nevada? Don't tell me," Robin said.

"Hey, you know what they say in the movies? Every now and then, you just have to say, WTF."

"What the fuck is that?"

"Exactly," Roger said.

"Say no more," came the response. With a few clicks and keystrokes, Robin's voice came back on the line. "Done deal, you can write your own ticket."

"It's a pleasure doing business with you," Roger replied.

***

That evening, all eyes turned to watch the gleaming white sports car pull into the parking lot. All eyes turned back to what they had been looking at before as the gray-bearded geezer climbed out of said sports car. *Typical*, he thought to himself as he walked to the door.

He rang the bell at the appointed time in the specified manner. Allie met him, and they did a quick walk through the place. One thing that struck him was the signs that said condom use is mandatory. "That is a departure from back in the day," he observed. "At that time, safe sex was a fairly nebulous concept."

Allie nodded. "These days, you can't be too careful. What say we sit down and talk for a while?" She pointed to a table in a cozy corner in the back.

As they talked, he thought about that night years ago when they shared a connection, and he told her about the idea of sex work and how it appeared to be agreeing with her. "Are you happy?" he asked.

"I am," she said. "This is the most rewarding thing I have ever done. The sex is great, but for the most part, they want to talk and form some connection. Maybe it's their first time, and they need a confidence boost so they can go into their next experience excited, or maybe they have been single for a while and feel isolated. I feel like I make a difference in their lives."

As they sat and talked, a hand touched Allie's shoulder. She turned and looked, and there stood her friend Alice Modicum, all four feet eight inches of her. "What are you doing here?" Allie beamed when she saw who it was.

"I had a client cancel at the last minute," Alice said.

"It happens to the best of us," Allie said.

"I have something for you," Alice said as she reached into her handbag. "I took the scenic route to get here. I found this place out in the middle of freaking nowhere, and this lady was selling these amazing pickles. You have to try them. Seriously, I'm thinking of quitting sex work and going into business with her."

The room got deathly silent, and all eyes turned toward Alice. She looked around and grinned. "Kidding!" she said. The sound level in the room returned to normal as people started to breathe again and talk amongst themselves.

"Alice, I would like you to meet my friend, Craven Moorehead," Allie said. "But he also answers to Roger."

"Any friend of Allie's is a friend of mine," Alice said. "You know, I could use a good rogering right about now," she said with a mischievous wink.

"Nice to meet you, Alice," he said. "Allie tells me you are nothing short of the best in the business."

"Does she, now?" Alice said. "She is too generous."

"Oh, I trust Allie implicitly that she knows what she is talking about. Don't sell yourself short, Alice."

Alice glanced sideways at Allie, who rolled her eyes and shrugged. "Yeah, he's always like that.

"Anyway, I was about to show Roger around the dungeon," Allie said. "I thought it would be right up his alley."

Alice rolled her eyes and facepalmed. "I'm surrounded by looney tunes," she said. "But I have nothing better to do, and I'll bet you two are going to need a safety monitor. Why don't I join you? I can be anything from a spotter to a dungeon master."

The three of them went to a place where they could discuss the arrangements for a threesome. Once the particulars had been agreed to, Roger was glad he had cleared things with the financial institution. As they were about to head off to the dungeon, Alice called a halt to the proceedings. "Aren't we forgetting something?" she asked. "You know, something for my peace of mind."

Roger had to think for a minute. "Oh, right, the most important thing - the credit check," he said as he reached into his coat pocket and brought out a bulging envelope. "It's all right there, employment history, bank references, latest brokerage statement, and three years of tax returns," he said.

Alice was dumbfounded and had a look of *What in the actual fuck?* as she watched him prattle on as if he had good sense. "Show me your dick," she said flatly.

"That seems a bit personal," he replied.

Alice grabbed him by his lapels and pulled his face an inch from hers. "Show. Me. Your. DICK!"

"Fine, if you insist."

He lowered his pants, and Alice gloved up and studied his semi-flaccid organ from every conceivable angle with the detached professionalism of a clinical urologist. "Not bad," she said. Then she looked again at the envelope on the table. "Three years of tax returns in there?" she asked. He nodded. "I had better have a look," she said.

Allie could hardly keep from laughing out loud. She wasn't sure what she was enjoying more, the master class Alice was conducting in bullshitting a bullshitter or the fact that Roger was meeting his match in that department. "Oh, what the fuck," Alice said. "I'll take your word for it," and led the way to the play area.

As they followed Alice to the dungeon, Allie brought a hand beside her face and whispered an aside to Roger. "Nobody fucks with her."

"That's not what I've heard," he muttered under his breath.

They entered the room, and Roger had to admit he was impressed with the wide array of equipment and devices. "So, how would you like me?" Alice asked.

"Stripped down and chained up," Roger said.

"Works for me," Alice said. She shimmied out of her dress and stood there clad in only the skimpiest of black bikini briefs. "Do as you will," she said.

Roger raised Alice's hands above her head and fastened the leather cuffs around her wrists. He eyed her helpless form longingly. He had always had a thing for women who would willingly place themselves in a vulnerable position for him. He wasn't sure how he wanted to proceed. As he surveyed the array of implements available to stimulate or torture her, Allie offered to lend a hand.

"Let me pick," she said.

Roger decided to trust her judgment. Allie selected a flogger with long leather strands that made a wicked crack as they were flung in Alice's direction. She lashed her across the back, once, and again, harder.

"Ouch, that hurts," Alice said. "Why don't you pick on somebody your own size?"

"Oh, yeah? Well, I have a bone to pick with you, and I'm just getting started," Allie said. "Who do you think you are, barging in on my party? I saw him first," Allie said as she let the flogger once more find its mark.

"Fuck, what's this about?" Alice asked. "You are going too far."

"You want me to stop? Just say the word," Allie taunted.

"I wouldn't give you the satisfaction, you psycho bitch," Alice said.

Allie squinted at her and gave a long look at the straining girl's heaving belly. She raised the whip to strike, but Roger intervened with a hand to stop her as she was about to let it fly. "Take it easy," he said. "There is enough to go around, I think."

Allie shuddered at the thought of what she was about to do. "I don't know what that was about," she said.

Alice had fainted at the prospect of being lashed across her tender, quivering tummy by the clearly unhinged woman with the whip. Roger wrapped his arms around Alice's limp body and told Allie to undo the cuffs. As Alice slumped into his arms, he carried her to the padded table in the middle of the room. He patted her face to try to bring her around. "Are you okay?" he asked.

"Shut up and kiss me," Alice said. He gladly complied. "Lower, please," she implored.

There were a lot of good options lower, so Roger started to explore them all. As he did, Allie's eyes met Alice's. "I'm so sorry," Allie said. "I don't know what came over me."

"Shut up and kiss me," Alice said.

Allie was more than happy to oblige Alice. Roger noticed their interaction and was impressed. He had not seen this side of Allie but was more than a little intrigued. As the two women continued to go at it, Alice rolled off the table and traded places with Allie. She started to take the role of aggressor, and Allie surrendered to her advances. As Alice hungrily explored Allie's flesh, she looked up at Roger, who was standing in awe at the spectacle that was unfolding before him. Alice tossed her head back toward her hind quarters as if to say, "It's there for you, big boy," and Roger headed there. As the two women continued to be oblivious to anything but their two naked bodies, Roger applied a condom and procured a generous supply of lube. He evaluated the shortest distance between two points to be the tip of his engorged cock and the crack of Alice's bare butt. He reached out to spread her cheeks apart and exposed the tight hole, and he moved against it. Alice acknowledged his presence up her ass and continued to pleasure Allie. After a few determined thrusts, Roger let loose and released his grip on her ass. At the same time, Allie began to convulse in an intense release of orgasmic delight. Alice let her gather her wits about her, then told her to get off the table. Alice sprawled out on her back and reached for a fresh condom for Roger to put on. He did and got on top of Alice and slipped himself inside her. While he was doing that, Allie had found herself a strap-on dildo and was making preparations to mount her target. This was a new sensation for Roger, as he started to experience the sensation of a good rogering. "Pegging," he thought. "What a concept."

"I think we just made a Roger sandwich," Allie said.

"All he needs is a pickle," Alice said, reaching into the jar on the nightstand and popping one in his mouth.

"Yummy," Roger said.

The ladies were in complete agreement.

THE END

CHAPTER 26

"Religion is regarded by the common people as true, by the wise as false, and by the rulers as useful."
– Seneca

When we next met, Sophia had finished reading my latest story. "You found a way to bring your saga full circle. I'm impressed," she said.

"The ending needs some work," I observed. "But that is the direction things appear to be headed."

"Pegging?" Sophia asked.

"Google it," I replied.

"I did."

"And?"

"Your kink is not my kink."

"Yeah, I get that a lot."

"I see the artisanal pickle distribution chain is thriving," Sophia said.

"Yes, if you remember, Allie had intended to make her way by selling pickles before she answered another calling," I told her. "The mantel passed to another."

"He works in mysterious ways," she said.

"You might even call it arcane," I mused.

"I think I created a monster," she responded.

"You flatter me," I said. She gave me the look.

"It does appear as though you have some real affinity for this Alice person," Sophia commented.

"I can see how you might think so. I would say my real-life dealings with Alice Modicum left a little to be desired, but it wasn't her fault. I made a lot of demands on the scheduling in my hopes of keeping it on the down-low for all the good it did. Alice has a lot on her plate, and I'm just small potatoes. I wanted to find some closure and put it all behind me. Still, I find it hard to believe how she led me down the garden path with the promise of hot virtual dates being as good as the real thing, and I swallowed it hook, line, and sinker. Or was it sink, line, and... hooker?" I saw Sophia wince. "Was that mean?" I asked.

"That came across as kind of mean," Sophia said.

"Yeah, I guess so," I responded.

"Feel better?"

"A little."

"Have you heard from Roberta lately?" Sophia wanted to know.

"No, not for a few days," I said. "I have no idea where we go from here. I think it would take a miracle to salvage this marriage. The thing is, I'm not sure I want to at this point," I went on. "I'm getting used to the idea of being happily divorced. Maybe this is one of those things being allowed to happen because it's the best thing for both of us." I found myself wondering if it could be possible. "Do you think it could be?" I asked.

"Is that what you're thinking?" Sophia asked.

"Why do you always answer a question with another question?" I asked.

"Do I do that?" she smiled. I gave her the look. "Part of my reason for being here is to help you see for yourself what the answer might be and come to your own conclusions," she stated.

"Sometimes I feel like Craven Moorehead in the first story I wrote about him, where he is saying he hung in there to prove a point," I told her. "I think there is a lot of that going on here. Roberta and I both hold on to the idea that you stick with it come Hell or high water, and it's all to look good for others. But you have to consider all the damage high water can do and what Hell is really all about." I could see there were two possible outcomes to this situation; they both scared me. I realized I was the one who needed a sign to help me move on.

Sophia looked strangely serene the whole time I was talking. She appeared lost in thought as she tapped on her phone. Her eyes met mine through the camera. "I think it is time we meet face-to-face," she said. "I am speaking at a TED conference in Denver next week. We could arrange to get together, say, Thursday evening? Otherwise, I will be available all weekend."

"Tell me more," I said.

"I just think we could spend some quality time together. We know each other well enough now, I think. Don't you?"

"I'm intrigued to see what can come of it, should you take it into your head to make it happen," I said. Sophia was starting to get the look. *Oops*, I thought.

"I'll send you my schedule, and we can work out the details when it gets closer to the time," she said.

I was starting to think I might get such a sign.

***

Since telling off Stu and basically ducking anyone who had a connection with Roberta, I was getting used to the isolation I was experiencing. I decided to use the time for something constructive, like knocking down sacred cows. Fortunately, I have a platform for doing so. It was time to make a statement and show what the Devil's Advocate is all about.

Fundamentally Flawed

There is a reason why religious folk are portrayed in popular culture as vapid, toxic dumpster fires worthy of the scorn and ridicule of anyone capable of critical thinking. I once thought it had to do with bias on the part of the pseudo-intellectuals who run the media. It turns out it is because they are vapid, toxic dumpster fires worthy of scorn and ridicule by anyone capable of critical thinking. As it says in the good book, where two or three of my people are gathered, there the collective IQ will add up to a respectable golf score. Again, I paraphrase. But like Moses, well, okay, Charlton Heston said, "If there is a God, He did not mean this to be so."

Right about now, there is nothing I would rather do than stick it to all the self-righteous assholes with all of their preconceived notions of what God intended. My issue is not with faith but with the 'religious-industrial complex,' in particular the evangelical wing of it that seeks to exert undue influence over every aspect of people's lives. This is so they can extort money from the gullible; otherwise, they would have to get real jobs.

These organizations attempt to gaslight the addle-brained and the gutless into believing in a God who is all-powerful, who watches over them every minute of every day, who loves them and wants to spend all eternity with them, but who is looking for any reason to kick them out on a technicality. Only by joining their fellowship and pledging a significant percentage of their wealth can they hope to avoid an eternity of anguish and torment.

My biggest beef with the religious crowd, other than their contention that they are 'spirit filled' (well, they are filled with something, but I doubt it is spiritual), is their 'us vs. them' mentality. I have been around a few too many people who appear to want a version of religion that plays into their confirmation bias. I think about the most recent church I attended. I look around the congregation, and I wonder where the leaders of society are. The bankers, the captains of industry, those who build the infrastructure. Honestly, where is anyone between the ages of fifteen and sixty? Mostly, I see a bunch of virtue-signaling posers who wouldn't know a biblical principle if it bit them in the ass. Their religion only takes into itself and returns nothing of value to the world.

It is incredible to me how many evangelicals support a particular president with broad populist appeal. Even though he has no discernable familiarity with religious principles, he can do no wrong as far as they are concerned. But if I had done a tenth of the things this buffoon is not only credibly charged with but openly boasts about, they would be staging an intervention on me. But he is number one with them. Well, I guess I can hold up one finger in regard to him as well.

For supposedly being the province of right-wing politics, I was once in a protestant church which was so far left you couldn't tell where they ended, and the Democratic National Committee began. They were at the forefront of political correctness, as it was called at the time, and they could put the 'woke mob' to shame with how they weaponized it. They were among the first to 'go green' to stop climate change. They also take a revisionist approach in expunging any mention of masculine pronouns from the liturgy and music. After 10 years of being there, I was ready for a bit of peace on Earth and goodwill toward men.

I contend that the vast majority of religious people lack any real conviction in their ideals; they simply say what they say because they think that is what other religious people expect them to say. I remember a preacher who criticized a classic Christmas story because it contained references to ghosts, which did not align with his idea of what Christmas is about. For my part, I would rather be thought of as a heathen than a functional illiterate, but that's just me.

A lot of what passes for religious thought amounts to a bunch of superstitious nonsense. How many times do you hear someone sneeze, and the knee-jerk reaction is to say, 'God bless you?' That comes from an old wives' tale that evil spirits cause sneezes. Does anyone know why coffins are wider at the top than the bottom? It is because people once believed the devil lurks in corners, so coffins were made without any square corners so the devil wouldn't be able to reach the person inside. Wow, they thought of everything.

In the Middle Ages, there was an arm of the church known as the Spanish Inquisition, which could execute people for being a witch or even accused of being one. Not only would the unfortunate person be put to death, but also their 'familiar' animals, which were often cats, particularly black cats. This gave rise to the belief that black cats are bad luck, but also, in those days, led to a sharp decline in the population of these animals, which in turn led to the proliferation of rats. These rats were a significant contributing factor to the black plague of the 14th century. Thank you, Spanish Inquisition.

On the subject of sex and relationships, the standard appears to be 'do as I say and not as I do.' Scripture tells the story of a woman caught in the act of adultery. Of course, the person she was adulterating with was not mentioned. The Biblical standard of adultery is if a man sees a woman and wants her a bit too much, it's as good as doing it. I believe this standard exists to demonstrate that 'all have sinned,' as they say. Show me someone who can stand guiltless on that count, and I will show you someone who, in all likelihood, has flatlined brain-wave activity. Maybe it would be a good idea for the Catholics to let the priests get married, if not for the sake of being somewhat knowledgeable in counseling couples; at least they could see what Hell is like. And don't get me started on the damage caused by expecting human beings to live a chaste and celibate life. That looks like it has worked out so well.

I believe a big part of the church's attitude concerning sex is they view it as competition. This is also true of how they regard the mental health profession. It seems ironic, as there are few people who are more in need of competent mental health care than the religious crowd. To say nothing of a good screw once in a while.

The beginning of the end for me with involvement in a church came when one of the mainline protestant congregations we belonged to was taken over by a dissident faction, which ended up ousting the pastor. Apparently, this pastor wasn't 'red state' enough for their expectations. The chief complaint was that he wasn't willing to maintain a hard line on a particular social issue. I bet you can guess which one that is. Yeah, it has to do with sexual preference and gender fluidity. Some people are quite selective in their application of biblical principles. In my mind, it is very easy to be anti-whatever you are not.

A lot of true believers come down hard on the LGBTQ community because they don't know anyone there, or at least they think they don't. They might be surprised. But if I remember correctly, the Bible comes down pretty hard on people who have a casual attitude about getting divorced and remarried. It remains a sticking point with most Catholics to the extent they had to develop the whole concept of annulment so they can manufacture a way to say the marriage never actually happened. It's kind of like the system of indulgences, but they tend to treat it more like a 'mulligan.' But evangelicals, by and large, won't come down on those people because they could easily be some of us people, and you certainly don't want to alienate anyone you might actually care about. What's that they say about hating the sin but loving the sinner, and any among you who is without sin can cast the first stone? If I were part of the gay community, I don't think I would be feeling the love right now. Since I'm not gay, it isn't a big concern of mine, and I don't get hung up on it. Maybe I should, since it is becoming a topic of conversation. In any event, it got downright ugly there, and I felt it wasn't a good fit for me.

I once had a friend who took great care to grow his beard in accordance with the way the Old Testament described it needed to be. He commented to me once that at a gathering of his religious nut-case relatives, someone told him he looked like Saint Peter. I wanted to ask him if he was aware that none of these first-century religious leaders, including Jesus himself, ever had the opportunity to sit for portraits. In fact, most of what we think we know about these people's appearance, and the nature of Heaven and Hell for that matter, comes from Renaissance artists (oh, and by the way, a lot of them were gay – just saying). I wouldn't be surprised if this person's cohorts think that Jesus was a White Anglo-Saxon Protestant who spoke the King James version of English. Verily.

In most churches, women set the tone, and they want to emphasize an image of Jesus as an effeminate figure clutching a lamb to his bosom. This is not the image I have of the leader the warrior kings of the Middle Ages believed in. Unfortunately, the church isn't promoting that version of Jesus. And why not? Because in most churches, the women have taken over the presentation, and they want a version of Jesus to whom they can sing love songs.

I have a suggestion for all the true believers out there. You can hold whatever closely held beliefs you want, but don't try to force them on others. If you want someone to follow your way, show us something in your life that proves the way you believe and conduct yourself is better than what I have. That would be a reason to do it your way, more than all the self-aggrandizing posturing could ever do. If you insist on taking the literal hermeneutic of scripture, you would have to believe it was taken down as dictated from on High to perfect secretaries and passed down intact through all the permutations of language through time. If it wasn't, you have to allow for personal bias on the part of the writers and the possibility that humanity is not a perfectible species.

Had I not drunk the Kool-Aid early in life, I would doubtless have made different choices in which paths to follow. I would have been more concerned about my own economic viability rather than putting my wants and needs behind everything else. I would have resisted the mindset that material wealth is not spiritual. After all, you can't pour from an empty cup. I would be less of a sheep and more willing to use my God-given intellect to find answers to the questions that religious folks can't or won't address. It would be a mistake to say these people are divorced from reality. In fact, they have never made reality's acquaintance.

In a world where truth is subject to interpretation, who is to say which interpretation is more valid? Then, the choice is not between good and evil but between different forms of evil.

***

Having edited this piece to something that could be considered more than a screed and less than a manifesto, I decided to hit publish and let the chips fall where they may.

After this post went up on Devil's Advocate, I saw a response from none other than Dr. John Daniel. He was in the mood to call me out on some of my assertions. "You appear to be hostile toward religion," he stated.

I felt like I struck gold. Now I have this asshole right where I want him. "It's not religion per se that I'm hostile toward; it's religious idiots and the people who enable them," I replied. I thought this would be an excellent opportunity to challenge him to a debate. I was more than willing to have him on a live stream to discuss our differences. But I suspected he would be reluctant to do so, and for good reason. I was particularly eager to engage him in a discussion of his antiquated beliefs about marriage and family, such as his statement about people questioning if they are married to the wrong person. His stock answer is if you are married, you are married to the right person. I could go on and on about how that is a crock. People get married for all kinds of reasons, and they are not always in line with a philosophy of Biblical principles. I wanted to bring up all of the high-profile preachers who have been caught up in scandals over the years. It makes me wonder why I even try.

CHAPTER 27

"There are more things in Heaven and Earth, Horatio, than are dreamt of in your philosophy."
– Shakespeare

After I dashed off my response to Dr. Daniel, my phone rang. It was Roberta. "Can we talk?" she asked.

"Sure," I said. "What's on your mind?"

"How are we going to resolve this?" she asked. "Have you given it any thought? Why can't we talk about the real issues between us?"

"Of course, I've thought about it," I replied. "The reason I seldom address issues is because I live in fear of triggering you into a psychotic episode. Nowhere is that truer than on the subject of sex. I am at a loss to figure out where you are at with things. It's like your sexuality is nonexistent, and if you see it in others, you prefer not to deal with it."

"What do you want from me? What do you need me to do?" Roberta asked.

"I've tried to tell you, but you always dismiss it," I said. "I've asked you to try things like sensual movement or acting out scenarios like a chance encounter at a business conference or a night on the town, and you appear to be spooked by it."

"That's just dumb," she responded. "Aren't I enough for you the way I am?"

"How do you imagine you are enough when you give me next to nothing?" I was getting exasperated. "You know how when we go to a wine tasting event, and you say no matter what kind of wine there is, all you notice is the alcohol? Well, it's the same way with sexuality. All you can detect is porn. I'm not sure if I'm more put off by the fact you see it that way or the fact you are so proud of doing so.

"The issue I see is that I don't share your view that sex is some sickness. I have been listening to people with a more sex-positive view who say it is an essential human function and it is normal and healthy. The problem with your worldview is that you can't see any form of eroticism away from the confines of some outmoded definition of morality, and you have become unable to make any distinction between the two. You have done everything in your power to make me feel bad about myself for being a man with male characteristics. You don't realize that it's those same characteristics that made it possible for me to get aroused at all with you. Now, things have deteriorated to the point that I can't function in that capacity. So, you got it done. How do you like the result?

"It all comes down to how you see yourself," I continued. "I think your reluctance is due to your self-image or self-esteem issues. But you use your religious masquerade to hide those. You go through the motions and call it lovemaking, but if I try to do anything to add spice or playfulness to it, you treat it like I have a sickness. I don't ask a lot, but I have feelings and desires that I would like to explore, situations that would add mystery and intrigue to the same old same old, but you don't want to go there. And then you think you can lie there like a bump on a log and expect me to get turned on? You are one to talk about unrealistic fantasies," I snapped. "That bell stopped ringing for me a long time ago. As far as I'm concerned..."

I stopped short of saying the one thing I knew there would be no coming back from, but there was one thing that I knew for my own sake I needed to say: "I don't have a life with you, I have an existence, and it's not enough. I have decided that I am going to live my life as an adult, and I am going to do it with you or without you. If you don't enthusiastically consent to do the things that make me feel like a man, then I will find someone who will. And as long as I am discreet about it, you have no right to complain because you left me with no alternative."

There was a long pause, after which I thought I heard Roberta crying. "Goodbye, Alex," she said and hung up the phone.

That was intense. I hated to say some of those things, even though I may have been thinking about them for some time. But I had, for all practical purposes, ended it if it wasn't already. At least I had my get-together with Sophia to occupy my mind.

After that exchange ended, I heard a ping on the email that I thought I might as well check. It was from Dr. Daniel. I didn't bother to read what he had to say. I was in vent mode, and I let him have it: "Your theory about being married to the wrong person just hit rock bottom, along with the last 26 years of my life," I wrote him. "That sad era has come to a flaming end, and so much the better.

"Honestly, the snow will fly in Hell before I believe a word out of your mouth. If you want to debate me on a live stream, bring it. I would love to verbally kick your ass up between your shoulder blades, you goofy old bastard. As far as I'm concerned, you can **go fuck yourself!**"

I figured I had spoken my piece with him, and it was abundantly clear to me that I had indeed torched one bridge after another lately. I turned my attention to thoughts about what I was heading into with my planned hookup with Sophia.

***

I made my way to the convention center where the conference was held. As I roamed the lobby, I saw a poster highlighting the fact that not only was Sophia Angelique a speaker at the conference, but she was, in fact, the featured speaker. She never mentioned that. I decided I had better be prepared to wait for her to get away from all the attendees who would want a word with her.

As I sat in the lounge waiting for Sophia to show up, I tried to comprehend all the events that had transpired lately. It was making my head spin. I thought about how I hadn't been with another woman in what felt like ages, my recent adventure (or misadventure) with Sue Nami notwithstanding. Now, I'm not at all sure what will come of this. I'm apprehensive but hopeful, too. It is a surreal feeling.

Sophia walked in, and I couldn't believe how ravishing she looked. The old song by the Hollies about a long, cool woman in a black dress came to mind. She was stunning. We hugged and sat down, and we ordered drinks. "I've really been looking forward to this," Sophia said.

"Me too," I replied as if I had to say it. "How is the conference going?"

"These things are always a hassle," she said. "But I'm learning a lot from the other presenters. I hope I can contribute as much as I'm getting back."

"I don't see how you can miss," I said. "So, how do we want to proceed? Are you ready for dinner?"

"Right now, I just want to get acquainted with you, maybe over appetizers, possibly followed by room service?" she winked.

She doesn't waste time, I thought to myself. We sat and talked about how far we had come in our discussions, exploring topics related to sexuality and adult relationships. I recalled the times she had dressed somewhat provocatively and how comfortable I always felt in her presence. After we had made small talk and flirted for a while, I asked her, "What did you have in mind?"

"I have something special planned for this evening. But I need a little time to prepare." She handed me a small envelope with a room key card inside. "Give me twenty minutes, then come on up, and come on in."

The minutes went by in a blur. I could only imagine what she was up to, but I was sure it was something amazing. Finally, I figured that by the time I got to her door, enough time would have passed. I slipped the card in the slot and went inside.

The lighting in the room was subdued, and she had several artificial candles flickering on the table and nightstand. Sophia was sitting in an oversized chair with her legs pulled up in front of her and wrapped in some sort of cover, her face hidden behind her folded arms. Music started to play; I remember from the time she appeared in her belly dance outfit. She opened the wrap from around her, and once again, I was looking at her in that fantastic costume. She looked even more ravishing in person, the flickering light playing off her skin, her lithe form gracefully moving toward me. She smiled, took my hands, led me to the chair, and sat me down. She started to move to the music, which had switched to the tune *Midnight at the Oasis* by Maria Muldaur, about a woman who wanted to be a belly dancer for a man who could be her sheik. Sophia moved with all the graceful and sinewy movements of an accomplished professional dancer. The incredible beauty of this fantastic woman transfixed me. I was enjoying her, and she was enjoying being enjoyed. "Don't be shy," she whispered, making what appeared like an unmistakable suggestion that I should let my eyes, my hands, and my lips roam.

"You are stunning," I said as I reached out and placed my hands on her hips. She continued to sway and shimmy, bringing her magnificent abdomen inches from my face. I couldn't resist leaning in to kiss her lovely navel, and as I did, she executed a perfect belly roll. She told me to make myself comfortable. She motioned for me to remove some of my clothing. I complied and asked if she minded if I moved to the bed.

"Not at all," she said.

Once I was sitting on the edge of the bed, she came to me, leaned in, and kissed me full on the mouth. Then she began to remove her clothing, starting with the hip scarf, giving me a look at even more of her creamy skin. Next to go was the skirt, showing her lean, lovely legs. She reached behind her back, unclasped the top of the costume, and let her breasts come into full view. I stood up and finished undressing myself, and we embraced and kissed with a passion I had never experienced. She eased me back onto the bed on my back and straddled me after removing the last of her garments. She leaned forward to let her breasts lightly brush my torso, arching her back so that her nipples were within reach of my lips. I latched on to one and began to suck lightly. She stretched out on top of me and rolled over so that I was now on top of her, and we were face-to-face. The thought occurred to me that this may be as close to Heaven as I ever get, and it's fine with me. "This is everything I have ever wanted," I said. "All I need is for someone to make me feel like the things I want are okay, that I can feel passion without guilt and shame."

"It's all fine," Sophia said. "Do anything you want, and I do mean anything!" She closed her eyes, tilted her head back, and parted her lips slightly as if waiting for my kiss.

By now, my engorged member was a heat-seeking missile locked onto its target. There was no turning back now. I thrust forward and took the plunge…

At least, I'm all but certain I would have had I not woken up at that precise moment. *What the hell?* I thought. I was sweating as I found myself alone in my bed at home. I have had vivid dreams before, usually connected to a sense of regret over a long-ago missed opportunity, but this was like nothing I had ever felt. It was as if I was experiencing another cosmic force situation. I started to wonder if Sophia was in cahoots with these same powers of the universe that had tormented me lately. As skeptical as I have always been about such things, I didn't think I could put it past her, particularly in light of my recent experiences with Alice and all the near misses we had.

I got up and made coffee and gathered my wits about me. I was still shaken by what I had gone through. I figured that forewarned is forearmed, and I would have this experience to serve as a guide when our actual 'date' occurred, which was still five days away. As I sat there amid the twisted, burning wreckage of my life, I decided to enjoy the anticipation and the memory of what I had just experienced and use it as a guide to see what could come of it.

In the meantime, I decided to continue with preparations for publishing my short stories. I had decided to go for it. I mean, what do I have to lose at this point? All that remained was to write the boilerplate BS about how these are fictional works and any similarity to actual persons living or brain-dead is a lucky accident. The dedication would no doubt be to those naive fools, by which I mean fans of absurdist fiction, who labor under the delusion that marriage, as it is practiced in our culture, is in any way designed to benefit men. I was becoming engrossed in thinking about the writing opportunities and the anticipation of good times ahead.

Then the doorbell rang.

I opened the door, and there stood a police officer with a concerned look on her face. "Good morning, sir. Are you Alex Anderson?" she asked.

I nodded, and she said, "Sir, there has been a traffic accident. Your wife is in St. Anthony's Hospital. Her condition is critical."

CHAPTER 28

"Hell is when the person you are meets the person you might have been."
– Anonymous

On my way to the hospital, I called Roberta's friend Eileen. She would undoubtedly spin up a prayer chain for Roberta. I didn't know if it would do any good, but I figured it couldn't hurt. Once I got to the hospital, I asked at the nurse's station to see Roberta, and they took me there. I saw Roberta in bed with monitors connected. It didn't look good.

I had a lot of thinking to do. The police officer told me it was possible the crash was deliberate. They didn't find skid marks to make it look like she had tried to avoid colliding with the abutment. Given her mental state and other health issues, both emotional and physical, I couldn't put it past her.

While I was sitting there, Eileen came in. I tried to imagine what Roberta might have said to her about our situation and status. If she said anything, Eileen wasn't letting on. I felt somewhat guilty over the fact that I have often wanted to keep Eileen at arm's length. She had been Roberta's friend for a long time. She knew what I was going through and sat with me silently, holding my hand. "You have to know God has a purpose for you and believe you are serving that," she said.

"How will I know I am accomplishing His purpose?" I asked her.

"Results," she said.

That blew me away. I was ready to brush her off, but it could be she had my back there. Normally, I would be tempted to tell Eileen to STFU and GTFO, but her presence was a source of comfort at that moment.

I decided to get some air and let Eileen have some time with Roberta. I stepped out into the hallway and saw Stu. He was coming for a visit, and when he saw me, he stopped. I wanted to find a way to talk to him. I extended a hand toward him, and we hugged it out. "There's a thing called tough love," I told him. "Maybe I was too tough on you."

Stu and I found a place to sit down in the waiting area. "The thing is, either Heaven is real, or it isn't," I told him. "I like to think it is, and I think that when we get there, we are all going to find out we were wrong about some things. I simply don't want you to be one of those who has to answer for pushing people away when those are the people who most need to hear what you have to say."

Stu asked how Roberta was doing. I told him I wasn't sure. "They are watching to see how she responds. So far, she hasn't regained consciousness. All we can do is watch and wait. But thanks for coming. It means a lot."

I got back to Roberta's room just as Eileen was leaving. Before she left, she scribbled a note and left it with me. It read Joel 2:25. I made a mental note to look it up soon.

Since I have been here, I have encountered Eileen and Stu, and it has gone better than I expected. One meeting I wasn't looking forward to was with Jason and possibly Freddie if he even bothered to show up. I would have to come to terms with one or both of them before this was all over. I was not looking forward to having to deal with Jason. We have had a lot to move past with each other over the years, and it was going to be a herculean effort to resolve our issues. I tried to imagine the things I would say to him, which had been festering in my mind for a number of years. Things like while I didn't adopt him, I did all the things a father should do in the course of raising him, paying the bills, providing a roof over his head and food on the table, all of which I didn't have to do, but did because it was implied in marrying his mother, which I also didn't have to do, but did because I said I would.

I began to feel uncomfortable in my gut. I was keenly aware that I had said some nasty things to Roberta recently, and I hoped I would have a chance to apologize.

I thought about my comment to Stu about tough love. Maybe I am experiencing this here. Perhaps it was a way of getting my attention. I thought about Roberta and what she was facing on the road to recovery. This is one of those times when people like to offer thoughts and prayers.

A short time later, a man dressed all in black, like a priest or a chaplain, stood in the doorway and asked if I would like to talk. I said sure. I was ready to speak with anyone who might have some answers to any or all of the questions swirling around my mind.

"I see all kinds of people in these situations, and I like to give them their space to discuss their faith or not. Are you open to talking about it?" he asked.

"I'm honestly not sure where I am at with that right now," I responded. "I have a tremendous capacity for faith, but I need some direction in what to put my faith behind right now."

"Many people experience a crisis of faith," he stated.

"I think mine has devolved into a chronic malaise," I said. "It has been going on for years. You probably wouldn't guess it to know of my recent actions, but I consider myself to be an ideologically committed Christian."

"It's not unusual for people, even Christians, to be angry with God at a time like this," he said.

"My quarrel is not with God," I replied. "It's with the people who claim to be speaking for Him as if they have a fucking clue. No offense intended."

"None taken," he said.

I started explaining our situation, what we had been going through, the possibility of our marriage ending, and the difficulties we had come through.

"The fact you are here says a lot," he told me.

"People can be so disingenuous at times like this. I'm not sure I believe all the thoughts and prayers and manufactured piety add up to a fart in a hurricane," I said. "No offense."

"None taken," the chaplain replied. "Scripture tells us, the effective, fervent prayer of a righteous man avails much," he went on.

"That lets me out," I said. "I certainly don't have any claim to righteous behavior of late."

"Is this a confession?" he asked.

"Just a statement of fact," I offered. "I know she is unhappy, and it's my fault. Plus, the last time we talked, I said some god-awful nasty things. I have messed things up big time, and I can't begin to think Roberta would have any interest in taking me back. I feel like the biggest screw-up of all time."

The chaplain grew thoughtful. "When I was an idealistic younger person, I had a poster with a poem on it which said, among other things, 'If you compare yourself with others, you may become vain or bitter, for always there will be greater and lesser persons than yourself.' That can apply to screw-ups, too, I'm sure. Some notorious scoundrels have turned out to be some of the greatest saints. You don't need to look much further than Saul of Tarsus or Simon Peter to figure that out."

"Doesn't the same poem say something like, 'Be at peace with God, whatever you conceive Him to be?'" I asked.

"Indeed, it does," he responded. "How do you conceptualize God?"

"Lately, I have been experiencing a lot of roadblocks which I have been laying off on cosmic forces or a universal master-mind that appears to be intent on seeing that I don't wander too far astray from some preordained path, not that I have a clue what that is supposed to be," I started to explain. "I have always had this vague sense of God as a 'father figure,' or even a heavenly father. But a loving father is something I honestly can't conceptualize. I'm sure the struggle has a lot to do with my relationship with my dad. Any idea of a loving father doesn't register with me. I haven't thought much about my feelings toward Dad in recent years. We had a lot of tough times, and I felt like I had a lot to forgive, not that he ever acknowledged his need for my forgiveness or asked for it. I simply gave it to avoid having to carry the baggage." (*How's that working out?* I asked myself. *Shut up!* I said to myself.)

"That's a starting point," he said.

"Well, that is about as much as I can do at this point. I'm all there is left of my immediate family. We have left a lot of things unsaid and undone."

"If God can use the likes of Peter and Paul, with all of their character flaws, who can say what you could accomplish?" he added.

"I would have to want to, wouldn't I?" I asked.

"That comes with soul-searching, which you have to do on your own. Just remember, sometimes the way to the mountaintop is through the garbage dump."

"That's one I haven't heard before," I said.

"I just made it up," the chaplain replied. "Who knows? Maybe I'll get quoted in a book someday."

"Fat chance," I said.

"Oh, well," he said. "In the meantime, I'll be praying for both of you, and so will a lot of others, whether you are aware of it or not."

"That's good to know," I replied. "I do appreciate you coming to talk. I guess I needed it. I'm dumping a lot on you, sorry," I said.

"That's what I'm here for," said the chaplain as he walked out the door. "Otherwise, I'd have to get a real job."

Crud, I thought. *Karma's a bitch.* I guess maybe you never know who is reading your blogs.

As I sat with Roberta, I began to wallow in self-imposed grief over what a disappointment I had been to her. I thought about all of the nasty things I said to her the last time we spoke. The one saving grace I thought of is that I hadn't said that one thing that I couldn't take back: that I felt that one night spent with Alice Modicum would be hotter than anything I had experienced with Roberta in the last two decades. I thought about what I honestly wanted out of this situation. Did I want to be free to hook up with a sex worker like Allie if anyone like her even existed? Or Sophia. I thought about the things I had learned from her, how she almost instinctively told me the thing I needed to hear at any given time. It was uncanny. And what about going to a brothel and hanging out with any number of compliant sex workers? Is that what I wanted out of life? While it might be a nice dream, it's clearly not a sustainable lifestyle, at least not for someone of my limited means. Plus, none of it is real. On the 1 - 10 rating system those ladies use, I'm little more than a number to the left of three zeros, and it's unlikely I would ever be a 10.

I thought again about what Sophia had said earlier about depression. I told her I would do something about it, but I've been dragging my feet at the thought of finding someone who knows about diagnosing and treating it. I made a mental note to follow through.

As if I weren't dealing with enough, I was beginning to come to the sad realization that my eagerly anticipated rendezvous with Sophia was never going to happen. I couldn't imagine going through with it right now, not with my wife fighting to hang on and my feelings of responsibility for her being in that situation. I knew I would have to tell Sophia; I wasn't sure how I would break the news. Mostly, I think I wanted to hang on to the fantasy a little while longer. Eventually, I knew I had to say something, so I sent her a text saying a family emergency had come up and it was likely I would have to miss our meeting. "Understood," came her reply, followed by some thoughtful face and praying hands emojis.

This was taking on the feel of a bad dream. How I wished I could swap this reality for the dream about Sophia I had earlier. It made me think that Sophia might very well have insinuated herself into my psyche and manipulated my feelings and impulses. I caught myself wondering if she could have the power to do such a thing, and if so, what is the source of this power? Is she a malevolent spirit hellbent on my destruction? Or is she an agent of a higher authority, one intent upon communicating to me in no uncertain terms what I am becoming, or perhaps, have already become? I almost chuckled at the thought of it, but isn't delivering messages from on High the purpose of angelic beings, after all? That's when it hit me. Sophia Angelique – angel of wisdom. O. M. F-ing. G. Are you kidding me? Here's my answer. This is where everything had been leading to. Everything happens for a reason.

I took Roberta's hand in mine, determined to make things right between us. When I did, a feeling of peace came over me, which was almost eerie. Then Roberta's hand squeezed mine, and I knew. She was going to be okay, and we would have a chance to put things right. I no longer had any regrets about not being able to meet up with Sophia. I was beginning to understand what miracles are all about.

I texted Sophia again: "I won't be meeting with you at all. I got a better offer."

"I thought you might," Sophia responded with a wink. The torrent of thumbs-up, hearts, and kissy-face emojis that followed told me she was expecting this outcome. You have to wonder.

CHAPTER 29

"Falling down is not a failure. Failure comes when you stay where you have fallen."
– Socrates

Roberta and I began to connect in ways that wouldn't have appeared possible only a few weeks earlier. She endured a long period of physical therapy, which we followed up with other physical therapy and various fun activities, by which I mean sex. We started to have date nights and do some of the things we enjoyed when we first started seeing each other.

I managed to patch things up with Stu, and we continued our friendship. I saw him in the bookstore one day, setting up a display of books on Buddhism. I will admit to being shocked. "What's this?" I asked him.

"Well, my new girlfriend says we should be open to other viewpoints," he replied. I was shocked to hear Stu had a girlfriend. To tell you the truth, I could not have been more surprised if he had told me he had just received his doctorate in evolutionary biology.

"Who's the lucky lady?" I asked.

"Oh, I think you know her. She's an Asian lady who spends a lot of time at the coffee shop. Sue is her name." Well, Sue continues to be full of surprises, and straightening out Stu will keep her busy for years to come.

One day, Roberta and I took a stroll and stopped by the Home for Helpless Pets shelter. We found a ton of cats who needed good homes. A few reminded us of cats we had over the years. We wished we could take in all of them, a feeling reminiscent of the old days in our relationship when everything appeared to be possible. Suddenly, I got an inspiration. The owners of Roasters & Readers wanted to sell the establishment lock, stock, and barrel, and there might be an opportunity. Stu said he would like to have the bookstore but had no idea what to do with the coffee shop. What if Roberta and I buy the coffee shop and turn it into a cat café where people can come and visit with therapy animals to calm their nerves and enjoy the company of some charming, furry friends? Think of the CATastrophes!

We were faced with the challenges of obtaining financing, business licenses, health and safety inspections, etc., etc., ad infinitum. To my amazement, the process all fell into place as smooth as silk. I guess these things happen when you follow your calling. Stu and Sue even supported the idea.

Sue decided to go back to school to become an actual accountant. She took a part-time job in our coffee shop as a barista. I wasn't entirely sure she was a cat person, so I checked with her on it. "Yes, I love cats. We had them all the time where I grew up. They're delicious," she told me, then said, "I'm probably just messing with you."

It is a well-documented fact that in ancient Egypt, cats were worshipped as gods. I have been told and have no reason to doubt that cats have never forgotten this.

I got help with my condition of clinical depression. Sophia, as usual, had hit the nail on the head. I started treatment and am doing much better. There's nothing like the combination of serotonin reuptake inhibitors and a wise guardian angel.

***

I never contacted Sophia again, nor any of my other friends from JOI. I didn't need it. I didn't really want to either, I found. I didn't harbor any resentment or hard feelings for any of them; I simply found I had moved on in my journey of illumination. I'm not even sure if Sophia still occupies my plane of existence, but I'm sure she is out there somewhere, helping others who can benefit from her wisdom.

I never published my sexy short stories. I figured there was no point in them unless they would help someone—maybe someone like me who needed some guidance and inspiration to open up about their feelings. I wasn't sure what that might look like.

Eileen Tudor-Wright became an animal rights activist after she rescued a stray Siberian Husky with symptoms of some unknown trauma.

Dr. John Daniel went and fucked himself. At least, that is what he said to begin with until an internal investigation by his organization revealed that he directed his personal masseur to do it as a condition of his employment. This revelation effectively scuttled his ministry, and he was forced to get a job doping horses under the direction of an ethically challenged trainer at a popular racetrack.

Alice Modicum mounted a bid to run for governor of Nevada. She lost the election by a mere 69 votes. Numerous recounts followed, but curiously, while the vote total of each one varied, the margin of defeat was always the same: 69 votes. Perhaps the universe was trying to tell her something.

Diane Marie also ventured into politics, being elected to the United States Senate, where she gave advice and consent (wink) to numerous chief executives from every imaginable party affiliation. She served with distinction for many years before moving on to head up the newly formed Department of If It Feels Good Do It in President Allie Moorehead's cabinet.

Speaking of Allie, one might wonder how a fictional character from an unpublished short story managed to get elected President of the United States, but as we all know, stranger things have happened.

I discontinued my blog so I could concentrate on creating content for a Y'allScreen channel called Herding Cats. The channel is about life in the cat café. As you might guess, it has been one catastrophe after another. Things couldn't be better.

Roberta and I both started working on our health and physical conditioning. I made a conscious effort to exercise regularly and eat right. The biggest thing was I stopped drinking altogether. After a short while,

I found I didn't miss it at all. Roberta also started going for long walks and reigning in her sweet tooth. Between us, we managed to lose enough weight so that we didn't need to worry when we drove over a small bridge, the kind with gross vehicle weight restrictions posted on it. At least we are no longer the gross part of the vehicle weight.

I had mentioned to Roberta some time ago about my thing for belly dancers. She was not enthused about it at the time, mainly, I think, because she interpreted it to mean I wanted a skinny Minnie in a stunningly revealing costume. While I had an appreciation for such things, it was not the primary motivating factor for me. I told her the outfit might just as well consist of yoga pants, a tank top, and a sash around the waist. The main thing for me was the willingness to perform and feel good about herself in the process. It's the old idea of being comfortable in your own skin. Besides, she might find the movements to be good exercise. Something must have registered with her because a few weeks later, she took me to the den and had me sit down on the floor. Then, as the tune *Midnight at the Oasis* played, she removed her robe and stood in an elegant outfit which, while revealing only a minimal amount of skin, the fact that she wanted me to pay attention to her in it and the movements she made had the effect of getting me turned on, and by that, I mean hard. After a brief demo of the moves she had worked to master, we became, shall I say, otherwise engaged. It was, quite honestly, one of the sexiest things I have ever experienced. If you want details, you will have to ask Roberta.

I told Roberta I wanted her to show me how to experience fun, excitement, and passion within the framework of what she was comfortable with. That brought on a whole new level of communication and openness between us. "I know erotica isn't your cup of tea," I told Roberta. "But if you could keep from making the stories all about you and realize I am trying to express energy and a passion that I want to experience with you in a completely intimate way and keep it only between us. There must be some way we can have fun, adventure, and sexiness while connecting without judgment and condemnation." She said she would approach it with an open mind, which was all I asked of her.

There was a minor dust-up when I suggested calling the café the Colfax Avenue Cat House. Stu appeared hesitant about it, saying he thought it was a dumb-headed idea. Roberta expressed a much lower opinion of it. She said absolutely not. Sue didn't see what the big deal was until Roberta told her. Then Sue looked amused. I think she got that I was messing with them.

Well, that's my story, and I'm sticking to it. Had I experienced the Grace of God? I don't want to speculate, but if I had, it would be fitting, as no one could have been less deserving of it than I was.

One evening, Roberta and I went out for tea and ice cream. It was like we were 20 years younger, and life held infinite possibilities. As we finished, Roberta said, "I have the strangest craving for a pickle."

He does indeed work in mysterious ways. It is positively arcane.

"I will restore the years that the locusts have eaten."
– God

The End

Thank you for reading. If you enjoyed this book, please leave a review here, https://www.amazon.com/dp/B0D9TW8HXP and look for my other books on Amazon as well.

ACKNOWLEDGMENTS

First, I must recognize my collaborator, Diane Marie, as my definitive muse. It is truly an honor and a privilege to call her my friend.

To Alice Little, who provided much of the inspiration for the life of sex workers. Everything she touches turns to gold. Or something hard and shiny.

To Nicole Emma, who gave the TEDx talk on YouTube, which was a reference in the story. I learned a great deal from it.

To all the stuffed-shirt preachers and holier-than-thou-rollers who made a major theme of this story possible, and it could be argued, necessary.

To all those I know who have been a source of help, encouragement, and support in my writing endeavors. Both of you.

ABOUT THE AUTHOR

Mack Stout is a writer of humorous essays, memoirs and stories that attempt to give the reader a perspective on life that says, "Lighten up and enjoy the journey." When life gets you down, you need to remember that we are all in this together. By realizing that others have been there, you can find clarity and hope that your situation has meaning.

Mack recently transitioned from being a snowbird in the foothills of Montana to his residence in Mesa, Arizona. Check out his blog at www.mackstout.com

OTHER BOOKS BY MACK STOUT

Gold Diggers, Bean Counters, and Miss Management:

Too Young to Retire, Too Old to Change Jobs in a Hostile Work Environment

Jerks for Whom I Have Worked:

Learning to Steer Clear of Bad Bosses

Available on Amazon.com

www.ingramcontent.com/pod-product-compliance
Lightning Source LLC
Chambersburg PA
CBHW030657260626
47157CB00007B/2690